Justice for All

Justice for All

A Novel

Christy Kyser Truitt

DUNHAM
books

Nashville

Justice for All Copyright © 2013 Christy Kyser Truitt.
All rights reserved.

No part of this book may be reproduced in any form or by any means, electronic, mechanical, photocopying, scanning, or otherwise, without permission in writing from the publisher, except by a reviewer who may quote brief passages in a review. Unless otherwise noted, Scripture quotations from the Life Application Study Bible, NIV copyright Tyndale Publishers, Carol Stream, Illinois. For information on licensing or special sales, please contact:

Dunham Books
63 Music Square East
Nashville, Tennessee 37203
www.dunhamgroupinc.com

This book is a work of fiction and, as such, is a product of the author's imagination, experience, and research. No resemblance anyone living is intended

ISBN: 978-1-939447-24-1
Ebook ISBN: 978-1-939447-25-8

Printed in the United States of America

To Rexena Barrington – save me a seat. Brian, Abby, Billy, and Trent, you are my inhales and exhales.

CHAPTER

1

K.D. rehearsed the opening line over and over in her mind, practicing the delivery, the pace, knowing the importance of timing. Low black heels, with scuffed areas blackened with marker, clicked along the tile as she checked her lipstick in a framed picture of George Washington. She adjusted the frayed waistline of her skirt, lips moving without sound as she clipped down the hall. As she turned into courtroom three, K.D. bumped into the security guard.

"Morning, Miss Jennings. A little late I see…"

K.D. held up a hand to discourage conversation, scared to break the cadence of thought. She glanced around the courtroom, surprised to find it empty, but then spied the object of her mental exercises. Squaring her shoulders, she marched right up to tap him on the shoulder, confident she'd get him this time.

He turned to glare at her. "Where have you been? You were supposed to be here an hour ago."

"Sorry about that, Ingram, but I have a very important question."

He raised caterpillar eyebrows in what seemed like exasperation.

She leaned forward, hesitated, and then continued in determination. "What do you call a lawyer with an IQ of 70?"

Her grizzled boss rolled his eyes and returned to placing files into his tattered briefcase.

K.D. grinned. "A judge. Get it? A lawyer with an IQ of 70 is a judge." She pulled back, waited on at least a hint of a smile, but received no response. "Oh come on, Ingram, you know that was funny. I've been practicing all morning."

Someone cleared his throat from across the courtroom. K.D. winced and slowly turned her head to see the judge straightening in his chair, glaring down from the bench. Now she could have sworn that seat was empty two seconds ago.

"Sorry, Your Honor, I didn't see you up there. I was, uh, trying to, well um..."

"Miss Jennings, you are Mr. Ingram's legal assistant, correct?"

Heat climbed K.D.'s neck. "Yes sir." *At least I was. I heard they were hiring at the Piggly Wiggly. Maybe I'll ease on over there.*

"Young lady, it would serve you well to find some respect for the court."

K.D. bristled. "I have respect, Your Honor. I'm going to law school at night just so I can cross this rail here and argue a case before you."

"Law school, huh?" K. D. wasn't sure, but she could have sworn he mumbled, "have mercy," under his breath.

"Yes sir. I..." Ingram silenced her with a sharp look.

The judge snorted. "Maybe you'll learn the civility associated with a court of law." The judge stacked some papers and stood up to leave, but paused at the door and pointed a finger, his black robe draped around a thick wrist. "Besides, it's my understanding only legal assistants' IQs top out at 45." The door shut on his chuckle.

The state of Alabama and the American flag flanked the now-empty judge's bench with a gold-plated justice seal on the wall above the chair. The railing between the audience and lawyer's region could have guarded Jericho with as much access as she had as a legal assistant to a jury on the other side.

But one day....

K.D. inhaled through her nose, straightening at the thought of arguing a case before her peers. America, land of the free, home of the brave. The place where a trailer-park girl with mud-caked toes could become a lawyer. A childhood spent arguing imaginary cases before tree stumps, the judge a knotty pine tree, all now within her reach. That is if her attempts at humor didn't get her fired.

K.D. turned to find Ingram heading out the door and hurried to catch up. "Okay okay. Sorry I was late. I thought the judge would deliberate awhile so I didn't think it was a big deal. If you'd bother to carry a cell phone, I might could have let you know."

"You didn't think, which is your biggest problem to begin with."

K.D. ignored the jab as her pantyhose grabbed her skirt like Velcro. "Come on, Ingram, lighten up. I'm sorry about the joke. I wanted to make you smile. I know how much you needed this verdict, but from the looks of your otherwise cheerful expression, it must not have gone well." She glanced down to talk to her boss, seeing as she stood a good six inches over him. Ingram kept his eyes straight, but walked like he had to use the restroom. K.D. almost lost a shoe keeping up with him.

"We won. And I didn't laugh because your joke wasn't funny. They never are."

K.D. grabbed his arm to stop his marathon pace. "We won? Well, gracious, Ingram, that's good news. Why don't you hurt that face of yours with a smile?"

Ingram turned and marched toward the bathroom with a penguin's gait. Either the bum knee was acting up again or he really did have to use the facilities. He turned at the open door. "I said we won. I didn't say we'd be able to collect. The defendant filed a bankruptcy petition this morning. Gave me the papers right after the verdict. All we have is a judgment with no cash. Our client can't even pay for the expert witnesses. I'll let you do the math." He let the door swing shut on his sour expression.

K.D. exhaled. A favorable judgment was a minimum of twenty thousand dollars, the most single winning they'd received in two years. Gone with one signature on a Chapter Seven document. They'd be lower than well-digger boots on the list of creditors. And expert witnesses? K.D. remembered an erosion-control expert, a surveyor. Hundreds of dollars rolled through her head. Either they paid out of pocket or risked an insolvent reputation. Hard to pay out of a pocket full of holes. K.D. leaned against the wall and waited.

She pasted a smile across her face as her boss rejoined the walk. Ornery was a generous description of Ezra Ingram, the man she'd grown to love like a father the last couple of years, but K.D. had never seen him so down. Ingram grunted at the security guard on their way out, slammed in the face by an Alabama determined to hang onto the heat. Silence lined the hazy block to the office, and a shifting wind brought a strong garlic smell from the Chinese restaurant which fronted their building.

As they entered the firm's reception area, K.D. decided against another joke, sure her attempts at humor would only sour his mood further. "Want some water?" Ingram didn't answer as he disappeared down the hall, and she took that as a yes.

A roach scurried toward the shoe molding, and K.D. let it pass, sympathizing with its home inside the walls and stained industrial carpet. When Ingram first hung the shingle thirty years ago, the building held prominence with its close proximity to the county courthouse. Now it barely held up at all as termites feasted on the shaky infrastructure. Thank goodness for the rent from the Chinese restaurant, even if it meant her stomach growled over the smell of sesame chicken every day at noon.

K.D. turned into the small kitchen, chose the "World's Best Boss" mug from the cabinet and turned on the faucet. A knock on the office door startled her, and she spilled water onto her blue polyester blouse. Grabbing a brown paper towel that felt more like sandpaper, K.D. called out, "Come in! Be right with you."

She rounded the corner to a man who looked to be around forty, with spindly arms wrestling with a toddler on his hip. The baby shrieked in terror at the sight of K.D. and monkey-climbing up the man's auto-mechanic shirt. K.D. looked behind her to see if Ingram came down the hall, as he was the one to scare little kids and puppy dogs, not her. But it remained only her and the man.

"Can I help you?"

The little girl bellowed at the sound of K.D.'s voice. The man shushed her, but only succeeded in raising the volume. He looked at K.D. with pleading eyes. "I'm sorry. Can you give me a sec? Gabby's terrified of strangers."

K.D. remained in place until she realized he meant for *her* to leave, not the other way around. *Excuse me, whose office is this?* "Oh, yeah sure."

"Where's my water?" Ingram's voice boomed down the hall, pushing Gabby over the precipice of hysteria.

K.D. held up a finger. "I'll be right back." She walked to Ingram's office, handing him the mug.

"What in all things holy is that noise?"

"A guy with his little girl. Probably meant to find the Chinese place and took a wrong door. I didn't have time to ask him before the kid opened a mouth the size of the Grand Canyon." K.D. cocked an ear, hearing hiccups through the open door, but no screams. "Let me try this again. Be right back."

She eased back to the reception area, peeking around the corner until the daddy gave her the okay sign with a nod. The baby narrowed shockingly blue eyes at K.D. while sucking on the tip of her thumb.

"I'm sorry about that. Gabby gets real scared a strangers. Takes her a while to warm up to folks."

K.D. offered a smile. "I see that. Were you looking for the Chinese place? Folks come in the back way to the building, think we're it. It's actually in the front of the building."

"No, I'm not looking to eat. My name's Buck Murdock. My wife, Shelly Anne, got tied up at work. She waits tables over at the Waffle Iron." His voice trailed off. K.D. noticed large hands, too big for such a little man, stroking the back of his daughter's blonde curls.

"Nice to meet you. I'm K.D. Jennings. What can I do for you?"

"Katie?"

"No, it's actually the letter K and the letter D, but it sounds like Katie."

"Oh, well, that Mr. Ingram represented my boss down at the auto plant, when those rednecks sued him for shooting their dog. Dern coon hound wouldn't stay on his own property, kept chewing up boss's chickens at his farm. I'da shot him too. Mr. Ingram looked after boss and countersued for lost property or something like that."

"Loss of property, I would imagine."

"Yeah, that's it. Danged if he didn't get the case dropped and my boss a coupla hundred dollars for his chickens. Like on Judge Judy or something."

Gabby whimpered against her daddy's shoulder, and K.D. wondered if this train would ever find the station.

"How can we help you, Mr. Murdock?"

"I want to sue the doctor that killed my boy."

"Pardon?"

Buck shifted Gabby to another bony hip. "You mind if I sit down?"

"Of course not. I'm sorry I didn't offer before. Can I get you some coffee? Water?" She'd offer soda, only Ingram cut that out of the budget. She missed her Dr Peppers.

Buck held out a pink sheet of paper. "I almost forgot. I found this in the hall outside your office." He sat on the 1970s sofa, green and orange plaid, and locked Gabby into the crook of an arm. Her eyelids drooped into sleep.

"Eviction notice!" K.D. clapped a hand over her mouth, embarrassed for having said the words out loud. They must have walked right over the paper on the way in. Even sub-leasing the front of their building to the restaurant didn't cover the rent. As Clear Point, Alabama sunk deeper into an economic recession, so did the firm's bank account with few real estate closings or property disputes to line the trough. Without today's settlement, K.D. feared postponing law school yet again until she could find another job.

"I got one of them one time. Make sure they give you thirty days. Law says they gotta give you that." He missed the irony of offering legal advice in an attorney's office and also seemed unfazed at the thought of soliciting an attorney with an eviction notice outside the door.

K.D. folded the paper and put it in the lap drawer of her desk. "You were saying?"

Buck cleared his throat, adjusting Gabby in his arms. "My boy played running back over at the county high school last few years. Best player in the state. Heck, probably in the country. A lot of folks said he coulda won Mr. Football his senior year."

"Mr. Football? Is that some sort of pageant?" She knew the South loved its sports, but a beauty contest seemed a little ridiculous.

The man looked at her like she sprouted three heads. "No ma'am, Mr. Football is an award given by Alabama sports writers to the best high school football player in the state. Everybody knew of Bo."

"Bo?"

"My son. Named him after Bo Jackson, 'cept I think he was faster. Bo Jackson played for the Raiders, won the Heisman." He tilted his head, adopting a simpleton's voice. "You do know who Bo Jackson is, doncha?"

K.D. stopped short of rolling her eyes. "Yes, I'm familiar with Bo Jackson." *Wasn't he in a movie or something?*

"Well, anyways, my boy fainted during practice after getting hit by a strong safety. The doc at the emergency room said he had a concussion, but he had a heat stroke before they got the scans back." Buck's words faltered at the last sentence.

K.D. chewed on the inside of her cheek. "I'm real sorry for your loss, Mr. Murdock, but I'm afraid we don't do malpractice or wrongful death suits. We'll be happy to make a referral." She turned at the sound of Ingram entering the room.

"Of course we do those types of suits, Miss Jennings. Good

afternoon, sir. I'm Ezra Ingram. Why don't you and that precious little girl go on back to my office and get settled. I'll get Miss Jennings here to run up to the restaurant and get you a drink. Coke? Sprite?"

K.D. frowned and crossed her arms over her chest as Ingram walked over to the man and shook his hand like he was visiting royalty.

"Buck Murdock, Mr. Ingram. No, nothing for me, thank you. Boss said you were the right one to help me."

"Indeed I am, sir. Go on make yourself at home. Last door on your right. I'll join you in a second."

K.D. left her mouth hanging open as the little man walked down the hall with Gabby's head lolling against his shoulder. Ingram turned to her with a grin as out of place as a polar bear in the Gulf.

"What were you doing, Ingram, listening against the wall? We don't do that kind of litigation."

"Keep your voice down." Ingram gestured with both hands. "We do now. Didn't I hear him hand you an eviction notice? Do you know what a case like this can do for us?"

K.D. retrieved the paper from the desk and handed it over. Ingram pulled his bifocals down from his forehead and scanned the document. "The man's right. We'll have at least thirty days. But if we become counsel of choice in a wrongful death suit, I can get my ex-wife to hold off on the eviction. Don't you understand? Cases like these usually go to the big guns, not to folks like us. I could go kiss every one of those chickens for bringing Mr. Murdock to my door."

"But we're not qualified, Ingram."

His eye twitched, and K.D. knew she was close to a line she shouldn't cross, but one she often did. "Young lady, we're as qualified as the next guy. Where's your faith, gal? Don't you realize we could buy our own office building from the winnings of this case *and* tell the ex-wife to shove it? I know you had to charge books this semester. Your bonus would take care of law school *plus* your books."

"How'd you know I had to charge my books?"

Ingram waved her off. "I have my ways. I know all about you mooning over that law student."

"How could you…" She stopped, knowing the futility. Ingram knew way too much of her personal business, but more out of protectiveness than nosiness. She let it slide, but she didn't *moon*, for goodness sakes. Although his brown eyes often distracted her in class, and the way his mouth turned down in concentration… "Well, couldn't you just be nice to your ex-wife? That'd be a lot easier."

"Impossible to be nice to somebody so mean. Bad enough she got the building in the divorce. Just because her daddy…"

"How much you talking about?" K.D. cut him off before he lost himself in the black hole of divorce reminiscing. She could only handle so much chatter about the ex's family, a lineage dating back to Henry Hudson or Ponce De Leon or some other explorer who knocked up the ex's great-great-great Indian grandmother on his way to greater glory.

"Depends. A million. Maybe more."

K.D.'s eyes grew the expanse of her face. "Really."

Ingram rubbed his hands together like a cartoon villain. "A jury would eat that man up. He looks pitiful, a father losing his only son. Folks around here treat football players like gods. Nobody would go up against that tradition, especially in the South. Malpractice insurance'll settle before you can charge your next books."

"But you don't even know anything about the case."

"And I won't if you keep flapping your gums out here while Buck back there changes his mind. Come on."

K.D. walked behind Ingram, acknowledging the possibility that things seemed almost too good to be true. She never trusted anything that made Ingram giddy, and the man was practically skipping. She stopped and hurried back to her desk for a pen and note pad. At the top she wrote, "Malpractice Law for Dummies" and re-joined Ingram and their new best friends.

CHAPTER

2

K.D. took the loveseat against the far wall, allowing Buck and his sleeping daughter the solitary chair in front of Ingram's desk.

Ingram leaned forward, his pen twirling among sausage fingers. "Now, let's start from the beginning."

"Like I was saying, Bo was a real talent in football. He was solid, six feet about 245 pounds of pure muscle. Recreation leagues always made him play up because if he touched the ball, he scored. Folks complained about his size, saying he needed to be in the older leagues. Fine with us. He coulda played high school in the seventh grade if they'd a let him. He started as a sophomore, first game ran for over 200 yards, course one of 'em was a punt return."

K.D. felt her eyes glaze over from the white noise of athletic banter. Buck's voice held strong, as if talking about his son's abilities kept him alive.

"So, he had a lot of promise, did he?" Ingram's joy over the case wrestled with a sympathetic tone.

"Promise? How 'bout guaranteed? Bo was gonna be the first one in my family to go to college. We talked to different recruiters every day and visited just about every SEC school during his sophomore year. Boy probably coulda gone pro with a little college experience behind him. No tellin' how much money he'd a made in his career.

Millions just to sign him."

K.D. circled the word "millions" on her notepad. *Millions because he could run fast, and here I am maxing out my credit card with law school.*

Ingram wrote a few lines, his pen scratching against the yellow legal pad. "Tell me what happened during practice."

"It was right before school started. Coach Camp was running two a days."

"Excuse me, two a days? What's that?" K.D. interjected, wanting to contribute *something* to the interview.

Both men looked at her again as though she'd sprouted horns. Maybe she'd keep her mouth shut and take notes.

Buck laughed a little. "Not much on sports, are you?"

Um, no, because I have more important things to do with my time than scream at men in zebra shirts blowing whistles at no-necked Neanderthals degrading one another's mamas.

"Two a days are when Coach has practice in the mornings and late afternoons, as in two practices a day. You try to stay outta the better heat, but in Alabama, there's no getting around it. Plus, most of your games are in 90 plus degrees anyway so you gotta get used to it. My wife and I were at work when Coach called to tell us Bo had fainted and they were taking him to the hospital. They were running a CAT scan when we got there so we had to wait." Buck's voice trailed off.

K.D. wrote down some questions: Who gave consent for the CAT scan since Bo was a minor? Date of practice? Talk to Coach, to players. "What was the doctor's name? And who was Bo's football coach?"

"Dr. Jackson Thomas. Always thought it was weird to have two last names. Talked funny too. Mark Camp is still the head coach. Won state last year. Like I was saying, once the test got done, we were able to go back in the ER and wait on the results with Bo in his stall, I think they call it. You know, the area where they pull the curtain around you? We hadn't even sat down before alarms started going off, the nurse told us we had to leave. We found out later Bo's temperature had shot up to 107. He die…," Buck choked over the word and then cleared his throat, "left us before they could get the ice bags on him."

Time stalled. Buck's voice shook and faltered at the last sentence. He bowed over Gabby's head, hesitating in her blonde curls. She stirred in sleep, burying deeper into the curve of his neck. He cleared his throat again.

The hum of the florescent light provided the only noise while the Glade vanilla outlets puffed a bakery smell through the room. K.D. caught Ingram's eyes over Buck's shoulders as even he honored the man's grief with a genuine look of sympathy.

After a few seconds, the man collected himself, ran a hand over the weathered skin and scratchy stubble of his face. "I've worked in the heat my entire life over at the Tire and Service center. Shop fans don't do nothing, but stir hot air. I know a thing or two about heat strokes, 'bout had one myself playing church league softball. When a player passes out in fall practice, first thing you do is treat 'em for heat. Any moron knows that."

K.D. kept quiet, not wanting to reaffirm her already established position of a moron when it came to athletics.

Ingram sat back in his chair, the wood squeaking as his weight shifted. He stroked his chin, deep in thought. "Sounds pretty cut and dried to me. First thing we'll do is order the medical reports from Dr. Thomas and the hospital. They'll drag their feet getting them to us, but we have to start somewhere. When did your son die?"

"Be two years next month. Got the call about three forty-five or so in the afternoon. Bo passed at five twenty-eight. He had just turned seventeen. I wanted to sue the doctor straight away, but my wife wouldn't let me. Wouldn't even talk about it. To be honest with ya, she wasn't real happy 'bout me being here today."

A young man's life reduced to numbers, a pin prick stuck in a father's memories. How else would such an insignificant time of day like five twenty-eight become the detonator to one family's happiness? In a blink, life as they knew it changed forever. A thought struck K.D., and she leaned forward. "Excuse me, Mr. Murdock, did you say two years ago?"

"That's right. Be two years this month."

"Ingram, statute of limitations runs out after two years."

Ingram nodded. "She's right. We can't wait for the records, Mr. Murdock. I'll need to file the suit in the next few days." He scribbled on the legal pad, and then pointed his pen at Buck. "Let me warn you. The insurance company's lawyer is going to tear into your son. They'll find every Tylenol, every Motrin, every allergy pill the boy ever took to try to twist this thing around. You best tell me now if the boy did any drugs or had any medical condition."

Buck sat up straight, adjusted Gabby in his arms. "My boy never did no drugs, Mr. Ingram. I'd swear to that. He was a good boy. Never knew of any health conditions either."

Ingram breathed out. "Good. My apologies for being blunt, but you can expect worse from the other side, particularly if they choose not to settle. We have to file suit before the two year anniversary of your son's death, meaning I'm going into this blind. So if there's anything I need to know, now's the time to tell me."

Buck shook his head. "No sir. I told you all I know."

"Very well. I'll write up the complaint against the doctor, hospital and Coach Camp."

"Why Coach Camp?"

"Well, it would really be against the school system, but he'd be liable as the representative."

Buck was already shaking his head. "Don't put in Coach Camp. He did everything right by calling the ambulance and getting Bo to the hospital. He loved my boy. I can't sue him." Buck's voice rose with each word, rousing Gabby from her slumber. She jerked up her head, looked around the room, and began to scream.

Buck stood, almost dropping the kid while shooting Ingram a stern look. "I mean it, Mr. Ingram. I know you're some fancy lawyer and all, but you don't mess with Coach Camp. He's a good man. A deacon at the church. He's gotten more of our boys to college on scholarship than anybody."

K.D. almost snorted at the fancy lawyer comment. Guess Buck didn't notice the water damage to the hall sheet rock or had chosen to forget the eviction notice.

Ingram raised his hands and his voice, trying to be heard over Gabby's wails. "Okay, Mr. Murdock. You're the client. We'll file a complaint against Dr. Thomas and County General as soon as possible. Come with me up front, let's fill out some paperwork." Ingram turned to K.D. "Take the baby, so we can finish up here. I'm sure Mr. Murdock needs to be getting home."

Buck walked over and dumped a screaming Gabby into K.D.'s arms. K.D. looked up in terror at Ingram with no idea of what to do with a baby.

Buck patted his daughter's back. "She always wakes up like this. Just walk her around. She'll be fine."

"Yeah, K.D. Just walk her around. We won't be but a second." Ingram seemed to revel in her situation as a grin tugged on his mouth.

Ingram guided Buck out of the room, shutting the door on K.D. and the screaming baby. K.D. tried to remember if she'd ever even held one and came up with nothing. Who leaves their toddler with a stranger? Especially one who didn't even know what a two-a-day was or thought Mr. Football was a beauty pageant?

"There, there. No crying. It's okay."

Maybe she should sit down. There would be less of a fall if she dropped the kid. K.D. sat Gabby on her knee, supporting her with hands under arm pits. The baby reached out and grabbed K.D.'s chain around her neck. The crying abruptly stopped.

"Okay, maybe I can do this. You like my necklace?" About that time, Gabby yanked on the chain, pulling it tight around K.D.'s neck. She disentangled her fingers from the necklace before the kid decapitated her. Gabby's face scrunched up in preparation for a wail.

"No, no, no, don't cry again." K.D. whirled around in search of something, anything, to distract the baby, and grabbed a fringed pillow, brushing it against the baby's face by accident. Gabby opened her mouth with a contagious giggle, laughing over and over until K.D. joined her. "Okay, we can do this." She kept tickling Gabby's nose.

"Well, look at who likes babies. You're a natural, K.D."

K.D. frowned at Ingram as the two men re-entered the room and then smiled at Gabby. "Kid's cute when she's not screaming." Gabby launched herself at her daddy who caught her with one arm before she hit the floor.

"Oops." K.D. winced.

Buck hoisted Gabby in his arms. "It's okay. There's a reason God made chillen full of rubber instead of bone."

She stood and walked to hand Buck the diaper bag. "You all done?"

Ingram nodded. "I left the contract on your desk. Buck went ahead and signed it, but you'll need to run over to the Waffle Iron tomorrow to get his wife's signature since she's the administrator of Bo's estate. She's working lunch, but Buck said things wind down around 1:30 or so." K.D. was quick to nod, knowing she'd get lunch money from Ingram since she'd be at the Waffle Iron anyway. She could taste the smothered, covered hash browns already.

Buck pulled the diaper bag over his shoulder. "You never said how much this case is gonna cost me. I can't pay you much, but I'll give you all I can."

Ingram looked pained for a moment and cleared his throat. "Won't cost you a penny. We take the case on contingency, meaning if you lose, you're not out any money. We'll take a percentage of the settlement, usually fifty percent. Once we get the contract back from your wife, we'll proceed with filing the complaint. Best bet would be the insurance company'll take one look at this and settle immediately. We'll be in touch."

K.D. looked hard at Ingram, wondering how they were going to finance this case without a proverbial penny between the two of them. If a case involving a blown-out catfish pond cost them a couple of thousand, which they had to pay because the defendant filed bankruptcy, how in the world could they finance a wrongful death suit?

Buck shook Ingram's hand over Gabby, whose eyes were still locked on K.D. She walked them out the front door, returned to Ingram's office, and waited until he finished three pages of scribbles before speaking. "Well?"

He slowly raised his head with a smile. "If the stars line up, we may finally have found the Emerald City, Dorothy. As long as the kid didn't have some undiagnosed condition or took illegal drugs, the case seems open and shut to me. I remember when this Dr. Jackson moved to Alabama about the time of this case, now that I think about it. Seems like I heard him speak at a chamber lunch or breakfast or something. Moved here from upstate New York, said he wanted a warmer climate. Fool had probably never even heard of a heat stroke except from some medical school class he'd long forgotten about."

"What's the first step?"

"I'll write up the complaint tonight, walk it over to the courthouse first thing in the morning. Then we'll request the medical records. They'll drag their feet and then bury us in a bunch of discovery nonsense. They'll deny all allegations, file a motion to dismiss, and the judge will then dismiss their motion. There are probably a few more back and forths I'm forgetting about, but you get the idea. We'll bump chests for a while, but there was a time I benched over two hundred." Ingram puffed out his chest, pushed his bifocals onto his forehead and actually winked at her. K.D. caught a glimpse of Ingram in his lawyering prime. She smiled at the color in his face.

"You got everything you need for class? Need me to review any cases with you?"

The dichotomy of Ingram fascinated K.D. One minute, he'd yap about easy million-dollar lawsuits, throwing baby Gabby in her arms in chauvinistic fashion, and the next, he'd offer to help with class or pay off her credit card. Beneath the armadillo hide beat the heart of a true gentleman.

K.D. would much rather stay with Ingram and start to work on the Murdock case. But then again, the seating chart had Trip Folsom beside her. His muddy river eyes brought a smile across her face before she returned to the conversation with Ingram.

Maybe she did moon a little.

"I think I'm good. I was able to review my notes last night. I'll be back in the morning to proof the complaint before you take it over. Why you don't insist that your ex-wife put in Internet connection is beyond me. You could then file your complaints online."

"How would I flirt with all the clerks if I filed online?"

"Gross, Ingram. Miss Betty's gotta be a hundred and three."

He smiled. "Beggars can't be choosers. You go on to class. The complaint will be on your desk in the morning. And K.D.?"

She turned at the door, pulling her purse over her shoulder. "Yeah?"

Ingram stood and walked over, hand on the door. "If you'd pay more attention to your professor instead of that Folsom boy, you might learn a thing or two. You bother to tell him what your initials stand for yet?"

"How did you know his name…" Ingram shut the door, but she could hear his laughter. She shook her head and smiled as she walked down the hall.

CHAPTER

3

K.D. slid into the nearest bathroom even though class had started five minutes prior. The cracked mirror was as much a hot mess as the reflection in it. K.D. tore through her shoulder bag, pushing aside gas receipts, a pocket calendar she never used, a nail file she should use, and scores of other trash-worthy items until she tunneled down to the brush.

Yanking out her ponytail holder, K.D. battled the mass of blonde curls, roadblocks of tangles reaching past her shoulders. She held it back up, liking the way her deep-green eyes jumped out when not hidden by a blanket of hair. Then again, if she left it down, especially brushed, she might be able to pull off a sexier look if she pouted her lips just right.

Lips. Ugh. K.D. searched for lip gloss, finding first some melted Chapstick and then her tube of Plum Perfect, swiping it across her lips.

"Good grief, Jennings. Get a grip." K.D. shook her head at the reflection. She compromised, grabbed a headband from the purse and dammed up the mass of curls. The water spot remained on her faux-silk button down, courtesy of *Mr. Know It All Athletics* Buck Murdock.

K.D. sighed, tucked the shirt in the waist of her skirt, and gave up on appearance. So what if Trip Folsom looked like he stepped off of an Abercrombie and Fitch walkway? They were friends, study mates, late night coffee runners. So what if the color of his eyes reminded her of the muddy creek that ran behind her trailer, the sanctuary from her mother's depression?

So what?

K.D. tiptoed down the tiled hallway and eased open the classroom door, hoping to spot Trip beside her empty seat and not bring down the wrath of Professor Elliott. Again.

No such luck.

"Well, Miss Jennings. So glad you could join us this evening." The professor stopped and looked at his watch. "Although ten minutes ago would have been more appropriate. Please let me know if we need to adjust the class schedule to accommodate you. I'm sure the other forty-odd students who managed to get here on time wouldn't mind."

The class chuckled, and K.D. cringed. She scanned the room, landing on Trip.

K.D. squared her shoulders and walked toward her seat. "Sorry about that, Mr. Elliott. You wouldn't believe the traffic. Took me thirty minutes to get through two red lights. And don't get me started on the deer population. I had to wait out Bambi's family reunion just to get in the parking lot." K.D. rambled across the classroom, knowing she should shut up, but nerves and babbling always took precedence over common sense.

The professor glared at her. "Are you quite done? I'm sure Miss Henry would like to finish enlightening us about who bears the burden in a motion for summary judgment. Or better yet, why don't you allow us the wisdom of your musings over the burden of proof?"

K.D. stopped and adjusted her satchel on her shoulder. "I'd be happy to. The party moving for summary judgment always bears the initial responsibility of identifying the basis for its motion according to Rule 56 (c). The movant can meet this burden by presenting evidence showing there is no dispute of material fact or by displaying the non-moving party has failed to present evidence in support of some element of its case." K.D. smiled.

Professor Elliott nodded. "Yes, er um, logical explanation, Miss Jennings. Now, I'm sure Miss Henry would appreciate the opportunity to continue with her assessment of the case. Would you so oblige us the courtesy of your attention?"

K.D. eased into her seat and nodded her head. She retrieved a notebook from her bag and clicked her multi-colored pen.

Trip knocked his knee against her, rubbing a hand over his mouth to hide the smile. She grinned back. He typed something on his Notepad and turned the screen toward her. "Not everyone gets your jokes," she read as the professor returned his attention to dismembering Miss Henry's explanation of what issues of fact were genuine, what made an issue material, and who must prove what.

K.D. opened a spiral notebook and wrote back in purple, "Their loss." She settled into her seat and tuned into the student's interpretation of last night's readings, her pen scratching while Trip's fingers flew over the keys. She blocked out thoughts of Ingram alone in the office, cobbling together a lawsuit, her mother locked inside the iron walls of depression, knowing she should have called her before class, and Trip beside her, smelling musky like a prom date.

K.D. emerged from the academic cocoon some three hours later, stretching her arms to encourage blood flow while grimacing at her watch.

Trip touched her arm. "Come on, let's get out of here before Professor Know-It-All keeps you after class and thrashes his ruler against your palm." He grabbed her satchel from the floor, took her elbow and tunneled them through the departing students. She didn't look back for fear the teacher would see her and make her write one hundred times while standing on one foot, "I will not be late for class."

The night air washed over them as they emerged into its soupy arms. The parking lot loomed under hazy light poles, as ominous as some horror movie.

K.D. touched Trip's arm. "Thanks for the rescue. Guess I'll see you Thursday." The day sat heavy on her shoulders.

"Nuh uh, not so fast."

"Nuh uh? What are you, twelve?"

"You owe me an Espresso Con Panna, grande I might add." Trip grinned under the stingy light. He actually looked twelve, with tossed brown hair left askew from a hand running through it every other second during class.

"For what?" She played dumb, knowing full well she owed him the coffee, but unsure how she'd pay for it.

Trip lowered his laptop case to the sidewalk, folding his arms. Shirt sleeves rolled up. Just enough hair on his arms to scream masculinity and not Sasquatch.

"You're not getting out of this one, Jennings. You bet me last class I'd be unable to answer one of Elliott's questions directly. And what did he ask me?"

"How can the nonmoving party avoid summary judgment?"

"And I said…" Trip's tone indicated he clearly enjoyed the conversation.

K.D. sighed, eyes up at the star-soaked night and mumbled, "You said the nonmoving party must do more than simply show some metaphysical doubt as to material facts."

Trip took her chin in his fingers, moving her head to look him in the eyes. "I'm sorry. I couldn't quite understand what you said."

K.D. squared her shoulders at his grinning face. "You heard exactly what I said. You were right. I lost the bet. But you gotta settle for McDonald's Café instead of Starbucks. Unless you can wait 'til pay day."

Trip grinned. "What are you twelve?"

She picked up his laptop case and pulled him toward the

parking lot. "McDonald's beats Starbucks in taste tests anyway. Least that's what the commercials say. Come on, there's one right around the corner. We'll walk."

"Yes ma'am. But I don't want to talk school. Let's leave our stuff in the cars."

Not talk school? K.D. forced her feet to keep moving. What would they talk about if not about summary judgments and movant behaviors? She thought she remembered Trip being an athlete, tennis or golf or something, two more sports about which she knew nothing. Cute ditties about life at home were out. Nobody wanted to hear about her easing into the front door, ear cocked, wondering if Mom had bathed that day or spent hours watching reruns of *One Day at a Time* on DVD, the full set purchased off HSN when K.D. wasn't looking. Or of her childhood friend Annie and the escapades they'd encounter roaming the woods through the trailer park. Good memories. It would be even better ones if Annie were a real person and not the neighbor's dog.

Trip shut the door of his Audi convertible, locking it with a button on the key chain. "Aren't you going to put your satchel up?"

"No, I'll take it with me. Somebody's gotta finance this expensive outing." She glanced over at her rusted Chevy at the darkened end of the lot.

The two walked along the sidewalk, away from the former elementary school that now housed the Franklin Abram Brantley School of Law. Although a thirty-minute haul from her house, FAB was the only portal she could afford to a better life. Well, at least to the maximum credit card limit. Her low-rent undergraduate degree just about put her under, taking years to pay off, and now here she started all over again, older than most of her classmates. Definitely older than Trip.

Though this time, she'd emerge a lawyer. Maybe she could buy a camisole and embroider the letter "J" on the bodice so she could cloak herself in justice every day.

"What's so funny?"

K.D. kept smiling. "Nothing." She tilted her head, looking up at Trip. "Say, what's a fancy guy like you doing in a place like this?"

"Are you coming onto me, Jennings?"

She laughed out loud. "Does a frog have wings and only jump to itch his butt?"

"I don't get it."

"Me? Come onto you? That would be a no. Seriously, you have money. Nobody finances Polo shirts and foreign convertibles to show off at the FAB. Why aren't you at Cumberland or the University of Alabama? Or Harvard for that matter?"

The two moved through a darkened patch of sidewalk, into more streetlights. The yellow glow circled Trip's head, and K.D. noticed a scar along his eyebrow. She made a mental note to dredge it out later should she reach a conversational abyss. Crickets chirped through the alleyways between buildings as they navigated the chopped-up concrete. A few cars drove down the highway of an otherwise slightly larger than small town.

"I could, I guess, but I hated asking my uncle to pay for it. Cumberland would be about thirty-five grand a year. I mean, he could afford it and all, but I hated to ask. Not that FAB's much cheaper, but at least I can live with him and save that way. My aunt's the one who insisted on the new car." He paused and pulled at his shirt, "the name-brand clothes. They couldn't have children so now they get to be parents to a twenty-seven year old."

Twenty-seven. So Trip was only a year younger than she was.

"Your aunt and uncle?"

Trip glanced down at K.D. "I guess we really don't know much about each other, do we? I mean aside from the fact you made a 34 on your ACT and sailed through your LSATs while I took mine twice before setting a score. Other than that, I don't know anything about you. How'd you end up at FAB? With your brain, you probably could have gotten a scholarship anywhere."

She thought of the crumpled up applications, a future on the other end of quality education left for the garbage man to pick up. "Too many obligations here. FAB will do fine for the kind of law I'll have to practice."

"What law is that?"

Survival, she thought. Out loud, she said, "This and that. I wouldn't have the money for living expenses if I moved somewhere else. Guess I'm lucky FAB is close enough I can live at home even if they don't offer financial support." She paused and looked up at Trip. "Hey, do you know how to tell if it's cold outside?"

"There you go again."

"There I go again what?"

"Whenever the conversation gets too personal, you start making jokes."

"I do not"

"Yes you do. I asked you one time what your favorite game was to play as a kid. I told you mine was Battleship. You answered by asking me how you can tell the difference between a monkey and a preacher."

"I can't help it if I have a sense of humor, Trip." K.D. kept her eyes ahead, her tone light in spite of the arrow hanging off the truth.

"Okay, I'll play along. How do you tell if it's cold outside?"

"If the lawyer has his hands in his own pockets." She glanced ahead. "Guess it was funnier in my brain. Come on. Let's get you some caffeine so I can drill you some more on Rule 56(c)." K.D. churned long legs across the McDonald's parking lot.

Trip half jogged to keep up. "Nuh uh. No law school conversation. My brain can't take anymore. Do they have lattes at Mickey D's or is it straight black mud?"

"Probably just mud. Would serve you right for being so smug. Come on, you can tell me more about this benevolent uncle of yours."

Trip grinned. The man always smiled. "Only if you tell me what your initials stand for."

K.D. narrowed her eyes at him and walked through the door, fighting the urge to turn around and run.

CHAPTER

4

The cashier took their order with a pop of gum and a roll of the eyes. K.D. didn't blame her. Late weeknights at McDonald's could have been her only option as well, but K.D. slugged through debt and a not-so-perfect home life to make sure that didn't happen.

She hauled the satchel onto the counter, digging for her wallet when Trip finished paying for their order.

"Wait a minute. You won the bet, fair and square. I'm a woman of my word, and it's my time to pay."

"My mama would haunt my dreams if I ever let a lady pay for a meal. Besides, it's enough to hear you admit to losing. Even I'm not mean enough to make you pay on top of that."

K.D. laughed. "Well in that case, I'll take an order of fries and change that water to a large Dr Pepper."

Trip handed over the extra bills, and the mascara-smudged cashier returned his change with a tattooed hand. The two made their way through the almost-empty restaurant, choosing a booth several down from an older man sipping coffee and reading a newspaper. Trip jumped back up almost immediately to retrieve their order, returning with his coffee and K.D.'s snack.

"I'll share my fries. It's the least I can do since I was supposed to pay anyway."

"No thanks. My aunt cooked a ginormous meal before class. I appreciate her doing that, but man it makes staying awake pretty difficult. Roast, new potatoes, gravy, field peas. I don't think I'll eat for days."

K.D.'s stomach rumbled in memory of the apple she ate for breakfast. She ran late for court and then in walked the so-called case of a lifetime, eating up her afternoon and leaving no seconds for her own lunch. Oh well, she could afford to miss a few meals. K.D. pulled in her stomach, reaching for a fry.

"Tell me about this aunt and uncle of yours. You said something about your mom haunting your dreams. I mean, I guess I don't mean to pry."

Trip's eyes clouded, and he looked away.

"I'm sorry," K.D. stammered. "I do that all the time. My boss tells me I need to think before I speak, but sometimes the words run out way too fast for my brain to catch up."

"Yeah, you're real good about getting into other people's business while not disclosing any of your own."

"Touché. You wanna tell me about your family?"

Trip added some cream and sugar to his coffee before speaking. "It's okay. It still seems like a bad dream. My parents were killed in a car accident. Actually, it was the night of my college graduation about five years ago. They had taken me out to dinner. A drunk ran a red light and suddenly, I became an orphan at twenty-two years old." Trip stirred his coffee as if searching for an answer in the swirling of cream into black.

K.D.'s thoughts circled her head, scrambling to find the right words to say at such a tender moment. "I'm sure sorry about that." She wished she were better in these times, more feminine and empathetic, but her crowded life didn't leave room for thoughtful responses.

The man in the booth turned a page of his newspaper and tattoo girl took another straggler's order while Trip seemed lost in his coffee. Finally, he cleared his throat. "Thanks. They were good people. Gone way too soon. Bad thing was, they had a lot of debt I didn't know about. Debt accumulated from paying for my college tuition. Life insurance took care of it, but didn't leave anything for law school. I worked for a few years, trying to save enough money. That's when my uncle stepped in."

A group of teenagers, or maybe early twenties, entered the door beside their booth, obviously drunk. One girl sauntered by them in a mini-skirt, determined to leave little to the imagination. The girl winked at Trip with long-lashed eyes, smiling with cherry-painted lips. Trip glanced at her legs, following them as she walked by. K.D. felt the roll of belly over her waistband and dropped the French fry in her hand.

A cleared throat regained his attention. "So you moved down here to be with your uncle. Where are you from?"

"We're all from up North. My aunt and uncle moved several years ago to Alabama, wanting a warmer climate. When my parents died, my uncle offered to pay for any law school I wanted to attend. There was one big problem."

"What's that?" The French fries sung to K.D., but she resisted as the long-legged mini-skirted hussy seemed to smirk at her over Trip's shoulder.

"Not everyone graduates summa cum laude from college like someone I know." Trip reached over and grabbed a fry, pointing it at K.D. before taking a bite.

"I should have never told you that." She smiled at the back of the young girl. She might have long, thin legs, but K.D. had a few brain cells. Pretty smart ones at that. She grabbed a fry and took a bite.

"Well, my LSAT scores didn't leave many options for law school. It seemed logical to enroll at FAB since my uncle and aunt live here. It's not that bad a drive. What about you? Why would someone as smart as you end up at FAB?"

K.D. widened her eyes, almost choking. She swallowed some Dr Pepper, wondering how to redirect the conversation away from her. This was not the time to come clean on all the dust bunnies in the closet. The cluster of teenagers took care of it for her when an amorphous guy in a letterman's jacket bumped their booth, knocking K.D.'s shoulder and causing her to spill the drink all over her blouse.

Trip immediately jumped up. "Hey, buddy. Shouldn't you apologize to the lady?"

K.D. grabbed his arm. "Trip, it's okay. Come on."

The linebacker wannabe turned, hitting a trash bin, beer fumes shooting from his mouth. "What's that, Preppy?" He spoke with a lisp, either from alcohol consumption or the missing front tooth.

"I said, you knocked over my friend's drink. At the very least you owe her an apology."

The guy turned a bald head to the group. "Preppy here says I owe this little lady an apology. Wadda y'all think 'bout that?"

Miss Hoochy America grabbed his tree-trunk arms, apparently the only one of the group with any sense, because the six others hooted for "Meat" to kick his tail. "Come on, Meat. This guy's not worth it. Be like swatting a skeeter." But she batted her eyes at Trip while delivering the insult.

K.D. stood. "Look, Mr. Meat. Why don't you and your juvenile delinquent friends join arms and skip away on the Yellow Brick Road, destination Oz, and look for your brains, courage, and hearts along the way. Your predisposition of size and strength obviously left little room for neurological activity, synapses blended together with sinew and muscles in steroidic retardation, allowing impulses to slide off into an abyss of testosteronic proportions."

K.D. pushed on his arm while Meat seemed two sentences behind her, nudging him and the group out the door. "Go on. Put one group of metatarsals in front of the other. Go on, you can do it." The group seemed mesmerized by K.D.'s high-dollar words. As the door closed on them, Meat asked, "What's a meta, meteeta, you know, what she said?"

Trip sat down at the booth. "I could have had him, you know."

K.D. joined him, grabbed some napkins and blotted her already water-stained blouse. "I'm sure you could have, Lancelot. But I'm afraid both of us would have ended up another grease stain on the floor. Alcohol and steroids don't blend well together. Makes for a very Goliath-like approach to argument resolutions."

Trip leaned back in the booth as chivalry and common sense wrestled inside him. "I wish you would have let me handle it."

"Think of it as good cop/bad cop. You came in, threatened him with physical violence. I countered by confusing his miniscule brain with big words. Between the two of us, our friend Meat had no chance. I'd say we made a pretty good team."

Trip smiled, and K.D. relaxed. Having grown up the better part of her life with only her mom, she was inexperienced in soothing the male ego.

"Speaking of big words. Testeronic? Steroidic?"

"You've never heard of testeronic? It's the highest level of testosterone the body can maintain." K.D. swiped the rest of her almost-cold fries to hide her smile.

"I may not be as smart as you, but even I know there is no such word as testeronic or steroidic."

"Yeah, but poor Meat would never know that." K.D. bore an arm down into her satchel, searching for her cell phone. Seeing a missed call and the dwindling hour, she said, "I need to step outside for a minute and make a phone call."

"Sure. I'll meet you out front."

K.D. put her trash into the paper bag and wadded it up to throw away. Stepping outside, she sat on a concrete bench and dialed home. One ring. Two rings. Three rings. "Come on, Mama," K.D. pleaded.

"Hello?"

K.D. exhaled. "Hey Mama. I'm sorry I didn't call after class, but I decided to stop for a Dr Pepper before driving home. How are you?"

A TV show blared in the background, but K.D. couldn't decipher the program. "Fine fine. I took Sophia for a walk after dinner. I can't believe how hot it is, even at night. When I got home, I got worried about you when you didn't call. I hate you driving those back roads so late at night. Reminded me of when I hollered myself hoarse for you as a child when the streetlights came on."

Lydia Jennings sounded lucid, in control, even upbeat. Not the sad, desperate voice reaching out from the pit of manic depression. K.D. hated leaving her alone, but had no alternative. Their Shih-Tzu Sophia provided companionship, but it wasn't like she could dial 911 if Mom tried to kill herself again. She squeezed her eyes shut to a childhood memory of slashed wrists and blood. Days later, she came home from school to a mom crumpled on the floor with bandaged wrists and no husband. He'd taken off when the weight grew unbearable.

K.D. didn't have the luxury.

"I know. I'm real sorry. We had a big opportunity come to the office today so Ingram had me tied up with that." And a two-year-old screaming baby named Gabby. "Then I was late for class. Anyway, I'm finishing up now and about to head home."

"Okay, honey. Drive carefully. I'll try to wait up."

"No, don't worry about that. I'll wake you up when I get home. Okay?"

"Okay. I will. I love you, baby."

Tears moistened K.D.'s eyes. Baby. She couldn't remember the last time she felt like a baby or even like a child. Probably the day her daddy walked out for good, leaving a little girl struggling with third grade math in charge of a woman who wouldn't get out of bed to pack her lunch.

"Love you too, Mama." Trip exited the McDonald's, refreshed coffee in one hand and a drink in the other. "I gotta go. I'll be home in a few." K.D. hit the call end button and turned.

He handed K.D. the Dr Pepper. "Thought I'd refresh your drink since our buddy decided your blouse was thirstier than you."

"Thanks."

The two walked in silence, sipping their sodas, content to let the thick air envelope body and thought. Trip touched K.D.'s arms, moving her to his other side, away from the road. She smiled, thinking his mama sure raised a proper gentleman, one quick to stand against injustice or drunken football players.

Then her heart weighted a bit, considering his mama didn't wait for him at home as hers did. Even with her health issues, the days of lucidity were better than having no mama at all. Her arms were accessible, her touch a reach away. Even in a depressed state, K.D. would often crawl into her mama's bed as a child, burrowing under a thin arm until it rested on her hip, sleeping under a mother's touch.

She chanced a glance at Trip whose eyes remained steeled ahead as if lost in memories. His brown hair lifted in the humid breeze, causing him to toss his head to the side to clear the vision. He sipped his coffee, streetlights illuminating soft lips and a strong jaw line. The scar ruined an otherwise perfect face. Well, that and ears which stuck out a little too far. He was lanky, thin and…solid. Not in build, but in character. Or so he seemed. K.D. knew from experience even the most solid men walked out on their families. She turned her head, allowing the headlights of oncoming traffic to radiate her thoughts into a million pieces.

Trip grabbed her arm. "Whoa, slow down."

"Sorry. I just need to get home. It's been a long day."

He looked down at her with kind eyes. "Why don't you tell me about it?"

K.D. shook her head. "I can't. I signed a document when I joined the firm I wouldn't discuss our cases outside the office unless with interested parties."

"Well, I'm interested."

K.D. smiled at him. "You know what I mean. But I will say this. We signed a case today that's gonna bury us for the next few months. Between work and studying, I'll be non-existent."

Trip laughed as they turned into the FAB parking lot, deserted save their two vehicles. "You mean non-existent as opposed to all the other opportunities we've had to spend time together outside class? You'd have to disappear altogether to threaten our almost non-existent friendship."

"True. But then again, how would you pass Civil Procedure if I disappeared all together?" They laughed together. "Thanks for the Dr Pepper. I'll see you next week."

"Hang on. I'll walk you to your car."

K.D.'s satchel slipped off her shoulder, causing her to keel over as it caught on the crook of her arm. "No, that's okay. You already passed your chivalronic duty tonight. I can walk across the parking lot by myself." She turned and walked away, reluctant for the evening to end, but knowing it must.

"There is no such word as chivalronic!" Trip yelled after her. K.D. waved a hand over her shoulder and kept walking, wishing he'd get in his car before she had to hip-bump hers to open the driver's side. She glanced back at him leaning against his convertible. Luckily, one bump freed the jam, and the car started on the second try. The fates lined with her side.

It was a good night.

CHAPTER

5

"Welcome to Waffle Iron!" The orange-shirted, pink-haired waitress sang out over a coffee pot as K.D. entered the swinging door. The smell of burgers and fries assaulted her nose while grease layered her skin within the first three steps into the building. "Have a seat, Hon, at one of them tables over there." She gestured to a few empty booths in the corner. "We'll be with ya in a sec."

K.D. slid into the booth, peeled off a napkin from the steel container, and wiped off the water rings on the tabletop. Drumming her nails, she turned her attention to the carwash out the window and watched a truck pull into one of the bins. A long-limbed cowboy hopped out, along with a mangy cur dog. He inserted some change, released the wand, and clumps of mud broke off the tire rims and swirled across the concrete. He sprayed water at the dog who yelped and barked, dancing around in circles.

"Can I help ya?"

K.D. looked up into punctuation lines of stress surrounding tired blue eyes. A stained, white rectangle badge stitched to an orange blouse read "Shelly Anne" with "thirteen years of service" below it.

Bingo.

"Mrs. Murdock?"

"How'd you know my name?"

K.D. stood and held out her hand. "I'm K.D. Jennings. I work at Ingram Law Firm, and your husband stopped by our office yesterday and acquired our services. Mr. Ingram sent me over to obtain your signature on the representation agreement. As administrator of your son's estate, we need your signature to proceed."

Shelly Anne looked over K.D.'s shoulder, seemingly lost in the car wash next door. K.D. turned to see what was so fascinating, only to watch the same cowboy call to his dog who hopped into the cab before the black Chevy drove off.

"Mrs. Murdock?"

Tear-rimmed eyes returned their attention to K.D. "I'm sorry. Bo had a truck like that. Only got to drive it a few months before… before." Misery swallowed the rest of the sentence.

K.D. reached out and touched her bare arm. "I'm so sorry for your loss."

Awkward silence followed until Shelly Anne cleared her throat. "Give me a few minutes. I'm due a break. Can I get ya some coffee or something?"

"A Dr Pepper'll be fine. Thanks." Suddenly the smothered, covered hash browns she craved yesterday didn't seem enticing. K.D. returned to her seat, staring out the window until Shelly Anne rejoined her with drinks.

The two sat in silence as K.D. sipped her Dr Pepper, and Shelly Anne stared into her coffee cup. Finally, unable to stand it any longer, K.D. spoke. "Like I said, we met with Buck yesterday. Given the fact your son was killed almost two years ago, we've got to act quickly. Statute of limitations expires at the two-year anniversary. My boss, Ezra Ingram, walked the suit over this morning to file at the courthouse, but we'll need your signature on the representation agreement in order to proceed." She reached into her bag and pulled out some papers. "I can wait while you glance through them now if you have time." Ingram had told her before he left for the courthouse not to return without the agreement.

Shelly Anne raised her coffee mug to her lips, but did not sip. Instead she pressed the cup against her chin as if the heat would burn her skin and remind her to breathe. Her eyes bore into K.D. without seeming to look at anything. They were a bold blue rimmed with sorrow. "Did Buck tell you that boy could run? I don't mean fast. I mean like lightning. Came out of the womb in a hurry to get somewhere. Once he landed on a football field, it was like he finally found traction, found his purpose. Hard to believe something you were born to do would be the very thing to take you away."

K.D. offered a small smile. "Your husband believes it was the ER doctor who killed your son, not football."

Shelly Anne lowered the cup, a small half-moon of red on her chin. "Whatever it was, he's gone. One minute, that giant of a boy kissed my cheek and told me he'd see me after practice. Seemed like a blink later, he was gone." She reached across the table and took the document, eyes roaming over the page.

She glanced up. "Looks pretty straight forward, but we're simple country folks. How do we know there's not some fancy lawyer speak in here, make us look stupid to our family and friends?"

Why did the word fancy keep cropping up in conversations with the Murdocks? As if any kind of higher education automatically put you on a greater social level than a Waffle Iron waitress. Guess she didn't notice the mended cuff of K.D.'s shirt or the fact that she wore no jewelry. She could tell her a story or two about gorging herself on muscadines because Mama didn't cook supper, one time so many she threw up for an hour.

Then again, every time she thought of obtaining a Juris Doctorate, she did feel a little fancy.

"We're not here to take advantage of you, Mrs. Murdock."

"Call me Shelly Anne."

"Shelly Anne. We live and work in this community just like you. The agreement is straightforward and from what we can tell from talking to your husband, we have a pretty good case. You don't pay any money out of pocket. We finance the lawsuit which, between you and me, can run us up in the $100,000 range. Mr. Ingram wouldn't pursue this if he didn't think he had a good chance of winning." K.D. barely squeaked out the $100,000 figure, still in disbelief as to how they'd come up with it.

Shelly Anne straightened in her seat, hardening her expression. "Oh, we must have a case. Right after Bo died, a lawyer, Mr. Cookson I think was his name, called us up, offering the same thing you are now. Called us the other day, as a matter of fact. Said he had medical people that worked in his office. Used the word expedite a lot. Said if we went with him, he could get us a settlement quicker and would spend more money than what you just said to make sure we got more money from that doctor. Why should we go with you and not him?"

Bart Cookson. The slimiest of ambulance chasers this side of the Mississippi and up to the Mason-Dixon Line. Ingram warned her they'd be hearing from him, but K.D. was shocked to hear he'd approach the Murdocks with the dirt still fresh on Bo's grave.

"I'm not here to rattle sabers with Mr. Cookson, Shelly Anne. All I can tell you is your husband approached us yesterday so he must believe in Mr. Ingram for a reason. We might not handle many cases like these," *or any cases* K.D. refrained from adding, "but I can promise you there's not a better attorney to serve you than Ezra Ingram."

Shelly Anne returned to the document for a few more minutes. "Fifty percent, huh? Buck said that Ingram fella mentioned he'd ask for a couple million. Seems like a lot of money you be makin' off my boy." Her voice sounded skeptical, and K.D. wasn't sure if that was directed at the estimated settlement or the fact that they'd get fifty percent. Either way Shelly Anne sounded offended.

"The fee is standard, Mrs. Murdock." K.D. tried to keep her tone neutral, but failed. As much as she sympathized with the woman, she wouldn't sit by and let her insinuate Ingram was greedy in his fee. Especially when he'd be hocking about everything he owned to finance the trial.

Shelly Anne frowned at her, about to speak when someone hollered her name. "Register's stuck again," the Pepto-Bismol-haired waitress hollered over the sound of grease splatters.

"I'll be right back." Shelly Anne exited the booth, straightening the brown polyester skirt and patting down wisps of drugstore-blonde hair escaping from the paper hat with the letters WI in front.

Please don't let my big mouth screw this up. K.D. sent up a prayer, knowing she probably ruined the case with her direct tone before it ever started. Shelly Anne had looked at her with gamma ray eyes as if ticked off by her defense of Ingram.

A few minutes later, Shelly Anne eased back into the booth, and K.D. held up a hand. "Mrs. Murdock, please forgive me if I offended…"

"I said call me Shelly Anne."

"Shelly Anne, I apologize. Sometimes my mouth works too fast for my brain."

"Nothing wrong with that. Over thinking things is what can get us in trouble sometimes, keep us from doing the first thing on our hearts to do. You're loyal. I like that." Shelly Anne took out a pen and tapped it against the counter a few times, chewing on her lip. "The thing is, I wasn't questioning how much your firm wanted from the settlement or even how much the settlement would be."

"A half-million dollars is a lot of money for your family, Shelly Anne."

Ocean-blue eyes, whites raked with red, looked hard at K.D. "Money don't bring back my boy. How do you put a price on someone so special? I'd sell my soul to smell his dirty football uniform again, to feel his sweaty hair against my face when he'd kiss me after practice. Hold him one more time. Tell him I love him. You can't put money on that, Miss Jennings."

K.D. was surprised to find tears in her own eyes and blinked rapidly. She couldn't remember the last time she cried. "No, I suppose you can't. Must mean a lot to have little Gabby."

"Why is it people say that? She was a year old when Bo died and half my church would say 'Thank God you have Gabby.' Like one child takes the place of another. What a stupid thing to say."

"Stupid or not, she gave you something to live for." K.D. didn't mean to sound so harsh.

Shelly Anne picked back up her coffee, this time taking a sip. "You're right about that. I'd a thrown myself in the ground with Bo if it weren't for Gabby. I'll never forget when I found out I was pregnant with her, I cried and cried right there in that bathroom, holding onto one of them test sticks you pee on. Must have stayed in there thirty minutes before someone came looking for me. I was thirty-five years old. What business did I have with another baby?" She told K.D. how Buck picked her up and twirled her around upon hearing the news. "Bo was even worse. Said he couldn't wait to have a little sister to spoil. You couldn't convince him it would be a boy. He named her Gabrielle. After the angel Gabriel."

"She's sure got a voice you could hear from heaven."

Shelly Anne smiled at her. "Buck told me y'all took a few minutes to warm up to each other. But said he about had to peel her off you when he left. Guess you got a way with kids."

K.D. snorted. "Hardly. More like I get away from kids as quickly as possible. I almost dropped her when I gave her back to him. But she's awfully cute. I can see how she'd be something to live for."

Shelly Anne's gaze turned toward the window again, the mid-afternoon sun washing over a face too old for her age. With a sigh, she clicked her pen and signed her name to the document, sliding it across the table to K.D.

"My husband needs this more than me. I don't really care who's to blame, you know? I got no animosity toward that doctor. It's not like he took a gun out and shot my boy. But Buck needs somewhere to point the finger. Somewhere to direct all his rage. Maybe when this is over, we can figure out how to be a family again." She paused for a minute and then smiled for the first time. "I think I'm gonna like you. I'm sick to death of everyone treating me like I'm gonna break. Like I'm some fractured crystal that will fall apart if someone says the wrong thing. You don't strike me as someone who'll do that."

"I can guarantee you I'll say the wrong thing twice in one breath, Shelly Anne. You can bet your waffle iron on that. But I'll always speak the truth."

Shelly Anne laughed, a small one. "Is that all you need from me?"

K.D. already liked her back. "Yep. Mr. Ingram will be in touch soon. He'll need to meet with both you and your husband to go over the events of the day. Also, we'll need to get both your signatures on a release for the hospital records."

"How long's all this gonna take?"

"Hard to say."

It was hard to say because K.D. had no idea, having never participated in a wrongful death suit, but she kept that piece of news to herself. "I do know they will try to drag this out, hoping to outlast us. The insurance attorneys have deep pockets, Shelly Anne. They'll bury us in a minutia of paper, ninety percent of which we'll never use. And then, when we persevere, they'll throw some dollar figures out, hoping it will all go away. But if everything your husband said can be backed up with evidence, we'll make them pay, and more importantly keep this doctor from ever hurting another kid." K.D. hoped Shelly Anne didn't watch any *Law and Order* reruns, because she was pretty sure most of her answer came from one of the episodes.

"Well, you got my signature. Guess that means we're here to help however we can." She stood, once again adjusting the waistline of her skirt. "I gotta get back to work. Can I get you another Dr Pepper?"

K.D. rattled the ice in her cup. "Sure. And how 'bout some

smothered/covered while you're at it." Once Shelly Anne signed the document, the knots inside K.D.'s stomach untied, leaving a gnawing growl.

"You got it. Be right back."

Placing the documents back in the satchel, K.D. settled into the booth, thinking the last thing she needed was hash browns covered in cheese, but wanting some comfort in calories following the heartbreaking conversation.

Ingram would laugh out loud when she told him she had made a friend. K.D. smiled over at Shelly Anne as she walked toward the table with a plate full of feel-good, placing it down. She also handed K.D. a piece of torn paper with an address and directions scribbled in black pen. "You come on out to the house tomorrow around noon; bring anything we need to go over. That Mr. Ingram's welcome too. I always cook a big lunch on Saturdays. Come break some bread with us."

K.D. thought about two cases she had to review before Tuesday's class, each over seventy-five pages. "I'd love to."

Shelly Anne smiled before turning away, her true beauty peeking around the corner of sadness.

K.D. took a bite of hash browns, about to close her eyes as the cheese melted in her mouth, when in walked Trip with all ninety pounds of Delilah Henry, the student Professor Elliott about hacked to death last class. The food lodged in her throat when Trip held the door open for an older lady behind him, none other than Lydia Jennings, K.D.'s mom, who smiled and waved at her.

CHAPTER

6

"Honey, you okay?" Lydia rushed over to K.D., pounding her on the back as K.D. hacked and spewed hash browns into her napkin. Trip and Delilah stared over her mother's shoulder as K.D. waved them off.

She tried to answer that she was fine, only the semi-blocked wind pipe would not permit any noise. Tears streamed down her face as she tried to communicate with her hands to no avail.

"Here, drink some water." Trip leaned around her mom, thrusting a glass at her that was given by the pink-haired waitress. Everyone in the Waffle Iron seemed to have stopped to watch K.D.'s spiral into death. She did as she was told and swallowed a small sip of water which seemed to temper the cough-o-rama.

Lydia smoothed the curls off K.D.'s forehead and took the seat across from her, handing her a napkin. Delilah said something about the bathroom and walked off. Trip glanced from her mom to her as if expecting an introduction, only K.D. still couldn't talk so she waved a hand between the two.

Her mom smiled up at Trip. "She does this all the time, would choke on Jell-O as a child. Hello, I'm K.D.'s mother, Lydia Jennings."

For someone who three days ago wouldn't open a curtain, Lydia might as well have been receiving guests at Tara today. Trip, of course, offered his hand, sandwiching her frail one between his. After he let go, Lydia pulled down her sleeves to cover the scars on her wrists. "It's a pleasure to meet you, Mrs. Jennings. I'm Trip Folsom. K.D. lets me cheat off of her in law school."

Finally, K.D. found her voice after another sip of water. "Mom, what are you doing here?"

"I stopped by your office to see if you wanted to go to lunch, but I can see your lunch about did you in, sugah."

K.D. loved the sound of her mother's Deep South dialect, melodic and smooth, like a lullaby. Before her daddy left, when life ebbed and flowed in normalcy, Lydia would read K.D. stories at bedtime, the hum of *Goodnight Moon* lolling her into dreams of happily ever afters, her dad down the hall asleep in front of the cop series on television. "Resting my eyes," he'd always say before dozing off.

K.D. pushed her plate away, tossed her head toward Trip. "Trip's right, you know. He does cheat off me in class."

Delilah rejoined the group, lipstick freshly applied. "Are you okay, K.D.? That choking business is nothing to play with. I once had to do a Heimlich maneuver on a kid while I was a lifeguard. I *told* his mama he shouldn't swim while eating a hotdog."

K.D. could just imagine Delilah as Miss America, standing on stage and warning the world against the dangers of throwing Oscar Meyer into the pool. K.D. stopped her eyes from rolling around her sockets. "What brings you two here?"

"We're preparing for Tuesday's case. We thought it would be a good idea to role play, try to anticipate which obscure words Professor Elliott will scream at us, demanding the definition."

K.D. laughed. "Yeah, like 'What does *mean*, mean, Jennings?'"

"Exactly." Trip laughed with her. "I tried to call you, but you didn't answer. You want to join us? Wouldn't hurt to have three people yelling at the same time."

K.D. watched Delilah's face prune into a frown. She almost accepted to see if the girl would break out in tears. "No, I have to get back to work." She grabbed her purse, gesturing to her mom to join her. "Mom, you want to order something to go?"

Her mom looked between her and Trip with an unreadable expression. "No, I really wasn't that hungry. I had to go by the post office, and I thought I'd spend some time with you before I went back home." Lydia glanced at her watch. "I'll give you a ride back to the office unless you brought your car."

"Sure, I walked so a ride sounds good in this heat." K.D. turned back to Trip, forcing her eyes on the almost perfect couple. Trip was dressed in pressed khakis and a pin-striped button down and Delilah sported a sundress, seemingly unaffected by the heat. "Y'all have fun. I'll see you Tuesday."

Trip snorted. "Yeah, some kinda fun. Just make sure you're prepared too or who else is going to slide me her notebook when Elliott calls on me?"

They said their goodbyes to the couple as her mom exited to wait outside, and K.D. walked to the register to pay, asking Shelly Anne for the ticket.

"Naw, hash browns are on me. Besides, you didn't eat more than a bite. I'll see you out at the house tomorrow. You got the directions?"

K.D. nodded, holding up the note. "I do. Ingram will be delighted to know I won't expense my lunch today. I'll see you tomorrow around noon."

K.D. joined her mom as the mid-afternoon sun slapped them in the face. Lydia sighed. "Gracious, this heat's brutal. Come on, my car's down this way."

K.D. glanced at Lydia's smooth face, and the usual worry knot between her eyes loosened. K.D. looped her arm through her mom's. "I'm glad you came into town, Mama. You feeling good?"

"Are you asking if I took my medicine?"

K.D. felt chagrined, but nodded.

"Yes, I took my medicine. I was a good girl. As soon as I got up, I immediately turned on all the lights, drank a cup of coffee and even did that yoga DVD for about twenty minutes before I felt like my hip was about to pop out. How that Trudy Styler does those moves at her age is beyond me."

K.D. squeezed her arm. "I'm glad, Mama. When I get home later, we'll take Sophia on a walk, spend some time together. How's that sound?" She dropped into Lydia's broken-down Ford sedan, the heat almost melting her into the vinyl seats.

Lydia slipped into the driver's side, lifting her bare legs off the seat. She pulled a ragged towel from the back and placed it under her rear. A turn of the ignition brought a blast of hot, then cold air, and Lydia looked at K.D. with an all-knowing expression.

"What?" K.D. squirmed in her seat with no idea why she felt guilty.

"Why're you making all these plans to walk your mama around the block on a Friday night? You should march yourself right back into that Waffle Iron and kidnap that nice young man. What was his name? Trip?"

K.D. rolled her eyes, gesturing for her mom to move on. She wouldn't spend Friday night with Trip because he hadn't asked. Not that she would if he did. The first day she had walked into class, she checked the seating chart, and saw him next to her assigned seat. Their first argument over intra-state taxation sealed her affections, especially when he threw a cup of ice at her in defeat but with a smile. Secret feelings locked inside; the key thrown away. Trip's type remained a stratosphere away from her reach. Best that way. K.D. could feel sweat collect under her breasts, meandering down to the rolls on her stomach. Delilah probably never sweated in her life.

Plus K.D. knew the drill. Lydia may sound all encouraging now, but even the slightest hint K.D. ventured toward a life of her own sent her mom into a downward spiral of dependency, making relationships futile at best.

Lydia tried to wait her out, but when K.D. remained quiet, she reversed from the parking space. The two drove in silence for the few blocks to K.D.'s office. Lydia waved at everyone she passed;

having grown up in the town she sometimes went weeks without stepping foot on its sidewalks. Lately she seemed to rally, so much it seemed permanent. Not the uber-fanatical happiness which arched out of the mindless, dark days of depression, but more of an even peace, a hammock swing as compared to a roller coaster.

"What's on your agenda today, Mom?"

"I told Doris I'd help her organize the pantry. She got a hold of some Sunday papers and cut out all the coupons. Apparently there was a major buy-one-get-one on canned goods down at the Piggly Wiggly so she loaded up."

K.D. snorted. "Good ol' Doomsday Doris. I wonder if she's ever going to accept she has no control over the Apocalypse."

Lydia stared ahead with eyes gone to another place for a second. "Don't laugh at Doris, honey. Some folks only have the end to look forward to. At least it gives them something to plan for, some sort of purpose."

K.D. chewed on the thought, nodding her head. Doris and Lydia, as different in appearance as Mutt and Jeff, but each waiting for the end to come. Doris by stocking up her pantry with butter beans, and Lydia by pulling the covers over her head.

Shaking off the melancholy, K.D. said, "Sounds like a blast. Organizing canned peaches with Doris. Hate I have to miss it."

Sunshine splintered through age-old oaks which lined the main street of town. Low-slung tin roofs from a hair salon and café, with decades of rust, shadowed men playing checkers. Homes integrated the town, some operating beauty parlors through the front door. Children ran in sprinklers on the thirsty lawns of ranch-style homes while dogs trotted with tongues lolling out of their mouths. Time stood still in small-town Alabama, especially when the heat pressed down.

They drove past the high school and the football team taking a water break. Sweat poured down red faces as the boys in white practice jerseys kneeled on the chewed-up earth. One kid dumped an orange drink over his head. K.D. made a mental note to watch practice one day and talk to Coach What's His Name.

Lydia cleared her throat as she pulled in front of Ingram's building. "Well? You gonna tell me about this boy?"

K.D. collected her purse. "Mom, if you think there's something between me and Trip, you're like a tone-deaf kid in a singing competition."

"I don't get your jokes."

"You're wasting your time, Mama." K.D. leaned over and kissed her cheek.

Lydia waved her off with a laugh. "You are a silly girl, but K.D., listen to me, sugah. You don't have to put your life on hold for me. I'm going to get myself together." Her voice sounded confident even if it wavered a bit, her blue eyes clear and rested.

K.D. got out of the car, but leaned in through the open window. "I know you are, Mama. You're doing great, and I'm proud of you. But seriously, there's nothing between me and Trip. Miss Delilah Saves the World From Processed Meat over there is much more his type. We're just friends. Now, go on and get. I love you." She pushed off from the car and marched into the office before her mama could say another word. She heard the Ford's whine as Lydia reversed out of the parking space and chugged away.

K.D. yanked on the ancient door, her stomach rumbling in response to the smells emanating from the Chinese restaurant. Mrs. Gonzales waved from inside, so K.D. decided to expense some Sesame Chicken instead of the discarded Waffle Iron hash browns.

She held up a finger and hurried down the hall to make sure no one sat in the office reception room, not that they ever did. Finding it empty, she returned to the restaurant and placed her order, calling out, "Maria Gonzales! The only Mexican I know who cooks the best Chinese in the world!"

The squatty Hispanic woman flicked the towel at her after punching the keys on the register. "Now, K.D. I am the *only* person who cooks best Chinese. Ahora, desea un sweet tea con su comida?"

"Does a mosquito like a fat girl? Of course I want a sweet tea with my lunch." K.D. sat on the bar stool. "Where is everybody?"

"Slow day today. Your Mister Ingram has not even come to yell at me. Hang on one second. I'll be right back." She disappeared through the kitchen door, screaming at her husband to "dejar de ser tan vago!" K.D. picked out the word lazy, but little else from her rusty high school Spanish.

K.D. felt guilty, knowing Ingram was probably buried in the Murdock case. She stood when Maria returned.

"What? You not gonna eat with me?"

"I can't. Ingram and I are starting a new case, and I can't get behind. Plus I've got a lot of catching up to do for school. But give me a receipt. I'm gonna make Ingram pay for my lunch."

Maria wagged a finger at her. "You work too much. Spend too much time with your madre. Sin vida para alguien tan joven. You need a man."

"I understood the first and last, but not the middle."

"You, er, um, too little to have no life. I saw your madre ayer. She looks good. Good enough you get your own life."

K.D. gestured toward her ample hips. "Nothing little here, Mrs. Gonzales."

"No, not little. Young. You too young to have no life."

K.D. moved toward the door with a wave. Why did everyone have to nose-dive into her business? Maria Gonazales always seasoned her food with heavy doses of sympathy, loosening K.D.'s tongue on more than one occasion. She'd have to guard her words next time. "I hear you. Now I gotta go work so I can actually finance this life I don't have. See you later." She eased down the hall and into the office, one ear cocked for Ingram's bellows for taking too long with Shelly Anne Murdock. Hearing nothing, K.D. lowered her satchel beside the desk and opened the Styrofoam box of Sesame Chicken.

She bit into its savory goodness, allowing the sauce to coat the back of her throat before chasing it down with a swallow of tea. Mrs. Gonzales was right. She *was* the best Chinese cook in the whole world, not just one of Hispanic descent. K.D. had no idea what brought the tiny Mexican woman across the border, or what possessed her to open a Chinese restaurant, but right now, eating the bursting piñata of spices rolling around her mouth, she would have carried her over the Rio Grande herself if it meant eating these goods. Probably why K.D.'s pants left a red imprint around her waistline by the end of the day. K.D. took another bite. She could always do the yoga video with her mother tomorrow.

Wiping her hands, she opened the copy of the suit she had proofed hours earlier. Pretty straightforward. The plaintiff, Mr. and Mrs. Eugene "Buck" Murdock, alleged Dr. Jackson Thomas of County General Hospital acted with gross negligence resulting in the death of Eugene "Bo" Murdock Jr. K.D. had been impressed with Ingram's medical speak, using words she had to look up earlier when she read the suit. She had tried to praise him, but he was in such a hurry to get to the courthouse he merely hollered, "Get that Murdock woman's signature today so we can move forward," before slamming out of the office.

A rattling sound echoed down the hall, causing K.D. to jump after thinking she was alone. She took another bite of lunch, grabbed a napkin, and walked down the hall to see if Ingram wanted to share the takeout. His door cracked, K.D. eased it open, widening her eyes as two people jumped apart from the front of Ingram's desk.

"Oh, sorry Ingram, Ms. Ingram. I didn't realize anyone was here."

Ingram's ex-wife grimaced as her hands flew to her throat, fiddling with a strand of pearls. "Hello, um, Miss Jennings. Mr. Ingram and I were going over the terms of the eviction notice. He was, um, just, you know…" her voice trailed off as she looked to Ingram for rescue.

His face held a look in stark contrast to his ex-wife's embarrassed state. A haughty smile spread from ear to ear as he threw back his shoulders in ram-rod posture. "Madeline stopped by to give me another eviction notice. I was sharing with her the details of our upcoming lawsuit, propositioning her to see if she'd offer an extension."

"Propositioning?" K.D. cocked an eyebrow.

Ingram shook his head. "Not propositioning. Proposal. I offered a proposal." He waved his hand at K.D. when she snickered.

Madeline looked as if she'd like to jump out the window. She walked to the loveseat and collected her royal blue jacket which matched her skirt. She always looked dressed for tea although K.D. wondered how many in a town of 2,500 actually took tea. From what Ingram shared, the woman had never worked a day in her life, yet she drove around each day in a 7- series BMW, dressed like a corporate executive.

"Ezra, I'll look over your proposal and let you know my decision next week." She brushed by K.D., finding airs somewhere between Ingram's lips and the door.

K.D. extended her napkin. "Here you go. Your lipstick's smeared a little on this side."

Madeline snatched the napkin from K.D.'s outstretched hand and marched out of the office.

Turning around with a whistle, K.D. said, "I was going to offer you some of my takeout, but from the looks of it, you might have already had a bite for lunch."

Ingram hiked up his pants in exaggeration and sat down, making a play for the pile of work on his desk. "I'm a lawyer, K.D. Lawyer's communicate. It's how we make a living. You find out what works, and you deploy the winning tactics. You don't learn that from your FAB Law School. You learn it from the school of hard knocks."

"Whatever you say."

Ingram ignored the remark. "You get those papers signed?"

K.D. nodded. "I'm starting a file up front." She handed him the lunch receipt.

"This isn't the Waffle Iron."

"You said you'd reimburse me for lunch. You didn't say it had to be at the Waffle Iron." She turned to walk out of the office. "If you had meant only the Waffle Iron, you should have said that, being the great communicator and all." Shutting the door to Ingram's grunt, K.D. whistled down the hall to finish her Sesame Chicken and study for Tuesday's class. She couldn't afford to get behind because once they had the release form signed for the medical records, she knew the deluge of work would begin.

At least that's what happened on *Law and Order*.

CHAPTER 7

The alarm screamed across the tiny bedroom, strategically out of reach from K.D.'s flailing arms as she reached to cut it off. Too early. Way too early for anybody to be up on a Saturday, but K.D. knew she had minimal time to read over the case for Tuesday's class and try to anticipate which areas or obscure words Professor Elliott would glass in on. She kicked off the covers before she could burrow into them, dropped her legs over the twin bed and stretched long arms over her head.

What twenty-eight-year-old woman still lived with her mother? K.D. needed a place of her own. Or at the very least an upgrade from the twin bed she'd slept in since childhood. She'd ventured out once, trolling neighborhoods for affordable rentals, but price tags and obligations sent her scurrying back. Shag carpet now tickled her toes as she walked across the room to turn off the alarm.

Law school came first, though; K.D.'s only way to a better life was not only for herself, but for her mother too. The medication consumed the greater part of a monthly budget, but without it, her mother either stayed in bed for a week or charged everything she saw on the Home Shopping Network. K.D. would spend days returning things like dozens of cooking knives and facial scrubs.

Trendy clothes and a new comforter would wait. Grandma's hand-stitched quilt would do till then. Faded, worn, but functional.

Kind of like her life right now.

Rather than battle the hair knots, K.D. pulled the blonde mass into a ponytail, brushed her teeth and splashed cold water on her face. She changed into sweats and walked down the carpeted hall to the kitchen, not too far a journey in a single-wide trailer, and poured a cup of coffee her mom remembered to set the night before. Feeling the caffeine nudge her brain cells to function, K.D. folded onto the plaid couch, opened her case book, and began to read about when it was fair to subject a corporation to personal jurisdiction. If she had a penny for every time her eyes traveled over the word *jurisdiction,* she wouldn't have to worry about law school.

A knock on the door yanked K.D. from the rabbit hole of *International Shoe Co. vs. Washington.* Glancing in horror at the plastic clock on the wood-paneled wall, she realized she'd sat in the same spot for several hours, her bladder the size of a water reservoir. She half-rose from the couch, her joints screaming in protest when straightening her knees, and walked like Quasimodo to the door, opening it to a scowling Ingram on the other side.

He glanced up and down at her rumpled state. K.D. held up a hand. "I'm sorry. I'm sorry. I know we're due at the Murdocks to get those papers signed. I've been studying since six and didn't realize how much time had passed. I can hurry. Give me ten minutes." She gestured toward the kitchen which sat off the den. "There's coffee and a clean mug beside the pot. I'll be right back."

She left before he could say a word and waddled down the hall, holding her stomach so as not to empty her bladder all along the shag carpet. K.D. leaped into the shower, gasping as the ice cold water penetrated the fog of a Saturday morning buried in Civil Procedure. Stepping into her robe, K.D. moved over to her bedroom where she slid on a pair of jeans and a white shirt, slightly wrinkled from its lengthy stay in the laundry pile. She sniffed the underarm and grimaced.

Yanking a brush through her hair, K.D. skipped the makeup and left her hair wet. Besides, the Murdocks didn't seem the type to put out the dog for company, so she kept it simple. As she stepped out of the bedroom, K.D. glanced at her mother's closed door, realizing she had yet to hear from her. It was never a good sign when no light shone from beneath the door. K.D. cracked it open and waited for her eyes to adjust to the pitch-black room. Lydia had insisted on black-out curtains for her migraine days, even though K.D. wondered how much were headaches and how much simply depression.

Finally, her eyes focused on her mother's figure in the bed, knees drawn up with hands under her head like a child. "Mama, you okay?"

Lydia stirred, lifted her head slightly. She sighed and dropped it back down on the pillow. "I'm tired, K.D. I think I'll lay in bed for awhile."

K.D.'s heart stopped beating for a minute as a cold dread spread through her chest. The last time Lydia lay in darkness she didn't come out for days, eating little of what K.D. would leave on her bedside table. She should probably stay to make sure Mom got through the day okay, in case she needed something. Yet the flooring creaked from Ingram's pacing, and the Murdocks expected her down the road. K.D. chewed on the inside of one cheek.

"Can I get you some breakfast? How about oatmeal or cereal? You sure I can't open the curtains?"

Lydia curled up into a tighter ball. "No. I'm so tired. I just want to be left alone."

K.D. hesitated, unsure what to do until she heard Ingram clear his throat. "Okay, Mama. I got to do something for work for a little while, but I'll check on you later. Want me to get Doris to come over? Sit with you a while?"

"No. I told you I want to be left alone. Leave me alone, K.D."

Her sharp tone slapped K.D.'s heart back into rhythm. K.D. pulled the door, leaving it cracked so that a sliver of light lay across her mother's face. She hesitated before walking down the hall, face drawn in worry.

Ingram stood as K.D. slid on her sandals. "Everything okay?"

She forced a smile and walked into the kitchen. "Sure. Mom's not feeling great, but it's one of her headaches. Would you mind waiting for me in the car? I need to clean up the kitchen real quick. I'll be right out."

Ingram walked to the door and turned. "Does your mother need anything? She sounded sick or something. Should she see a doctor?"

The man could hear through rock.

The uncharacteristically soft tone gave K.D. pause. "No, she's fine. Just a headache. She gets them from time to time. Let me clean up the kitchen, and I'll be right out."

"Want some help with that?" Ingram's brow unfurled, his face managing to look almost nice and helpful.

Okay, enough with the Mr. Nice Guy. He was starting to freak her out. K.D. glared at him. "Why're you being so pleasant? Does this have something to do with your ex-wife?"

"I just thought you might need some help. You don't always have to be so stubborn."

"Well, if that isn't the pig calling the monkey ugly. Ingram, you wouldn't know your way around a kitchen holding a street map. No, I don't need any help, but I appreciate the offer. I won't be but a sec."

He hesitated, but then left the trailer. K.D. opened a few drawers and took out all sharp objects. Moving to the far corner, she retrieved a key from its magnetic holder against the fridge, unlocked a cabinet, and placed all the knives inside. She reached into the medicine cabinet, shook out Lydia's daily pills onto a napkin, locked the remaining vials in the cabinet, and shoved the key into her pocket. She poured some dog food into Sophia's bowl, wondering if Ingram

60

would shoot her for taking the dog out for a quick potty, but then realized Sophia was probably buried under Lydia's covers. The little dog never left her side during the darkened spells.

Ingram honked the horn, and K.D. headed outside.

"You sure this is the right way?"

K.D. flattened the wadded note across her legs, tracing the crude street drawings with her finger. "Yep. You took a right off Main, three blocks to county road twelve, then we're to look for…" K.D. leaned forward in the car seat. "There's the trailer she mentioned to look for the turn, although you can barely see it with all the kudzu. Should be a dirt road right up on the right. Slow down, Ingram, here it comes."

Ingram's face wrinkled in concentration as his vintage Cadillac eased over oak roots the size of speed bumps. The Murdock's driveway was nothing more than a pig trail meandering through pines, oak, and poplar trees. A flock of crows worthy of a Hitchcock movie raced from the woods, and Ingram and K.D. both ducked as if the birds had grazed their scalps. Mobile homes and cabins dotted the woods with no obvious path from the main road. Ingram stomped on the brakes before passing the Caddy under overhanging pine branches and kudzu.

"I'm not driving Hank through that. Get out and clear me a path."

"Wasn't Hank Aaron a trail blazer?" K.D. smiled at her recollection of at least some sports trivia.

"He was back in the day. This 1963 Cadillac Coup Deville and Hank Aaron were dynamite in their day, which is why I named my car after him. But one's dead and the other is an antique. Come on. Help me clear this road. Hank hasn't had a scratch on him his entire life. I'm not about to start now."

The two waded through mid-day Alabama heat, the air as thick as cheap make-up. K.D. grabbed a pine limb and bowed it back, twisting it around a larger limb. Ingram yanked on some kudzu hanging down, pulling the vines until they snapped. He tossed them aside, wiping his forehead with a monogrammed handkerchief he retrieved from a pocket. Even in the heat, Ingram wore a suit. They returned to the Caddy, Ingram's breathing labored as they pulled into a clearing filled with an old car and several chickens.

Buck emerged from under the hood, waving them toward a bare patch of yard. He wiped his hands on a bandana as they exited the car.

"Y'all find the place okay?"

Ingram grimaced at K.D. who shushed him with a look. She turned to Buck. "No problems at all. Thank you for the invitation." K.D. extended a hand, which Buck shook. Ingram kept his in his pockets, looking pointedly at Buck's grease-stained shirt, until K.D. elbowed his arm before Buck noticed. Ingram took his hand.

"Ya'll come on up, then. Be another thirty minutes or so before we eat. Shelly Anne said y'all had some more paperwork for us to sign. Gabby's sleeping so we'll have a little peace and quiet at least for a spell."

They followed Buck across the yard. He stopped every few steps, picking up plastic toys along the way. A chained yard dog barked from a shed where K.D. noticed the front of a black truck, a lot like the one Shelly Anne had stared at through the Waffle Iron window the day before.

It was Bo's truck peeking out from the darkened shrine.

The screen door opened to the manufactured home, and Shelly Anne stuck out an arm. "Glad y'all could make it. I got a roast cooking, should be ready soon. Too hot to sit outside so we'll have to keep quiet if we want Gabby to stay sleeping."

K.D. smiled at Shelly Anne, glad to see a somewhat relaxed face. Sorrow still colored her ocean-blue eyes, but with her hair pulled low at the neck she looked younger, a bit happier. She hugged K.D. who squeezed her back. "Thanks for having us. The only thing in my fridge was some leftover fried chicken from Piggly Wiggly. I wish you had let me bring something. I heat up a mean Sister Schubert yeast roll."

"Company don't bring nothing to my house when you're invited to eat. Come on inside."

The home was neat, picked up. Vacuum lines raked the carpet. The double-wide was spacious and homey with simple curtains on the windows, yellow lace along the bottoms, and sunshine beaming through their sheerness.

Shelly Anne gestured toward the kitchen, twice the size of K.D.'s. "Let's sit in here. I'll pour us some sweet tea, and y'all can tell us what we need to do to get this ball rolling."

Buck walked in behind them. "I tell you, for somebody who never wanted to file this suit, she sure is raring to go."

"If we're gonna do it, might as well get to it. No sense dragging our feet and making everybody miserable." Shelly Anne shot the words at her husband, her eyes like daggers. K.D. felt sorry for the little man who winced at the sharp response.

Ingram took a seat and gestured for the others to join him. Shelly Anne circled the table with a pitcher of tea, filling the waiting glasses of ice. K.D. took a sip to have something to do with her hands, waiting on the air to thaw between the two spouses. Obviously, words had exchanged prior to their arrival, and K.D. felt as if she'd turned on a movie thirty minutes after it started.

Taking the paperwork from his briefcase, Ingram shuffled around until he found the right one. "This here's a request to the hospital to release Bo's medical records. We'll ask for them all, and their attorneys will advise to send three times that amount."

"Why would they do that? Send you more than you asked for?" Shelly Anne joined them at the table.

"Big shots do that. Try to intimidate you. There are only two of us at our office so they know the more paperwork they send over, the more overwhelmed we might be. Then they'll swoop in, offer some ridiculous settlement, hoping we'll cave because they think we're some little peon office and you're just dumb country folk."

"We ain't dumb." Buck straightened in his seat.

Shelly Anne shushed her husband. "That ain't gonna happen, Mr. Ingram. If I'm gonna do this, I'm in it all the way. I'm not after some piddly settlement that won't mean nothing to them big shot insurance lawyers and rich doctor. I know where he lives. Over there in that fancy Riverwind subdivision. I drove by his house one time; saw his flashy cars. I don't care about the money. After we win, we'll give our share to the church, save for Gabby's college. Money won't bring my boy back so I could care less, but now that my mind's made up, I do think somebody needs to be accountable."

K.D. reached over and placed her hand over Shelly Anne's. "We're all in this together."

Shelly Anne patted her hand and loosened up a bit. "We've told some folks at the church, and they said they'd help in any way. If they do send over boxes of paperwork, bring 'em on. We might be simple folks, but we ain't stupid. We can help read through anything you need us to."

Buck stood and poured some more tea, swallowing in one gulp like a shot of whiskey.

Ingram laid the papers out and clicked open his pen. "Both of you sign here. I'll get the papers faxed over this afternoon, and hopefully the hospital will turn those around first of next week. Sometimes in the bigger medical facilities, you have to stay on them to get a response, but I know the administrator. She's a cousin of my ex-wife's and always had a crush on me. I can work that angle if I need to."

Shelly Anne caught K.D.'s eye with a raised brow, but K.D. refrained from an eye roll at Ingram's Casanova personality. As soon as word of his divorce got out, K.D. had spent the next week fielding phone calls from the lonely, the widowed, and the still-married-yet-would-love-to-be-with-a-lawyer. With the height and gait of a penguin, Ingram wasn't lying about his effect on the ladies. K.D. just couldn't figure out why.

Buck and Shelly Anne signed all the documents Ingram offered, never reading any of them. He gathered the papers together, knocking the ends against the table to straighten the pile and connected them with a clip.

Shelly Anne stood. "Let's try to eat before Gabby wakes up. K.D., if you'll grab the casserole out of the oven," she handed over two oven mitts, "Buck you slice up the roast."

Ingram cleared his throat. "How can I help?" He looked scared of the answer.

Shelly Anne smiled. "How about you butter the rolls?"

Ingram furrowed his brow as Shelly Anne handed him a basket, knife, and a tub of butter. K.D. bit back a smile, taking out a roll and demonstrating how to butter the top. She patted Ingram on the back as he did what he was told. K.D. retrieved the green bean casserole, and they all sat down to eat.

K.D.'s fork was mid-way to her mouth before Shelly Anne patted her other hand. "Buck'll say grace."

K.D. lowered her fork and bowed her head.

Buck cleared his throat. "Heavenly father, we ask your blessings over the food we're about to eat and the families represented at this table. Protect our loved ones, Lord. Take care of the ones who eat at Your table. Bless this food to the nourishment of our bodies and our bodies to your service. Give my boy a kiss for me. Amen."

The group offered an "Amen" and began to eat. K.D. swallowed the first bite over the lump formed in her throat.

"May I use your restroom?" K.D. wiped the corners of her mouth with a napkin and then placed it on her empty plate.

Shelly Anne gestured toward the den. "Go through there and

down the hall. First door's Gabby's room so be extra quiet cause she'll be waking up soon. Bathroom's the next room on the right."

K.D. tip toed past the toddler's room, hearing her stir and mumble behind the closed door. After using the bathroom and touching up her lipstick, she turned toward the den, but the open door across the hall caught her eye. Glancing down the hall to make sure no one saw her, she stepped toward the room, curiosity getting the better of her.

A full-sized bed with an NFL comforter and pillows the shape of footballs sat between two windows. A wall of shelves held at least thirty trophies of various sizes. K.D. stepped over, mesmerized at the accolades accumulated in Bo's short fifteen years. Little trophies for pee wee football participation on up to a few the size of her lower leg. She took down the largest, holding it with both hands.

"That's the junior high state championship trophy. They won it the year before he died."

K.D. jumped at the sound of Shelly Anne's voice. "I'm sorry. I was just, um…"

K.D. about dropped the trophy trying to put it back, but Shelly Anne took it from her and stared down at it. "Coach brought it over the day of the funeral, said they wanted us to have it. He knew they'd a never had that trophy if it weren't for Bo." She ran a finger over the engraved plate and sighed, placing it back on the shelf.

Shelly Anne looked around as tears filled her eyes. "I guess I should re-do the room, but I can't bring myself to do it. I keep thinking if I leave things just like they were, he'll come home one day, dumping his pads right by the front door like he always did. I'd yell at him to clean up and he'd swallow me in a big ol' sweaty hug." She breathed in as a tear escaped down her makeup-less face. She didn't bother to wipe it off, staring at her son's bed while the water clung to her chin. "I keep waiting on this to get easier. Time heals all wounds. What a load of crap. Maybe Buck's right. Maybe suing the doctor will help us find some closure."

K.D. noticed a framed photo on the desk cluttered with gum

wrappers, a Coke can and some school books. She picked the picture up, staring into the deep brown eyes of Bo Murdock in his football uniform, one knee in the dirt…dirt that now covered his grave.

"My goodness, he's handsome." K.D. could almost trace the veins in his arm as he gripped the football, could almost see the blood pumping through the flexed biceps. It was easy to speak of him in the present tense when looking at a photo so full of life.

Shelly Anne's smile caused the tear to drop. "Thank you. I think so. One of the hardest things to get used to after, after…. well the house got way too quiet. I used to fuss and fuss about how the girls would call the house, looking for Bo. We wouldn't allow him to use a cell phone except for emergencies. So he'd have to use the home phone for personal business. Thought we could protect him better that way." She paused and shook her head, blowing out her breath. "You wouldn't believe how bold those girls could be. This one girl argued with me about whether or not he was at practice. Didn't believe me when I said he wasn't home. My mama sure didn't raise me that way."

K.D. stared at the photo as a thought nudged into her brain. She returned it to the desk and then looked at Shelly Anne. "Didn't you say you knew where the doctor lived?"

Shelly Anne nodded.

"Can you tell me how to get there?"

"I can, but why?"

K.D. shrugged her shoulders. "Seeing Bo's room, I guess it makes him real to me. I'd like to put the opposition in the same context. Flesh and bones, you know? I mean, I know what the doctor and his wife look like from our file, but I'd like to see where he lives and all. Get an idea of who he really is." K.D.'s words stumbled to a halt, unsure how to further explain herself. How could she fight an opponent who existed only on paper? She wanted to assess him, burn his image in her mind to offset the monotony of discovery. A constant reminder of the enemy.

Shelly Anne chewed on her inside lip for a second before speaking. "I can do better than that. I'll go with you."

K.D. held up a hand. "I don't know, Shelly Anne. I'm not going to be doing anything but driving by. Ingram will have to take me to get my car so it'll be dark before we'll get back. Are you sure?"

"I'm sure. I told you we're in this all the way. I'd offer to take our car, but we only got one, and I'll have to leave that with Buck."

"Leave what with Buck?"

The two ladies jumped at Buck's voice from the doorway and turned to find him holding Gabby. At the sight of K.D., the toddler leaped from her daddy's arms and into K.D.'s, who barely caught her.

"Well, hey there little friend. Did you have a good nap?" K.D. asked as Gabby gummed a handful of K.D.'s blonde curls. The kid was growing on her.

Shelly Anne smiled at her husband. "Hon, you're gonna get some quality father-daughter time this afternoon. K.D. and I are gonna take a little trip." Shelly Anne turned and winked at her, who couldn't help but think this might not be her best idea.

CHAPTER

8

"I'll be right back." K.D. left Shelly Anne in the yard, feeling guilty for not inviting her inside her home, but not sure of how she'd find her mom. "I need to grab my purse. Won't be but a sec." She eased up the wooden steps and unlocked the door.

She stepped over the threshold, shutting the door behind her, and listened for any sign of her mother. Nothing. As she walked across the carpet, the creaks in the floor sounded like limbs snapping in a tornado against the silence of the house, the stillness taking her back to a place she longed to forget. A memory buried, but with a faint pulse.

Elementary school had been tough on K.D. Not because of intelligence, but more from learning to navigate her mother's moods. She'd made an A on a spelling test. Hard words, too, conjunctions that had always stumped her. The bus had dropped her off at the front of the trailer park, and K.D. ran all the way home in year-old shoes, two sizes too small. Leaping from the bottom step, she hurled into the trailer, hollering for her mother so she could show her the test. She found her in the bathroom, crumpled into a bloody pile the color of the ambulance sirens which soon came screaming to the home. Her daddy had left the next week. Nobody had heard a word from him since, leaving her with Doomsday Doris when Mom fell down the rabbit hole.

K.D. shook her head to rid herself of the memory. The door to her mother's room remained ajar, a wall of black on the other side of light.

"Mom?"

Silence.

K.D. slid open the door. "Mom? You okay?"

A figure stirred in the bed, and K.D. made out her mother's outline. "Go away, K.D. Leave me alone. My head hurts."

Lydia's voice drew a sigh of relief from K.D.; the memory of the suicide attempt still fresh in her mind. She knew the futility of arguing with her. "OK. Do you need anything? I have to run another errand, but it shouldn't take too long. Can I get you something to drink? You want some water?"

"No. I need to sleep."

Mom had already "slept" fourteen hours since last night. "Alright. I'll have my cell phone with me if you need to call. I shouldn't be long." K.D. left the door open, and the hall light on, hoping her mother wouldn't argue with a little illumination, something to help motivate her to join the day.

She didn't protest. In fact Lydia said nothing at all which was even worse.

K.D. scoured her bedroom, the den and kitchen, but couldn't find her bag. Her keys lay on the counter, but no purse. Maybe this wasn't such a good idea. Mama catatonic in the bedroom. K.D. with no license or cell phone. Signs everywhere for her to stay put. K.D. ran to the door to catch Ingram, to have him take Shelly Anne back home, but the Cadillac's tail lights disappeared around the corner of the trailer park road.

She sighed, locked the door behind her and then smiled at Shelly Anne. "We're going to have to be careful. I can't find my license anywhere, and I sure can't afford a ticket." She gestured toward her Chevette. She waved at Doris who stuck her head out her trailer door and looked Shelly Anne up and down before ducking back inside.

Shelly Anne raised a brow at the disappearing neighbor and then returned to K.D. "Want me to drive?"

"Nah. This car takes some getting used to. I'll drive her. You help me look out for the police." She forced a smile at Shelly Anne over the hood of her car, bumping the door a few times in order to open it. Shelly Anne tugged on hers to no avail. K.D. jogged around the car, gave the door a few hip bumps. "Told you."

The car chugged through town as K.D. cracked a window and apologized for the lack of air conditioning. She took a right past Johnson's hardware store and meandered along a few town streets whose names would never win creativity awards. Main Street. Dump Road, populated by city trash trucks. Station Street, where the silent train station sat empty. Sawmill Road was the one rebel in the bunch as the river sat at the end of the asphalt with no sawmill in sight.

A few modern subdivisions skirted the town, but even they were earmarked by either the developers or the geography – Johnson's Landing, Thomas Trestle, and the elaborate gateway to Riverwind.

Shelly Anne leaned forward in her seat. "How we gonna get in there? The gate's shut."

K.D. pulled over to the side of the road across from the entrance. Golden arches, like the entrance to the Wonka factory, spread across the cobbled road, flanked by azaleas wilting in the late-afternoon heat. A security guard sat chin to chest inside the gatehouse.

K.D. chewed on her lip a minute, glancing down the road. The sun meandered down the skyline, full from the day behind them as if in a hurry for night. "Well, we sure can't go in the proper way. Unless you know someone who lives in Riverwind."

Shelly Anne shook her head.

"Let's drive down the road a bit. Maybe there's a construction entrance or something."

The painted brick wall extended for at least a half a mile. They *could* pull off the road and casually walk through the neighborhoods as if they belonged, but it sure would be a hike. The road wound away from the elaborate subdivision, trees beginning to outnumber houses as they drove until finally bouncing onto decaying asphalt, two miles and a world away from Riverwind.

K.D. pulled into the dirt parking lot of a gas station, dust settling over the Chevette as the tires ground to a stop. She turned to Shelly Anne. "I need a Coke. You mind if we stop a sec while we come up with Plan B?" The sign read *Patsy's* over a lopsided building with what looked like a stapled-on tin roof. Two rectangular pumps rose from the ground like tombstones, rusted and useless, all of the numbers flipped halfway between slots. But the word "Open" flashed, and florescent lights shone through the murky windows. Shelly Anne agreed to a drink.

K.D. stopped at the door when she noticed Shelly Anne peering around the corner of the building. Joining her, K.D. saw nothing in the twilight but the back of the station, a sharp slope shouldering off into the river. A dock with very few teeth jutted out from the scarred bank, and a John boat rocked in a wave created by a passing ski boat.

An idea poked K.D.'s brain. "You know how to work a boat?"

Shelly Anne grinned as if reading her mind. "Does a fat man burp?"

"Good, I got an idea. If we can't do a ride by on the road, maybe we can go by river." She jogged back to the car and grabbed a scarf to tie around her mass of curls.

Before the two entered the store, Shelly Anne touched her arm. "Let me handle this. Follow my lead."

A cow bell tied to the door announced their arrival, and an elderly man, pale and bald, looked up from behind the register. K.D. grabbed a soda from the nearest cooler.

The store held three rows of various groceries, canned meat and meat byproducts, a line of candy, etc. Coolers circumnavigated the store with everything from sodas to buttermilk. Scorch marks climbed the cinderblock walls as if from a decades-ago fire.

Shelly Anne approached the man who switched off a crackling radio. "I'd like a word with Miss Patsy."

The old man palmed his chin, leathered skin scratching across stubble. "I don't know who *Miss* Patsy might be, but I'm Patsy. What can I do for you?"

"Oh, I'm sorry, Mr. Patsy."

He waved a hand. "Happens all the time. My mama expected a girl. Wanted to name her after Patsy Cline. You'd think I'da changed it to Pat or something, but no, Patsy kinda stuck with me. I guess if Johnny Cash can sing about a boy named Sue, I can hang onto Patsy alright. What can I do for you ladies?"

Shelly Anne gestured toward the window over his shoulder. "Well, Patsy, you see my friend K.D. here." She paused and laughed. "The truth is, this poor thing has lived here all her life, but hasn't ever been on the river, bless her heart. Can you believe that?"

K.D. started to protest, but Shelly Anne nudged her in the ribs with an elbow so she nodded. "Um, yeah, she's right. Hard to believe I could live here my whole life and never go on the river." She looked sideways at Shelly Anne who bit back a smile. K.D. handed Patsy some money for her drink.

Patsy looked at them with skepticism while counting out the change.

Shelly Anne talked fast and with her hands as if signing. "So you see, we were riding along and saw your boat out back. And I was, well, I was wondering if you wouldn't mind very much, if we could borrow your boat for about an hour, so I can show my friend here an Alabama sunset over the river." She looked at him with lowered lids.

Her tactics must have worked because Patsy's face grew red at her tone of voice. He cleared his throat. "I can't let you pretty ladies out there on the river this time of day, without protection. Wouldn't be fittin'. It'd be dark before you got back."

Shelly Anne leaned forward, her voice husky. "Oh come on now, Patsy. We won't be gone long. I was practically born on the river. Heck, by the way my mama talked, she found me in a brush basket caught in some reeds. I've fished every slough from here to Jackson. We'd go home and get my canoe if we had time, but it'd sure nuff be dark by then. We won't be long. We're just looking for a little adventure. You wouldn't be one to deny us a little fun would you?"

Good grief. K.D. thought Shelly Anne would start purring any time soon, but attempted to contribute something herself. "Please, Mr. Patsy? We'll be awfully careful." K.D. tried to bat her eyes, but only succeeded in locking her upper and lower lids, causing her to blink hard to free them.

Patsy's face lightened, and he pulled a set of keys from the bib pocket of his overalls. "Alright, but just in case you gals are some kinda delinquents or something, how about leaving your driver's license with me?"

K.D. panicked, thinking of her lost license, and then came up with a way out. "I tell you what, how about I leave you my car keys. That Chevy isn't worth much, but it's my only car. You can bet I'd come back for it."

Patsy thought for a minute, scratched his chin again, and then acquiesced. "Alright. That'll do." The two swapped keys. Patsy reached under the counter and extended a hand towel and bug-repellant lotion to the ladies. "Y'all better lather up. Those river skeeters don't play. Especially on pretty skin like yours. I'll be here 'till eight. Y'all make sure you're back by then."

Shelly Anne took the offering. "Thank you, Patsy. We shouldn't be more than an hour. Sun's about to set anyway." She leaned across the counter and kissed Patsy's weathered cheek. The man's mouth fell open and stayed there as they made their way outside.

K.D. held her laughter until the door shut, managing to make it down to the dock before exploding. "I can't believe how you flirted with that old man. Poor thing didn't know what to do. He'd a sold you the store for a dollar if you'd asked him."

Shelly Anne grinned. "It was mean of me, wasn't it? I'm glad you thought of the boat, though. If I remember right, the doctor's house is in the dead center of the subdivision, on the nicest lot. If we had parked and walked back, it would have been at least five or six miles. This shouldn't take us any time." She bent over the John boat, unlocked the chain and wiped the aluminum seats before offering K.D. her hand.

As K.D. stepped into the boat, she said, "You know, I really have been on the river. I grew up with a creek behind our home."

Shelly Anne arched an eyebrow.

"Maybe not *on* the river, but I've walked alongside it. Well, more like driven by it." She scowled at Shelly Anne's laughter. "I mean, it's not like I'm a complete indoor girl."

"Buck told me you didn't even know who Bo Jackson was."

"I did too! I watched *The Green Mile*. Just because I'm not athletic or even interested in wasting my time on watching football doesn't mean I'm a complete moron."

The two settled into their seats. K.D. looked around and then over her shoulder, rubbing bug repellant on her arms. "What now?"

Shelly Anne laughed. "Well, Miss Outdoor girl, how about taking that paddle there and shoving off from the dock while I check out the trolling motor?"

"Why do we need a paddle if we have a motor?"

"Not sure we'll need the motor. If I remember right, Riverwind starts just around this bank over there." Shelly Anne gestured with her hand toward a dark corner of land. "We'll probably just paddle, but I want to make sure the motor works as back up. You wouldn't be the first one to drop a paddle in the water on accident, even being outdoorsy and all." She snickered at her last comment.

K.D. shoved off, mumbling under her breath, "Why does everybody put so much stock in football and fishing? How hard can it be to paddle a boat?" After a few strokes which caused the boat to turn in circles, K.D. finally got the hang of it, matching Shelly Anne dip for dip, her muscles straining against the murky water.

The sound of chirping crickets filtered through the last remaining rays of light, and dusk settled over the pair as they skirted the river bank. A few eager stars made an early appearance, and for a minute, K.D. forgot the clandestine mission ahead.

She stopped paddling and looked up, breathed in the dank river, pine mixed with mud. Pleasant and organic. She breathed out, stress leaving her body. She couldn't remember the last time she'd spent time outdoors. Worries over Mama and finances cluttered her days, compounded by the unbelievable stress of law school. More than once she wanted to chuck her books and walk away from it all.

Sitting right here, she could almost pretend she had.

"Hard to believe somebody can look up at a night like this and not believe in God," Shelly Anne whispered from behind.

K.D. soaked up the comment, looking around the shadows of trees and underbrush. Something jumped into the water near her, maybe a turtle or some night creature. No fear. No worries about what lay in the dark below. Their purpose remained nothing more than to jump in the water at that very moment. Trust in whoever made the water. Made them. Acting on instinct alone with no plan or preparation.

Stupid turtles.

"Don't you agree?"

K.D. turned and nodded, pulling her fingers through the water, feelings its warm wetness against her skin. "Something smarter than me created all this, that's for sure."

A light blinked above. Probably an airplane. But then it dropped, fell, and burned down the black skyline.

"A falling star." Shelly Anne said from behind. "Quick. Make a wish."

K.D. didn't answer, but also didn't make a wish. She knew wishes served as much purpose as turtles jumping off riverbanks did.

"Did you make a wish?"

"You make a wish for me, Shelly Anne."

"Hey look." K.D. turned in the direction Shelly Anne pointed. Night had fallen fast and moonlight now shadowed a three-tiered dock, bigger than Shelly Anne's double-wide, encasing two boats and what looked to be several jet skis. "Why don't we tie off here? This is the doctor's house. I recognize the boat because he had it in the driveway when I came by last winter."

"We're not tying off anywhere, Shelly Anne. I'm not trespassing on the man's property who we're filing a lawsuit against. I told you we were just riding by. Or in this case, floating by." K.D. could make out the word *Life Saver* on the side of the pontoon boat.

"Oh come on. I want to get a closer look at the house." The two glided to the dock. K.D. startled, thinking she saw a man in the shadows, but it turned out to be life jackets hung along the wall. A strong wind blew across the water, freeing a clump of blonde hair across K.D.'s face. She loosened the scarf to fix it only to have the wind take the scarf from her hands. It floated through the air and landed on the dock. K.D. watched in horror as the wind picked it up again and blew it halfway up the yard.

She turned to Shelly Anne, her mouth wide open. "I have to get that scarf."

"Good. I want to get a better look at the house anyway."

"We're not looking at the house, Shelly Anne. I mean it. But I've got to find a way to get that scarf back."

"What's so important about a scarf?"

"It's my mom's, and she always puts her name and address on everything. If they find it, they could attach it to me. My law career would be over before it ever began."

Shelly Anne did not respond. K.D. turned in the dark. "I said…"

"Shhhh!" Shelly Anne's voice dropped to a frantic whisper. She pushed off from the dock, turning the boat around. "Dredge your paddle. Hurry!"

"What's that mean?"

"Pull it back against the water so we can turn around. Hurry.

Somebody's coming!"

A small light shone, what looked to be a cell phone, as a figure walked from the house toward the water, heading straight for them.

CHAPTER

9

"Do you think he saw us?" K.D. slid off her shoes, rolled up the legs of her jeans and stepped into the bathtub-warm river water. Shelly Anne exited the other side, and they pulled the boat onto the edge of the wooded lot next door to the doctor.

"I don't think so."

K.D. examined their options. "Okay, I'm thinking if I enter the property up by the house, I can move down the side of the yard until I'm closest to the scarf. Then we'll say our prayers, maybe change our wish on that falling star, and hope nobody sees me run out and get it. Better yet, why don't you stay in the boat and be ready to go when I haul tail it back?"

Shelly Anne was already shaking her head. "Nuh uh. I'm going with you."

K.D. sighed, recognizing the stubborn set of Shelly Anne's jaw. The two put back on their shoes and made their way around the blackened trees, briars scraping K.D.'s exposed ankles. She reached down and lowered her jeans. The ground stayed soft beneath their feet, the oaks stingy with their leaves as the fall wind tugged at their branches. Beads of sweat dotted K.D.'s upper lip and the bend of her elbow, the night hot and muggy. A mosquito whined in her ear. Keeping the faint light of the doctor's house in sight, they walked until Shelly Anne touched her arm, tossing her head toward the house.

"If I remember right, they have a detached garage with a breezeway leading to the house, probably into the kitchen. It was about Christmas when I drove by here last year, and they had a tree you could see from heaven. Kept their front blinds open so I know a formal room faces the road. I'm thinking some sort of family room must face the backyard."

K.D. stopped at the wrought-iron gate guarding the property line. She worried about motion sensors in the back of the house, but she wasn't close enough to see any along the roofline. The man who'd been heading toward the water, K.D. assumed it was the doctor, walked in circles around the yard, the low murmur of his voice reaching their ears, but not loud enough to decipher words. He ended the call and put the phone in his pocket. Walking up the back deck, he ran his fingers through his hair as if frustrated and walked into the house.

K.D. looked hard at Shelly Anne as she wiped sweat from her brow with the back of her hand. "You sure you want to do this? Could be pretty embarrassing if we get caught."

"You're the one who lost the scarf."

K.D. looked again at the house, inhaled, and exhaled through her nose. "Okay. I'm thinking we ease over to the carport and stop, look at things a little more closely. If the alarm doesn't go off or we don't get shot, we can scoot along the back deck. Then I grab my scarf and high tail it out of here. Ol' Patsy back there may call the cops on us if we don't get his boat back soon. That's if Dr. High and Mighty in there doesn't first. Come on, follow me."

K.D. opened the gate, stopping when it squealed.

"Shhh!" Shelly Anne whispered.

"I'm trying!" K.D. thought for a second, trying to find another entrance to the property. Seeing none, she leaned over and started spitting on the gate hinges.

"What are you doing, K.D.?"

She looked up at Shelly Ann. "Haven't you ever read *To Kill A Mockingbird*? In the movie version, when Scout and Jim want to spy on Boo Radley, they first had to get through a squeaky gate. They spit on it to loosen up the hinges. You try it."

Little House on the Prairie, Nancy Drew, Little Women, and eventually *Gone with the Wind* and *To Kill a Mockingbird*. Spines stacked beneath her childhood bed, the escape route to a different place.

Shelly Anne wrinkled her brow, but then moved her mouth around, gathering her saliva, and spit onto the gate. K.D. moved it back and forth in silence. "Come on."

Shelly Anne grimaced. "Forget what I said about you being an indoor girl. Gross."

They sprinted to the carport, their backs against the brick exterior. No flood lights came on. No guard dog charged. K.D. released the breath burning her lungs. They edged along the outside back of the carport as if walking the ledge of a tall building, the yard dark except for the distant light at the dock and the light filtering through various windows. At the breezeway, K.D. could make out a woman through the window on the door, whisking something in a bowl and placing it on the counter. She dipped a long finger into the mix and drew it to her mouth, closing her eyes as if savoring whatever it was she tasted.

K.D. gestured toward some boxwood that lined the back of the house. As soon as the woman turned from the window, the two ran for the next hideout, diving behind the bushes. K.D. winced as a branch scratched her face. She touched Shelly Anne's arm to give them a minute before making another move.

A door above them opened onto the deck. "Come on, Sissy. Go tee tee before supper," a man's voice called out.

The tap tap of a little dog's toenails raced across the deck and down the stairs. K.D. saw the white of a small Shih Tzu or Pomeranian turn around in circles in the yard, doing its business and barking in delight at being released from the house until it found K.D.'s scarf, upon which it pounced. K.D. and Shelly Anne exchanged wide-eyed glances, both curled up behind the bushes. The little dog sniffed the air and came right for them, the scarf between its teeth.

The man called out. "Sissy, come on. Mama's got supper cooked. Come back in the house."

Sissy sniffed the bush, pushing away a branch until her nose hit K.D.'s tennis shoe. K.D. reached out to take the scarf, but the dog began a tug-of-war, growling in play.

"Go on, Sissy. Go back to Daddy." K.D. whispered, tugging harder until she heard a rip.

"Sissy! Don't make me come down there! Leave the squirrels alone." The man's voice grew stern.

Shelly Anne leaned over to whisper, "Yeah, Sissy. Leave us squirrels alone. Please don't make him come down here. Please?"

The scarf tore in two, causing the dog to fall back on its haunches, a piece of fabric in its mouth. Sissy ran in a circle, and then by some miracle, danced away and up the deck.

"Daddy's little baby wanted to play, didn't you? We'll go out after supper. I'll get your toy…" The shut door ate the rest of the man's sing-songy voice as he wooed the dog indoors.

K.D.'s head leaned against the brick as her heart rate calmed to mild heart attack, relieved to know her end of the scarf contained Lydia's personal information. "Oh…my…goodness. Maybe we just experienced our one gimme of the night. This is by far the worst idea I've ever had."

Shelly Anne burst out laughing, throwing a hand over her mouth.

"I don't find one thing funny about this."

Small shoulders shook in silence, and Shelly Anne dropped her head onto her drawn up knees. Her muffled voice said, "Everything about this is funny, K.D. If you only knew how boring my life has been. Every minute swallowed in grief, sadness. Every day a chore to get out of bed. The weight unbearable half the time. I don't even like my husband anymore and can barely tolerate myself. But this…" She raised her head and gestured with her hand. "Is amazing. Here we are, two grown women sitting behind a hedge, hiding from a dog no bigger than fish bait. This, my friend, is hilarious. I don't even care if we get caught." The grin consumed her entire face as laughter tears filled her eyes.

K.D. grinned back in spite of herself. "Bite your tongue, girl. We should leave before something worse happens."

"No way I'm leaving without looking in that window."

K.D. sighed and inched out from behind the bush, exposing her head to ensure no outdoor animals or jail-breaking Pomeranians waited to shout their arrival. The coast seemed clear so they moved along the house, behind the bushes, until they came to the back deck.

The kitchen sat above them, but they'd have to climb a few stairs in order to see through the window. K.D. eased out of the bushes and onto the first step, crouched like the criminal she emulated. She could hear muffled voices through the window, male and female. She knew the couple had no children and lived alone in a house that could fit three families. Her research showed Dr. Thomas's wife, Frances, to be a philanthropic woman who dedicated the greater part of her life to domestic violence issues, hosting fundraisers for battered women's shelters both up North and now in Alabama. Their church directory photo showed a handsome couple, Frances regal with a long, slender neck and black coiffed hair. She wore pearls, but round dark eyes held a twinkle as if she knew the punch line already.

Frances crossed the window above K.D., who ducked lower on the step, reaching behind her to still Shelly Anne. She pointed and inched up another step to where she could straighten, ever so slowly, until she could look through the glass.

Frances's back was to her as she took something out of the oven. She opened the roasting pan, revealing a steaming whole chicken. K.D.'s stomach growled in response. Dr. Thomas entered the kitchen from the family room through an arched doorway. K.D. ducked on instinct, and then slowly rose back up again. He was shorter than his wife with a healthy head of white hair despite his sixty-four years. He walked up behind her and nuzzled her neck, hugging her intimately.

K.D.'s Judas heart softened toward the couple so obviously in love. She looked down at Shelly Anne.

"What, K.D.? I want to see."

Easing her down the step, K.D. gestured for them to return to the woods. "There's nothing to see. They were in the kitchen for half a second then went into the family room. We'd have to go up on the deck to look further. With all those windows, we'd surely be caught. Come on. Let's get Patsy's boat back."

"I want to see, K.D."

K.D. looked straight into Shelly Anne's eyes. "No you don't. Nothing will be served by this, Shelly Anne. Let's get 'em in the courtroom, not out here trespassing on their property."

Shelly Anne glanced at the house, but as if she sensed something more, allowed K.D. to take her arm, pulling her toward the woods. They walked in silence a few yards; K.D. wrestling with the intimate domestic scene. She didn't want to like this man and felt awful it had only taken half a second for her heart to tender toward the couple. Where was her loyalty? She'd come on behalf of Bo, to support Shelly Anne, and yet the scene she'd witnessed made her want to curl up on the couch with a blanket while Frances rubbed her head. Did she crave a normal mother so badly?

"Was the kitchen pretty? I bet they have granite counter tops."

"Gorgeous. Something straight out of a magazine. Stainless steel appliances, huge island in the middle, the works." She left out the image of Frances wearing jeans and a simple button down, appearing normal in every sense of the word. One flash into their home might not adequately portray either of them so K.D. refrained from offering Shelly Anne anymore. She had a right to her anger. Her son was dead, after all, and would never eat his mama's pot roast again, while Dr. and Mrs. Thomas munched happily on chicken. Maybe the lawsuit would allow Shelly Anne to one day cook in fancy ovens and sample mixes from a granite-covered kitchen island.

They lowered into the boat in silence, a sort of depressing ride home as compared to their previous muffled laughter behind the boxwood. Shelly Anne guided the boat alongside Patsy's dock and collected the towel and bug spray. The store was closed, but Patsy had left a note instructing them to put the key through the mail slot and to look for K.D.'s car keys on her driver's front tire.

The Chevette groaned to life, the front axle screaming in protest to the turning wheels as K.D. eased onto the highway. Shelly Anne didn't live too far from Patsy's, and K.D.'s heart dropped a bit more when she realized Shelly Anne had to drive past Riverwind every day on her way to the Waffle Iron.

Shelly Anne shifted in the seat beside her, drawing a knee onto the seat as she poked K.D. in the arm. "Hey, I gotta question for you. How old are you? About twenty-five?"

"Twenty-eight. Why?"

"How come you aren't married? You don't have a boyfriend or anything?"

"No, I'm not married. Never have been, and no prospects on the horizon." K.D.'s voice trailed off, unsure how to continue the conversation without disclosing too much information. Trip's eyes floated through her mind, the feel of his arm when she'd bump against him walking back from McDonald's the other night. How he moved her away from the street to place himself between her and danger. What a nice boyfriend he'd make.

For someone else.

"No one? But why?"

K.D. moved in her seat and cleared her throat. "I don't have time, to be honest with you. As you can tell by my wonderful trailer, we're not exactly swimming in money. My dad left when I was little, and my mom is sick a lot so I live with her. I'm going to law school at night, but I have to go in piece-meal when I can afford it. I go to school around my job."

"Don't you want a family?"

K.D. turned into the Murdock's clearing as the light came on outside the door. Did she want a family? She'd never considered herself a real kid-friendly person. Never enjoyed even holding a child until Gabby eased into her heart with her plate-sized blue eyes. K.D. had done enough caretaking to last a lifetime. "I don't know. I kind of like doing things on my own. Having nobody but myself to figure things out. Seems easier that way."

"You're too pretty to be all by yourself."

K.D. thought of her mama during a good day. Her blonde hair swept into a French twist, tiny tendrils twirling around her ears. The smell of White Shoulders perfume on K.D.'s pillow after she'd lain down with her. Pretty didn't make husbands stay.

"I'll be alright. I can take care of myself. Don't worry about me, Shelly Anne. But I do need to get home and check on my mother. I have a late night of studying ahead of me."

As Shelly Anne started to get out of the car, K.D. reached over and touched her arm. "Hey."

Shelly Anne stopped and turned.

"I just wanted to say thanks for going with me. I don't have many girl friends. I think I'd rather have a good one of those than some stubborn, smelly man any day. Besides, don't forget I have Ingram to boss me around. I'm good."

Shelly Anne patted her hand and exited the car. "Call me next week and let me know if you need help with anything. In the meantime, I'll try to think of some more laws we can break." She winked over her shoulder as she made her way toward the home.

K.D. drove through the quiet streets of town. No twenty-four-hour coffee shops glowed on the corners. Commerce at this hour consisted of a few gas stations and seedy bars outside the city limits. She kept an eye on the speed limit to avoid the attention of Clear Point's bored police. She turned into the trailer park, deep in thought, and the Chevette bounced over a few small rocks outside her trailer. K.D. turned off the ignition.

Her home remained dark and quiet. K.D. rounded the car to find Trip sitting on her doorstep, holding her purse.

CHAPTER 10

K.D. drew up short, startled.
"Trip."
One word uttered with a thousand questions behind it. *How did you find my house? Did you knock on the door? Did my mother answer it? Why are you here?*

Trip stood, dusted off the back of his khakis and walked down a step into the yard. He held out her purse, which she took, unable to even offer a thank you.

"Hope you don't mind me coming by. You left so fast out of the Waffle Iron yesterday you forgot your purse. I told that pink-haired waitress I'd hang onto it for you. Scary thing was, she gave it to me with no questions. Guess she saw us talking. Anyway, I tried to call your cell phone, but it rang from the bag." He smiled. Had he always had a slight dimple on his left cheek? Maybe it was a shadow. Please let it be a shadow. The man didn't need another endearing quality.

K.D. found her voice. "How'd you know where to bring it?" *Where was Miss Celery Stick Delilah?*

"Your driver's license and a little help from Garmin. Your next door neighbor said if I caused any trouble, she was calling the cops."

Her face flamed in the dark at the thought of Trip rummaging through her things and at Doris's nosiness.

As if he read her mind, Trip held up a hand. "I only looked in your wallet, at your license. The fact you eat beef jerky is completely your business."

Of course, an empty wrapper wadded in the bottom of her purse, probably along with tampons, weeks-old gum, and several past due bills.

K.D.'s face wrinkled in anger. "You could have kept it until class Tuesday. You didn't have to go digging through my stuff." A few late-night coffee runs and cell-phone study sessions didn't give him permission to delve into her personal life. Doomsday Doris probably peered at them right then through plastic blinds. Trip needed to stay at the peripheral and not barge into her inner circle. She jerked the purse under her arm and brushed past him.

Trip grabbed her arm. "Wait a minute, what's wrong? Are you mad at me for bringing your purse to you?"

K.D. stopped at the top step, her hand on the screen door. *I'm not mad at you for bringing me the purse. I'm mad at you and that silly, bone-headed Delilah for being so perfect and me, well, not so much. I'm mad because I want to like you, but can't. I'm mad because I'm...mad.* She inhaled deeply before speaking, gritting her teeth. "No, Trip, I appreciate you bringing my purse. I just wish you hadn't gone through my personal belongings, that's all." She knew at this point, she should invite him inside, act nicer for his effort, but she stood there, glaring at his confused expression made almost comical in the stingy glow of the street light with a shattered globe.

"I'm sorry, K.D., I..."

"Look, thanks for bringing my purse. I was worried about where it ended up. Not that there's much to steal as you found out, but I do need to go. My mom's sick, and I need to check on her. Besides, shouldn't you be with Delilah in one of your study groups built for two?"

"What are you talking about? I've only studied with Delilah once and invited you to come along, if you'll recall."

"I don't care about who you study with, Trip. Your business, not mine."

"I study with you, K.D." Trip frowned and shook his head as if trying to translate. "What is all this about Delilah anyway? You think we have something going on? Come on, she looks like a skinny, ten-year-old boy. Why would you think I had anything to do with her?"

"Maybe because y'all looked awfully cozy on your date at the Waffle Iron."

Trip snorted. "Who in the world takes a date to the Waffle Iron?"

Every boy in her graduating class including her last two dates, but K.D. kept the information to herself. She waved a hand, anxious for him to leave her home, her life, her reality. "Whatever. Listen, thanks for bringing the purse. I gotta get inside." She nodded her head at him to move along.

Trip stared off for a minute, a backdrop of peeling trailers and broken down cars hung behind his perfectly pressed shoulder. "Okay. Have a good evening, I guess." He shook his head and walked toward the car parked on the street. The Audi looked as out of place in the trailer park as glitter on a pile of dog mess. How had she missed it when she drove up? K.D. let him get as far as the car door, trying to bite her tongue from calling out to him.

She failed.

"Trip, wait." She walked toward him. "I'm sorry, I'm sorry. I'm tired, and I'm mean when I'm tired."

"You're mean all the time." He halfway grinned at her.

Maybe he wasn't horribly upset then. "I didn't say only when I'm tired. I merely pointed out the fact that when I'm tired, I'm mean. All other times are open for interpretation. Mean is actually a subjective term."

Trip leaned his elbows on the roof of his car and smiled at her. No, she did not imagine the dimple on his cheek.

Sigh.

"You can't bully me with your big words, Miss Jennings. But I do have a confession."

Oh no! Did he look in her side pocket and find her rocks? The ones she found that looked like Jesus and Mel Gibson in his *Lethal Weapon* years? Right next to her melted bubble gum Chapstick? And her mom's refilled prescription of anti-depressants?

"What do you need to confess?"

"I brought your purse because I wanted to see you. I had fun the other night at McDonald's. When we bought our books. Even when I picked you up in the rain, when your car broke down after class. You make me laugh, K.D. I found myself wanting a laugh tonight." His brown eyes softened under the florescent glare. He looked up and down the deserted street littered with kids' rusted bikes, balled up fast food bags and beer cans. "You want to take a walk?"

K.D. glanced back at her house.

"If your mom's sick, you can go check on her, but she didn't come to the door earlier when I knocked."

Okay, whew. Wait, she didn't answer the door? K.D. glanced back.

"We don't even have to go for a walk, K.D. We can hang out inside."

K.D. would put on a cheerleader uniform and lead a rah-rah for Professor Elliott before she'd let Trip inside. Instead, she looked back at him. "Mom's been a little under the weather. A head cold or something. She was probably just asleep when you knocked. She's a hard sleeper."

"Well, then? Want to go for a walk?" He must have noticed her hesitation. "I know it's late, and you're tired, but I'm here. You're here. I promise not to keep you long. I guess I, well, I guess I need some company." He toed the asphalt, scattering a few pebbles.

Something about his tone caught her attention, and she found herself nodding. "Sure, we can go for a walk. In fact, I know the place to go, but let me check on Mom first. Hang on a sec." K.D.

jogged up the steps, hurrying down the hall. After a few coherent answers and one final, "K.D., I said leave me alone," K.D. rejoined Trip on the street, motioning him to follow her around the trailer.

Trip looked hesitant. "I meant walk on the road, not in the pitch-black woods."

"Don't be such a sissy. Come on, I want to show you something. It's not far."

Doris's voice rang out through the darkness. "K.D., you okay? I got 911 dialed. All I gotta do is press enter."

K.D. winced and turned her head. "I'm fine, Doris. Just going for a walk with a friend. Mom's fine. The world's fine. No need to call the cops." She lowered her voice to Trip. "One time, after getting to know Doris and her propensity for paranoia, we bought her one of those all-purpose weather radios, seeing as how she's always concerned with natural disasters. Problem was, we forgot to input our zip code, and the radio broadcasted everything going on in the entire world from earthquakes to forest fires to volcanic eruptions. We found poor Doris the next morning in her bathtub with a mattress over her head, clutching a fire extinguisher."

The two laughed together as they tread along a darkened path. The crickets chirped, and their feet crunched along the leaves as two owls conversed among the limbs. K.D. hoped the wind wouldn't shift and toss the smell of trash bins their way. Trip reached out and took K.D.'s arm, threading it through his. Not so much in a "come on" kind of fashion, but more in a protective way. K.D. almost laughed at the consideration, thinking of the countless times she'd braved the woods alone as a child, desperate to be a princess running from danger, searching for her castle, anything to escape the reality that waited for her back in the trailer.

But there was never a prince. K.D. had no memory of princes.

"Right around this patch of poplar trees."

Trip looked at her strangely.

"What?"

"Sorry, you just don't strike me as a woodsy kind of girl who knows the names of trees. You seem kind of feminine to me."

Why did everybody say that? Just because she didn't know how to paddle a boat right away or the sophomore yardage of Bo Jackson's collegiate years didn't make her un-southern. Feminine, hah. K.D. looked down at her blouse and faded jeans. A hot mess, sure, but certainly not feminine.

"I can hang in the woods. Did it all the time growing up. Just because I prefer air conditioning to hundred-plus heat does not mean I'm a girly girl."

"Could have fooled me. Weren't you the one who freaked out over the mouse at school? You stopped the entire class by standing on your chair while I herded the poor creature out the door."

"Um, excuse me, but I was not the only one who freaked. I believe Professor Elliott ran out like a six year old getting immunization shots."

Trip laughed, snorted more like it. "You're right. He did. Man, if we survive this class it will be a miracle. Well, me anyway. I'm sure you'll pass with flying colors and minimal effort." Trip grew silent, staring sideways at her as they walked.

"What?"

"I don't know. You're such a contradiction. One minute you're dressed like you are now in your pretty blouse that looks like a Dutch milk maiden, with your hair all gathered up like that." He reached over and tucked a curl behind K.D.'s ear, leaving goose bumps in the wake. "Putting on your lipstick before you ever step foot anywhere. And the next minute you're shredding some poor soul's argument in class who lost the battle as soon as you stood up. I never know which K.D. I'm going to find."

Me either, K.D. refrained from saying out loud. She hoped the day she passed the bar would solve the lifelong puzzle of who she was meant to be. "Right now, I'm the girl who's going to show you something really pretty."

She pulled aside a veil of kudzu, exposing moonlight flinging diamonds along a black ribbon of water. The water moved rapidly, producing a soothing white noise over the stones — a balm for K.D.'s wounds that life would rake across her soul. Picture rocks abounded here, a new one each time she visited. The last looked just like Woody Woodpecker.

"Wow." Trip whispered the one word, peeking around a curtain of Spanish moss dripping from the oaks. He looked up as if to find the crowns, but the trees soared to heaven from mountain-sized trunks.

"Here. Come over here with me." K.D. took his hand, long fingers wrapped around hers, and guided him along the mud until they came to a band of rocks. Navigating around one, she showed him where erosion and time had carved out a curve in a larger stone, the perfect shape in which to sit and lean back. She did, pulling Trip down beside her.

He drew his knees up and wrapped his arms around them. K.D. watched his face relax as his eyes closed, and he breathed in deeply. The stress she noticed earlier washed from his face with the sound of the rushing water. She leaned back as well, enjoying his presence.

After three deep sighs which seemed to sink him deeper into the rock, K.D. broke the silence. "So what really brings you to my neck of the woods?"

Trip spoke without opening his eyes. "It's the anniversary of my parents' death."

The air stilled around them; pain washed from his mouth like the water traveling over rocks. He winced as if from a physical blow and then relaxed. K.D. reached over and touched his arm.

"I'm sorry. I know you must miss them." She left her touch on him, wishing she could find the right words to say as the shadowed clouds glided across the moon, casting them in darkness for a second before traveling on. "You want to talk about it?" Stupid. Obviously he did or else why would he have come to her?

"Not much to say. I guess I always get a little down this time of year. No matter how much I prepare for it, or pretend it's not there, no tactic really works. To be honest with you, this year I really had almost let it get by me." He lifted his head and turned to K.D. "Law school is the best remedy for sadness because I've been so stressed about Tuesday's case argument. Plus my aunt and uncle are going through something I can't help them with so things are kinda tense at home. I don't know, I mean, I didn't even remember what day it was until around dinner. It was like something tapped my shoulder, and when I looked at the clock, it was the precise moment we had gone through the red light."

"You want to tell me what happened?"

"Which part?"

"I meant about the accident, but you can talk to me about anything, Trip."

He shook his head. "I can't tell you about my uncle's business. I wish I could, but it's confidential."

"Okay. You wanna talk about the accident?"

Trip stared off into nothing, silent for so long K.D. wished she hadn't asked the question. Without turning his head, he finally spoke. "I do, but not tonight. One day. One day I want to tell you everything about my parents, what happened that night. But not tonight. I kind of just want to sit with you."

"Okay, if there's one thing I do well it is sit. Exercise, like running, walking? Not so much. But sit I can do." K.D. wished she'd shut up, but the corners of his mouth lifted slightly. What did he mean by one day? Would there be more days or nights like this? Did he want to spend more time with her outside of class? Why in the world would he want that when he had Miss Ninety-Pound America waiting to hang on his every word? And how could K.D. manage it among work, law school, and her mother?

The night enveloped them, swaddling them with heat and humidity. K.D. retrieved her hand and put both under her knees, then folded them in her lap before finally leaving them on the cool rock. Trip needed something. A tender touch? Maybe sympathetic words? She knew little about either. Instead, she gave him her presence like he'd asked; she stayed silent until she felt him staring at her.

K.D. turned, puzzled by an expression she couldn't read, but then Trip leaned toward her.

"K.D., would you mind if I…"

"Did you hear the one about the skunk?" K.D. fussed with her hair, barricading the space between her and Trip. Was he about to kiss her? Crazy. The man's talking about his dead parents, and she's wondering if he's about to kiss her. She must have misread him, but still…

He leaned back and smiled. "No, I didn't. Why don't you tell me?"

"I would, but it really stank."

Trip laughed again. The man always laughed. Even when he was sad or her jokes were not funny. He leaned over, knocking against her with his shoulder. "Good one. Or at least a good enough one." Trip looked at her intently, then reached over and fingered her necklace. "I need to buy you a charm for this. It's too thin a chain not to have something on it."

K.D. swallowed, unable to tell him of the charm in her bedroom drawer. The butterfly given by her father, flung off when he never returned. Discarded like he had discarded her. The chain served as a constant reminder of his abandonment and her determination to succeed in life in spite of it.

Trip didn't seem to require an answer. He looked at his watch, moving his arm until he caught enough moonlight to see the time. "Guess we better get back if your mom's sick."

No, I'd rather stay here with you. All I do is check on Mom.

K.D.'s mind switched over to Tuesday's school assignment, knowing she'd wake tomorrow with one foot off the couch, the case book across her face, and a line of drool down her cheek. If it had been a good day for her mom, she would have invited Trip in so they could study together, but not now when her mother hadn't bathed or seen daylight. Plus, she needed distance from Trip and his sadness and vulnerability. Her thoughts of what his lips must feel like. "Yeah, I'm beat. I'm hitting the sack as soon as I walk in the door."

Trip held out a hand to steady K.D. over the rocks, but she kept hers inside his as they entered the woods. He was being protective again. And for half a second, K.D. envisioned a prince.

CHAPTER

11

In the next few days, K.D. did not think of Trip's moonlit eyes once. Not during the horrific fight with her mother who refused for the third day to get out of bed and had the gall to accuse K.D. of not having time for her. Not in the office, during discussions with a dad who wanted to sue his neighbor because her dog bit his son. Although the dog was chained. In its own yard, and the kid, home because of a school suspension, had been shooting at it with a pellet gun.

Not once did K.D. think of Trip.

No, she thought of him multiple times. No matter what she did or how she busied herself, K.D. could not get the man off her mind. In class, he had successfully discussed the case of *International Shoe Co,* explaining the differences between interstate commerce and intrastate commerce and the effects on jurisdiction and the payment of taxes.

Eloquent. Confident. K.D. closed her eyes for half a second and pictured him before a jury, each member swaying to his opinion before the first sentence's conclusion.

Professor Elliot had then caught her off-guard when he asked, "Miss Jennings, what if the corporation showed by audit that no accounts receivable originated in said state?" She had no response, and his tirade drew a few snickers from the class. Trip had patted her knee when she sat down, making it all better.

Trip had called her various times a day, sharing something from his activities or funny jokes he found on the Internet, planting himself at the forefront of her thoughts.

"Give it up, Trip Folsom. You'll never be funnier than me." The smile would remain on her face long after she'd hang up the phone.

She had to find a grip, but when she entered the back office, she found instead the top of Ingram's head over boxes upon boxes which almost consumed the entire room.

"What in the world is all this?"

Ingram pushed up his bifocals, standing to be seen. "This is called careful what you wish for. Remember I called the hospital and requested Bo's medical records and all things pertaining to the emergency room from that day? Well, they obliged."

"All of this?" K.D. stood there, her mouth open, holding two cups of coffee with nowhere to set them down.

"I told you this would happen. Our job now is to sift through all the documents, copy exactly what we need, and go from there. Might take a while."

"I'll say." K.D. handed Ingram a cup of coffee. "Even if we dropped everything else and read the material twenty-four/seven, it would take us weeks to disseminate this information. What about temps? I'll bet I could get some of the law students in my class to help out." She thought of Trip and days spent working on an actual case together.

Ingram ran a hand over his face. "We can't hire temps. We don't have the money. As it is, I'm shaking sofa cushions to find spare change for the expert witness, which we're supposed to conference by some contraption called Skype. Plus, we can't let just anybody read over the materials or else we risk a breach of attorney/client privilege."

"I can help you with Skype. I did an extra credit course online and skyped with my project group. We'll have to go to the library, though, since your wife won't approve Internet service in the building."

"Ex-wife."

"Whatever. What time are we supposed to call him?"

"He said around two central time. He's in South Florida. We'll know more about his expenses after our meeting today. In the meantime, we need to get busy on all this." He gestured around the office.

K.D. bit her lower lip, her mind racing as her eyes traveled over at least fifteen boxes around the office, maybe twenty. "Hang on, I've got an idea."

She hurried down the hall, past the break-room door and the case study waiting on her desk. She yanked open the front door, and charged head first into a man who stabled her with an outstretched arm.

"I'm sorry, sir. I was in a hurry and didn't notice…Oh, Mr. Cookson." Bart Cookson. Or as K.D. liked to call him, Bart Crookson. The dirty ambulance chaser who'd already wooed the Murdocks following Bo's death and failed to get the case.

"Well, hello there pretty lady. I don't believe we've met, although you seem to know my name. I'd remember someone as beautiful as you." He took her hand and raised it up. K.D. jerked it back before it reached his lips.

"What can I do for you?"

Bart adjusted his tie and cleared his throat. "I'm here to see Ezra Ingram. He does still practice in this building, doesn't he? His ex-wife hasn't kicked him out yet?"

K.D. blocked the door, infuriated by Bart Cookson's knowledge of Ingram's personal business. Even inbred Southern hospitality could not move her out of the way for this dirt bag. "The law offices of Ezra Ingram are still in this establishment. I'll be happy to make you an appointment to see him as our firm does not accept walk-in clients."

Raucous laughter bounced off the interior hall of the building, loud enough to call Mrs. Gonzales out of the restaurant. K.D.

waved her back inside with a toss of her head.

"Touché, Miss Beautiful. Professional even when mad. I like it. Now look, I've driven all the way from Birmingham to see Mr. Ingram and won't be leaving until I do so. Since we both know I'm not here as a client, would you kindly move out of the way and allow me to wait in the lobby until Mr. Ingram can find time on his busy calendar to see me?" The man enunciated *time* like he talked to a simple-minded person.

K.D. had no choice but to move. She gestured toward the sitting area, wincing at the tear in the couch. "If you'll sit over here, I'll check with Mr. Ingram. But I have to warn you, he has a lot of client meetings today so I wouldn't count on seeing him any time soon."

Bart moved to her desk and picked up the nameplate. His fingers moved over the brass plate almost suggestively. "Why thank you for your consideration, Miss Jennings. K.D. is it? What a lovely name. I think I'll stand. Please inform Mr. Ingram I'm here at the request of the Murdocks. I'm sure that will get his attention."

K.D. masked her shock. "I'll be right back." Because he parted his oil-slicked hair right down the middle, she didn't even offer him coffee.

Restraining her legs from full gallop, K.D. eased into Ingram's office and shut the door. He sat cross-legged on the floor, an open box and mounds of files beside him. "Excuse me, Ingram?"

"Not now, K.D. Where've you been? Get down here and help me cull through this paperwork."

"Well, you see, Bart Cookson is in the lobby." K.D. winced, expecting the explosion. Ingram's visceral dislike of Bartholomew Cookson dated back to Cumberland Law School when the Crook was elected editor-in-chief of the Law Review, and Ingram was relegated to a lower editorial board committee, a suspect election at best due to the Crook's dalliances with the previous year's editor-in-chief.

A look somewhere between hatred and murder clawed across Ingram's face. If he hadn't been buried in folders and paper, K.D. felt certain he'd have thrown something. The piece of paper he held crumbled in his grip. Clenching his teeth, he breathed in and out of his nose which whistled.

After ten eternities, somewhat collected, he frowned at K.D. "What in all things holy does that fershtinkiner want?"

"You know I don't understand Yiddish anymore than you get my jokes."

"Loser. Why does this loser dirty my presence with his foulness?"

K.D. looked at the ground, the ceiling, anywhere but at Ingram. She fiddled with a box lid. Finally she spoke. "He, um, says he's here at the request of the Murdocks."

Ingram's brows shot up. He stood with great effort, scattering papers in his wake, and marched to the desk. He picked up the phone and looked at K.D. "What's the Murdock's phone number?"

K.D. shrugged her shoulders. "How am I supposed to know?" Then she remembered her cell phone where she had saved Shelly Anne's number for future law-breaking adventures. She called it out to Ingram who punched the phone with a finger.

One side of the conversation gave her enough information to know the Murdocks had indeed talked to Bart Cookson when he initiated the call, but they had not committed to anything or signed any paperwork. The conversation was enough to encourage the Crook to travel from Birmingham for evidentiary items so he must have received *some* encouragement.

Ingram hung up the phone and pointed a finger at K.D. "He's going to try to railroad me and steal our clients when we're not looking. But we're not going to let him. Keep your mouth shut and follow my lead." Ingram straightened, tucked in the tail of his shirt and strode to the front lobby as if accepting an award. K.D. didn't even have time to be offended at his tone.

"Why the Honorable Bart Cookson. Oh, pardon me. You

did lose the judgeship bid when that nasty rumor circled about a certain barista. What a shame you can't wear the judicial robe, as good as you look in black." Ingram smirked. "What in the world do I owe the pleasure for your company on this fine day?"

If Ingram rattled Bart, it didn't show. Bart extended a well-manicured hand, the cuff far enough back to show a sparkling Rolex. "Hello, Ezra. I was talking to my friends the Murdocks, and they mentioned you were counsel of choice for a lawsuit against the ER doctor who tended to their son. Congratulations. Mighty big case for a small firm such as yours. Madeline was telling me over lunch how close you were to taking down the shingle. I was surprised to hear you could afford such a case."

Ingram paused at his ex-wife's name, his eye twitched. He gestured for Bart to sit, which he obliged, choosing an arm chair rather than the tattered sofa. Ingram leaned against K.D.'s desk, giving him the height advantage he'd never have if Bart stood.

"Why thank you, Bart. That's very kind of you to drive all the way from Birmingham to offer your congratulations. Good to know someone else is picking up Madeline's lunch tab for a change."

The two squared off like a bull and a matador, only K.D. couldn't figure out yet which was which. She'd never seen Ingram wound so tight, and Bart oozed calm like tree sap.

Bart chuckled. "I'm here to do more than that, Ezra, although you can bet I'll give Madeline a call before I return to Birmingham. I would imagine right now your office back there is filled to the rim with documents. It's my understanding the lovely Miss Jennings here remains your only employee. I called the Murdocks the other day, as I have often since I learned of young Bo's early demise. When they mentioned you took the case, I offered them my assistance."

"You offered your assistance before the death certificate was signed, Mr. Crook, sorry, I mean Cookson." K.D. spat from the door frame leading to the firm's offices. "They turned you down."

Bart narrowed his eyes before easing into a smile. "Yes, I

certainly did. The Murdocks have a clear cut wrongful death suit in front of them. Someone should be held accountable for such an unfortunate circumstance. The Murdocks weren't comfortable dealing with someone from Birmingham even though I grew up here same as you, Ingram."

"What's your point, Bart? I'd like you to land this plane before you take up all the oxygen."

"My point, Ezra, is your office is not equipped to handle a case this size. You don't have the resources to peruse the discovery information alone, much less the finances to hire the medical experts to testify. I talked to the Murdocks this morning and told them we handle cases like this every day. I have medical experts on retainer. Their job, for me, is to work these cases. I don't have to go find them. I don't have to convince them. I simply assign them the work. Plus I have the money to finance the case until a successful jury decision. I'll let you assist, of course. You'll earn a referral fee, somewhere in the ball park of twenty percent. Think about it, Ezra. Twenty percent of a couple of million dollars is a lot of money."

"A couple of million?" K.D. spoke before thinking, earning a foul look from Ingram.

"What? You would ask for less? The boy's temperature was over a hundred degrees when he entered the emergency room. The fact the doctor did not treat for heat stroke immediately is obvious grounds for a favorable judgment. Southern juries love to award big punitive damages in medical cases, particularly ones involving small-town football heroes."

Ingram's expression remained unchanged. "I think it's time you go, Bart. If, and I emphasize the word if, I need some assistance in the case, I'll let you know. Until then, save your time and gas and stay in Birmingham. Everybody knows you don't even visit your own mother."

Bart Cookson's face clouded and his brow wrinkled. But it passed just as quickly, leaving behind the smirk he wore when he first entered the office. Offering a hand to Ingram, whose arms remained folded across his chest, he then turned to K.D. "Miss Jennings, it was a pleasure to meet you. I do hope you'll talk some sense into Ezra here. Sometimes his Superman mentality gets in the way of common sense. Y'all take care now." He turned and slithered out of the room.

After he shut the door, Ingram stalked down the hall. K.D. moved out of his way much as she would a locomotive. She left the office to continue on with the great idea she had earlier and headed for the Chinese restaurant and Maria Gonzales.

CHAPTER

12

"You want me to do *what*?"

K.D. leaned on the counter while Maria rolled silverware. "I want you to come down to the office for a few hours and help me and Ingram look through some boxes. We're preparing for a case and need help reading some of the documents."

"I don't read English bien, K.D."

K.D. picked up a fork, spoon, and knife and began to roll them into the white cloth napkin. "Maria Gonzales, you are lying through your beautiful white teeth. You have read through entire cases with me on more than one occasion, asking me questions and helping me prepare for class. Heck, you've done it so many times you should go to law school yourself. I know you read English good."

Maria kept rolling napkins as if working alone.

K.D. tapped her on the wrist with the blunt end of a knife.

"Maaaaria." She sang.

"I don't like him."

"Who? Ingram?"

"He says my food tastes like roasted cats. How does he know how roasted cats taste?"

"He's an old man who needs to increase his fiber intake which makes him cranky. You can't hold that against him. Please? Can you do it for me? We need to help this couple. A man and a woman, Buck and Shelly Anne Murdock, lost their son."

"How do you lose a son? They forgot where they put him?" Maria mumbled in Spanish, something about crazy Americans.

"They didn't *lose* him. That's American slang for die. Their son died in the emergency room of a heat stroke almost two years ago. The doctor misdiagnosed him. He could have been saved if the doctor had not made a mistake."

Maria looked up with round, tootsie-roll colored eyes. "Doctors can't make a mistake?"

"They can and do, but in cases like these, when the error is so egregious, they must be held accountable. And don't tell me you don't know what egregious means. You used the very word to describe how badly your husband cleaned the dishes."

Maria laughed. "I like that word. It confuses mi esposo, my husband."

"So you'll do it?"

Maria swept her arms toward the restaurant. "How am I to leave this? I'm busy, K.D."

The room remained empty at the mid-morning hour. Chinese art decorated the wood-paneled wall. Sunlight bounced off the always-shiny red vinyl booths. Fake ferns drooped over both sides of the half-wall which bisected the room.

K.D. stared pointedly at Maria who waved her hand. "Still. We're busy during lunch and then supper. No tengo tiempo."

K.D. placed her roll of silverware in the gray, plastic bucket and leaned over the counter. "You do too have time. Plus you know you want to. I can see it in your eyes." She playfully cupped Maria's chin who swatted away K.D.'s hand. "Hey, didn't the bank say they needed updated organizational papers on the restaurant in order to renew your loan?"

Maria shook her head. "I tell you too much information."

"Sooo, let us draw up your organizational papers. You help on this case. Win/win for both of us. Come on, it'll be fun." K.D. stopped short of a desperate tone. For one thing, Ingram was probably going to wring her neck when she told him she hired Maria Gonzales as her assistant. Even in trade, but she knew Maria would be a great asset. She could argue a case better than most trial lawyers. At least, she could when propped up on the counter of her kitchen while K.D. would pace the floor. "Come be with us in the afternoons. Let Lupe run the restaurant for a while."

A crash sounded on the other side of the kitchen door followed by a string of Spanish curses. Maria looked at K.D. "The man does drive me loco." A grin spread across her face. "I get to be a lawyer?"

"Close enough."

"I get to boss Mister Ingram around?"

"Don't push it. Come on."

Maria called out to her husband, Lupe, who forbid her to leave the restaurant before mopping the floor. "You mop the floors and handle lunch! Tu hagas algo para un cambio!" She grabbed her purse and stomped toward the door muttering, "You work for a change. Don't be telling me what to do."

K.D. ran to catch up, wanting to get ahead so Maria could wait in the lobby while she explained things to Ingram. Instead, Maria charged into the office and down the hall. K.D. caught up with her as she stood over Ingram. "Where you want me to start?"

"I beg your pardon?" Ingram scowled at Maria.

K.D. put her hands on Maria's shoulders, easing in front of her. "Ingram, hear me out. Maria said she could help us in the afternoons between the lunch and supper crowds." Ingram began to stand, but K.D. held up a hand. "Now, before you argue about breach of confidentiality, we're going to hire Maria in trade. She needs some organizational papers drawn up for the restaurant, which I'll do, and is willing to give us a few hours in the office in payment."

"The woman can't even speak English!"

Maria squared her hips. "You see? I told you!" She whirled and pointed at Ingram. "Puedo hablar inglés. Hablo mejor que usted? Cómo se atreve usted decir que no puedo hablar Inglés!"

Ingram pointed at K.D. "See?"

Why was everyone telling K.D. to see when she was the only one who could? Maria turned to leave, but K.D. grabbed her arm. "Hang on, hang on. Ingram, you need to apologize to Maria. She speaks as good English as both of us, but what's even better, she's an avid reader. She reads four books a week. Granted, they're Harlequin romance series, but she reads fast and can tell you anything from any of them. It's how she learned to speak English so good. Maria can plow through these documents quicker than both of us together." K.D. paused for effect before landing the final blow. "Do you *want* to lose this case to Bart Cookson?"

Ingram's pewter-colored eyes shot at her like lasers.

"Well do you? Because we can stand here for the next hour debating whether or not we can use Maria at no cost to the firm, or you can stop being so stubborn and let us get to work. What's it going to be?"

Ingram pushed his glasses up and rubbed his eyes. Without speaking, he waved them into the office.

K.D. clapped her hands together and gestured for Maria to put her purse by the fake ficus tree long in need of dusting. She wrote down the names Buck and Shelly Anne Murdock as well as Bo. K.D. also wrote down the date of Bo's death and handed the paper to Maria.

"We need to go through all of these boxes and take out any papers that have any of these names or this date on them. Just make a separate pile. These are our copies, so it doesn't matter if you take things out of the boxes. Why don't you start over here?" K.D. gestured to the other end of the room from Ingram.

Maria started for the corner, but stopped. "How we know who has looked at which box?"

K.D. smirked at Ingram in a "See? I told you she would be an asset" kind of way.

"That is a great question, Maria. Let's do this. I have a ton of pens in which you click for a certain color. Hang on, I'll be right back." She ran up to her desk, retrieved several pens, and returned to Ingram's office. "I use these in law school to help me remember which day of the week I took what notes. Maria, when you're through with a box, just write a check on top in red. Just depress the red like this." K.D. demonstrated.

"What if I want to be red?" Ingram sounded like a sulky two-year-old.

"Okay, then you be red. Maria, you be purple."

"I like purple."

"Wonderful. That way, we'll know who looked through which boxes."

Maria's brow wrinkled. "Why we need to know who looked through which boxes as long as the boxes are looked through by somebody?"

"Again, very good question." K.D. liked leading the discussion, teaching. Maybe she could give Professor Elliott a run for his money one day. "If we get to the end and don't find what we're looking for, it would be better for us to go through boxes someone else has looked through. A kind of fresh-eye approach. That way, we'll know who has looked at what. My color will be pink."

Her cell phone rang as K.D. lifted the lid off her first box. Trip's name lit up so she excused herself and walked out of the office and into the outer hall. Ingram's ears could hear through an atomic bomb shelter so the more distance the better.

"Hey Trip, I thought you were helping your uncle on his farm or something."

"I am so if I cut out, I'll call you back. I wanted to see if you had plans this evening."

K.D. smiled to where her whole face felt like teeth. "Nothing except studying. Why?"

"Good. I'd like to take you out on a date. A real date. Not a quick bite to eat after class or anything like that. I mean a fancy restaurant with a wait staff that's actually glad you're there as opposed to the drive-thru people who don't put the lids on the Cokes all the way."

K.D. thought of Maria and Ingram busy on the other side of the wall and how many hours stretched ahead of them. Plus, what would she wear? On a real date? She wanted to crack a joke, but her mind could only muster panic. A date? With Trip? "It might have to be late."

"I don't mind." He paused and then spoke. "I mean, how late is late?"

K.D. laughed. "You sound like Professor Elliott saying our argument depends on what our definition of is is."

"I mean, is it skip dinner and have dessert and coffee kind of late? Or is it when the stomach starts to growl, but short of when it actually starts feasting on your intestines kind of late?"

K.D. looked at her watch, giving herself a few more hours to work and invent a credible reason to leave. "To be safe, let's count on dessert and coffee. Is that okay?"

"Perfect."

"How um, should I, you know, dress?"

"Clothes, preferably."

"Trip. You know what I mean."

"Don't dress up. What you had on the other night when I came to your house would be fine."

Sure, if it wasn't at the bottom of a pile of clothes waiting on K.D. to find time to wash it. "I'll try to scrounge something together."

"Great. Text me when you're leaving work so I'll have an idea of when to pick you up."

"Okay. I'll see you later." K.D. depressed the call end button, wondering how in the world she could concentrate on medical records when Trip waited at the end of the day.

CHAPTER

13

K.D. tried to ease out of the office without a production. She had warned Ingram of her need to leave early, but he either ignored her or had turned the volume down on his hearing aid.

She jumped at the sound of his voice. "Where are you going?"

"I've got plans tonight. I told you. I'll be in early tomorrow. I promise." K.D. flung her purse over her shoulder and exited the room before he could protest. She almost shut the door on Maria's face. "No, no, no, Maria. You need to stay and help Ingram. He'll be here all night if you don't."

Maria fled toward the restaurant. "I won't stay with a man who's not my husband. It's not proper. Besides, I worked through lunch. Lupe has probably already left me and took my babies. You go. Go on your date. Your Mister Ingram will be fine."

"How'd you know I had a..." K.D.'s question was lost when Maria shut the restaurant door. Between her and Ingram, K.D.'s private life might as well be painted on a billboard. Drat Maria's high moral standards. Now Ingram would be working through the night with only the roaches for company. Guilt tugged her back, but thoughts of Trip tampered it down.

The Chevette wouldn't start on the first couple of tries, and K.D. feared calling Trip to pick her up at the office. "Please, baby,

Please start for Mama." She stroked the dashboard, stopping short of kissing it in encouragement. The car responded to her caress. K.D. could picture the cloud of black smoke from the exhaust pipe out back. She raced home, as fast as a car in its condition would allow, and pulled to a stop at her home as Doomsday Doris waved to get her attention.

"K.D., you be mindful of your water supply." The elderly woman stood by the concrete steps leading to her single-wide, one hand straining on a wobbly rail.

"Good evening to you too, Miss Doris."

Doris wagged a gnarled finger. "You'll thank me in November. Saw a program the other day about that Mayan calendar. Says this is the year, showed all kinda experts including that Nostradamus fella."

"I'll take a look at the supply as soon as I walk in the door. We try to keep at least a closet full of water bottles, but I'll check with Mom in case. Appreciate the warning." Surely God would forgive the tiny lie, but she didn't have time for a lecture on dehydration.

Doris lifted her hand in dismissal, allowing the screen door to snap shut on their conversation.

Mayan calendar. Nostradamus. Good grief.

K.D. opened the door to her mother at the kitchen table, eating from a bowl. The linoleum floor shined; a mop stood propped in the corner with a hint of lemon meeting her nose. The sink sat empty, no dirty dishes spilling onto the counter, only the ceramic frog holding an orange sponge in its mouth.

Lydia turned and smiled. "Hi, honey. You're home late."

K.D. slowed, approaching her mom like a stray dog. It was the first time she'd seen her vertical in days. "Hey, Mom. How're you feeling?"

Should she retrieve her mom's medicine from the cabinet? Give it to her without a word? Without starting an argument? Maybe she took the pill already. Which would explain her return to life. Then K.D. heard the TV in the background. Susan Lucci was selling makeup on the Home Shopping Network, which probably meant her mom came out of the abyss of depression by charging hundreds on K.D.'s credit card. The credit card she'd paid off last week.

K.D. would call tomorrow, report it missing again, and get a new number. Keep better tabs on it. In the meantime, she hoped the balance would at least allow for a grocery run as the cabinets offered a teaspoon of Nutella on the last piece of bread this morning. "Glad to see you out of bed."

"I feel fine. Took a shower and my medicine."

K.D. breathed a sigh of relief.

"Thought I'd watch a little TV before calling it a night." Lydia took another bite of soup from the chipped bowl.

"You'll be okay watching by yourself if I go out?" Please say yes. Please say yes. She'd already texted Trip who was probably on the way by now.

Her mom must have picked up on her tone and turned in her chair with a playful smile. "Go out? Where you going?"

K.D. stalled, scrambling to find some reason to explain why she'd be going out so late without actually telling a lie. "I um, well, you see." She took her mom's empty bowl to the sink and began to wash, watching the water swish around, not wanting to tell Lydia she had plans with Trip for fear she'd somehow sabotage the night.

"I see what?"

Finding no answer in the sink or whispered in her ear, K.D. sighed and turned. "Trip called and asked if I'd like to do something after work."

"Handsome Trip from the Waffle Iron? The one who looks like he should be on a recruiting brochure for Ivy League colleges?" Lydia raised suggestive eyebrows up and down.

K.D.'s face heated. "Yes, but don't get all excited. He probably needs help with class preparation or something and feels guilty about asking me all the time. It's probably his way of saying thanks." The words hollowed out as K.D. realized their truth. Trip probably did invite her out of guilt for all her help. Oh well, free food was free food. "I need to jump in the shower. I smell like Ingram's cigars."

K.D. stopped at the hallway and turned. "Trip's picking me up here. Is that okay?"

Her mom frowned, looking around the room. "I wish I'd a known. I would have picked up." She stood and began scraping crumbs from the round, plastic table into an open palm.

K.D. refrained from mentioning she had fully expected to find her mom curled up in a fetal position in the middle of her bed like she had the past few days. "Mom, the place looks fine. Do not put out the dog for this guy. He's a friend. Nothing more." At least for now. She didn't invite questions by elaborating. "If he can't like us for who we are, we don't need him anyway. We both know a clean house doesn't make a man stay."

Her mother frowned at her. "Not every man's your daddy, K.D. You go on and get ready. If I want to tidy things up, that's my business. Take your time. I'll entertain young Mr. Trip until you're ready."

The words branded K.D. in the rear as she took off for the bathroom. Her mama alone with Trip was one of her greatest fears.

K.D. spent too much time trying to cobble together something better than wrinkled jeans. She settled on a cotton blouse in deep purple, mostly because of the contrast with her blonde hair, which she took the time to straighten. Not that time was her friend at the moment, but she stole some just the same. Laying flat, her hair fell to her shoulder blades, tucked behind her ears. K.D. put down the brush and stared in the mirror.

Shoulders up, she could pass as tolerable. Blue eyes shone brightly with a few sleep-deprived lines of red marring the whites. K.D. reached for the Visine. She wished she made time to fix her hair more often as even she could concede its better qualities. The other qualities? The amount of body between her chin and toes? That was a different story. K.D. stepped back and turned from side to side. She pulled in her tummy so it didn't hang over the waistline of the faded jeans, wishing she could pull in her rear. She longed to be someone like Delilah, who would probably eschew a slice of chocolate cake and munch on a piece of lettuce for dessert. Oh well.

"Good man don't want skin and bones, K.D." Maria had told her often, the flab of her underarm jingling as they shared some bread pudding Maria had baked and snuck into the restaurant before Lupe got a whiff. "Lupe back there?" She gestured with her spoon. "He don't like it if I lose weight. Says I look sick. You don't worry about your trasero. Your, how do you say it? Junk in your car?"

K.D. laughed at the memory, using her bedroom mirror to slide small earrings in place. She thought of Maria and her slang translations while speaking to her reflection. "I don't have time to worry about the junk in my trunk, Maria." Voices carried down the hall. Trip's and her mother's. How long had they been talking? K.D. leaned toward the cracked door. Something about K.D. and colic, midnight car rides to get her to sleep. Thanks a lot, Mom.

K.D. glanced over the reflection one last time, sighed, and grabbed her purse. Peering out of the hall, she found Trip sitting on the sofa, accepting a glass of water from her mother.

"Hey, Trip. I'm sorry I didn't hear you come in."

He stared long and hard at her with no words — long enough for her to finger the hair already tucked behind her ear, straighten out imaginary wrinkles in her blouse, and still he stayed silent.

Lydia's mom spoke first. "K.D., honey, you look so pretty."

Trip cleared his throat. "You do. Artists would kill to have the ability to recreate the colors of your hair."

Heat climbed K.D.'s neck. "Oh please, Trip. You sound like a Hallmark card." She stopped herself from running back to her room and locking the door, barricading herself from all the scrutiny. She knew she wasn't *that* pretty.

"Hallmark or not. I've never seen your hair like that. I might need to take you to a fancy restaurant after all." He stood, placing his glass on a coaster. "I know you had a long day at work so if you want to get going we can."

Lydia stood too. "Trip, can I speak to K.D. alone for a minute?"

"Sure. I'll wait in the car. Thank you for the hospitality, Mrs. Jennings. I hope to see you again soon." Trip offered his megawatt smile before closing the door behind him.

K.D. turned to her mom, surprised to find tears in her eyes. "What is it? Do you feel bad?" Oh no, here it comes. *K.D. I really need you to stay home with me. I feel one of my headaches coming on and need you to rub that place in my shoulders. Run to the drug store. Cook me some soup. Wake me up every four hours because you're scared I quit breathing.* K.D. waited on any of the above to prevent her from having a life outside of caring for Lydia.

Lydia shook her head, wiping the corner of an eye with her finger. "No, no, nothing like that. I guess I haven't seen you take any time for yourself in so long. I just want you to know how pretty you are, and I love you. I hope you'll allow yourself to have fun."

Her tone shook K.D. a bit. It sounded as though she was saying her goodbyes. "Mom, you are feeling okay, right? I mean, we can stay here and watch TV with you."

Lydia shooed her toward the door. "Don't be silly. I'm fine. Truly. I'm sorry I got all sappy. A mother's greatest wish is for her daughter to see herself as her mother sees her." She paused and pressed a finger in the corner of an eye. "Or in your case, at least take the time for yourself. That's all. You go on and enjoy yourself. I won't even wait up."

"If you're sure."

"I'm sure. Go now."

K.D. obliged, allowing her mother to push her out the door. Trip waited by the passenger's side, and K.D. could feel Lydia's sigh as he opened the door for her. She slid onto the leather seats, admiring the glare of the radio numbers in florescent green. K.D.'s radio still had teeth she had to push in order to move a red bar over to the desired station. Trip entered the driver's side, and the air conditioner came on immediately upon the turn of the ignition.

"So, Mr. Mysterious, where are we going?"

"You'll see."

They drove in silence, K.D. almost losing the battle against drooping lids as jazz played through the XM radio. She didn't recognize the melody or the voice, but loved the way its soft baritone massaged her brain, pushing out stressful thoughts of school, work, and her mother, and leaving room for K.D. to enjoy the ride.

Streetlights had vanished before K.D. realized they cruised past the city limits. Asphalt rolled beside hills like dinosaur humps in the moonlight shadows. He turned onto a dirt path, coming to a stop before a gate.

"Is this your uncle's farm?"

Trip nodded his head, exiting the car. He looked shorter when standing in front of the massive iron gate as he fiddled with the lock, but he also looked at home swinging it open, stepping up on the lower rung to ride the gate until it banged against a rock — a flashback of a young boy. He ran back to the car, grinning.

"I never took you for a cow poke, Trip."

"No cows anymore. My uncle dabbled in them some for awhile, but it was really a hobby. Hang on a sec." The car eased through the gate, and Trip jumped out to lock it back before they continued down the winding dirt road along the pasture. "What were you saying? Oh, cows. No, but I did talk him into the horses. Do you know how to ride?"

K.D. shook her head.

"I grew up in rural New York State, on about a hundred acres. My aunt and mom did too. It was their family property. We had horses, chickens, sheep. I loved horses. I never showed them or anything. Just always loved to trail ride. Every time I'm on a horse, it's like I'm back where God wants man to be. Nature and beast. You probably think that's cheesy too."

Anything but cheesy, she wanted to say. Instead K.D. grinned.

"Like cheddar on toast. I hope you don't think you're getting me on a horse."

Trip pulled through an opened gate, stopping beside a barn illuminated by a flood light. K.D. stepped out into a star-soaked night, not a cloud to mar the brightness of a three-quarter moon. The land spread out before her, rolling shadowed hills dotted with pines and brush. Open pasture to the right behind yet another split-rail fence. A snort caused K.D. to spin around, face-to-nose with a huge chestnut horse.

She stepped back with a laugh, hand to her chest as the beast nudged her shoulder.

"That's Grady. Nothing but an oversized dog. He's searching for a sugar cube." Trip whistled softly, and Grady turned toward him. Trip extended the treat in his open palm on which Grady's massive lips clomped down.

K.D. stepped forward, determined not to be the sissy girl Trip claimed her to be. She reached out a hand, surprised at the softness of his neck. "Hi there, Grady. My, aren't you a big fella."

"To answer your question, you most certainly are going to ride him."

"I've never ridden a horse, Trip, and I'm not about to start now. You can forget that. I'll wait here if you want to ride. I'd love a little peace and quiet." K.D. looked around and spotted a hammock between two pines just off the barn. "See? I can go lie down. Relax for a spell. You go on ahead."

Trip shook his head. "Nope. If you're not comfortable riding alone, that's cool. You can ride with me." He was already walking toward the barn and returned carrying a blanket and saddle and some other contraption thrown over his shoulder. Trip showed her step by step how to saddle a horse, as if she'd ever need those skills again. "Here, you put the bit and the bridle on. Like this."

He guided her hands onto the iron, showing her how to maneuver it between Grady's lips and behind his teeth. "Doesn't this hurt?" K.D. asked.

"Not if it's in there properly. Grady is bridle trained. Some horses know where to go based on the pressure of your legs. Others, like Grady, pay attention to the reins. I'll show you once we get on. Whenever Dad would harness a horse, he'd say, 'Like a whip for the horse, a halter for the donkey, and a rod for the backs of fools.'"

"What's that mean?"

"It means a word aptly spoken is like apples of gold in settings of silver. It's from the Bible, Proverbs to be exact. Dad would always tell me to choose my words carefully, to use them as a guide. If I chose them foolishly, then it's like a whip for the horse rather than a gentle tug of the harness."

"I never took you for a Bible scholar."

Trip laughed, but it sounded a little hollow. "I could write the Ten Commandments about the time I could my own name. But somehow words from the Bible didn't sound as comforting coming from the preacher's mouth at my parent's funeral. What about you?"

"What about me what?"

"You and God. Are you a believer?"

She paused her hand on Grady's neck. "Sure, I believe in God. Did you not think I did?"

"I didn't know. You always seem so in control of things. Sometimes it's hard for folks who have it all together to lean on anyone, especially God."

K.D. snorted. "I most certainly do not have it all together, but I appreciate the compliment."

"Who said it was a compliment?" He smiled, but then it faded under the barn's floodlight. "I can tell you this: I don't know how folks get through hard times without the presence of God. Even when I was so mad at Him, I felt Him right beside me when my parents died."

K.D. patted Grady's neck for a moment, thinking of Buck and Shelly Anne, their gentle blessing before the meal. Her heart hurt for Trip, for Bo, for all the lives destroyed by death. Shelly Anne praised God for creating a nighttime sky, but did not hold a grudge against Him for taking Bo away so soon. Trip stood here, giving God credit for comfort while admitting to anger against Him. There were true relationships with God, while K.D. knew Him more like a distant relative everybody talked about, but whom she'd never met.

"I'll admit I don't think about it much. Too busy, I guess. I mean, I believe God exists and all; I believe in Jesus."

"I found that having God in your life is more than knowing Jesus, K.D. More than religion. It's about a relationship."

K.D. felt uncomfortable with the passion in his voice, his words echoing her very thoughts. She laughed nervously. "Maybe you can teach me more about that. The biggest relationship I have at the moment is with Professor Edwards, which is kind of sad now that I think about it."

In the silence, K.D. managed to harness the horse with Trip, but looked doubtfully at the saddle. "There is no way my fat rumpus is going to fit with you up there."

Trip's eyes cleared; a smile interrupted the seriousness on his face. "I'm too much of a gentleman to remark on the perfection of your rumpus. In regards to the saddle, you'll sit in it and I'll sit behind you. Or vice versa if you're more comfortable."

K.D. thought of being lead cowboy, the one in the saddle, and shook her head. "No, you sit in front of me with the reins. That way, I can tuck and roll when Grady here decides he's tired of hauling both of us around."

Trip laughed, pulling the reins over Grady's head. He walked him over to a stump and gestured for K.D. to join him. "Step up here. It'll be easier the first time to put your foot in the stirrup." He guided her foot up, holding onto her ankle. "Hold onto the saddle horn and swing the other leg over. You can slide over the saddle when you get up."

K.D. inhaled and obeyed his commands, embarrassed at the first failed attempt. Trip steadied her for another try, placing a hand on her hip to push over. He followed her in one fluid motion. Grady stayed still as Trip settled into the saddle. "You can either hold onto the back of the saddle or put your arms around my waist. However you're comfortable."

With a cluck of Trip's tongue, Grady moved away from the stump and toward an open gate. K.D. started to encircle Trip's waist, but thought better of it, grabbing the back of the saddle. They walked a few paces, enjoying the stillness of the night with only the sound of Grady's hooves to mar the quiet.

She inhaled his cologne, a scent she'd breathed many times in class, but never this close. What would it be like to circle her arms around his waist? To place her cheek against his back and mold herself against him? To simply ride and ride with no one to tell them to stop? Smiling in the darkness, K.D. settled behind the saddle.

They talked about everything and nothing. K.D. didn't expose details of her mother's mental illness, but shared about her father's abandonment.

"You mean you just came home one day, and he was gone?"

"Yep, that about sums it up."

"I can't even begin to relate." Trip glowed with descriptions of growing up with his parents, about his father's example of how to be a Godly man. Like Buck, the melancholy left his voice when he spoke of the time before their deaths, love kept alive through memories. K.D. could feel the cold northern winters he described, splitting logs on the farm, the simple country life.

"Some winters, the ice split huge trees right in half. Sounded like a war up on the mountain, canons firing at each other. First time I heard it, I had nightmares." Spring brought edible plants to the surface, and Trip described munching on dogtooth violets and wild apples.

"You ate flowers?" K.D. grimaced behind him.

"Sure. The roots especially are good. You can pull them right out of the ground, eat them on the spot."

"News to me." K.D. gnawed her lip for a minute and then spoke. "Why didn't you stay? Sounds like you really loved the outdoors, the whole living off the land thing. Why become a lawyer?"

"My dad decided not to go to college. He said the only education he needed lay between the covers of his Bible. I don't know. I guess I wanted to show him you could love the Lord, but pursue another calling. He cautioned me it would make entering heaven more challenging; the temptation to put too much stock on the things of the Earth more tangible. But I had such discontent in my heart after I graduated college. I knew I couldn't be happy as a farmer, as much as I love the outdoors. Circumstances changed, and here I am."

After several minutes of open pasture, Trip turned his head and said, "This a good pace?"

K.D. smirked toward his back, more confident in her horse-riding skills. "Sure. If you're a five year old." Girly girl. Feminine. Hah. She could handle the ride just fine.

Trip laughed. "Okay, then. Hold on." He kicked his heels into Grady's abdomen, and the horse lurched forward into a quicker pace. K.D. almost fell backward, and then threw her whole weight into Trip, circling her arms around his waist in terror. Grady stretched into full gallop, the wind blowing over her enough to whip hair all over her face, even guarded behind Trip's back. K.D. would not let go to clear her eyes, but instead squeezed them shut.

The run lasted for eternity, arms numb from the tight embrace. Trip finally pulled back the reigns, guiding Grady with soothing words until he dropped into a steady walk. Trip hollered, "Whoooeee," like any good cowboy would do at the conclusion of a race. K.D., on the other hand, stayed glued to his back.

He patted her hands. "Are you okay?"

Silence, but she somehow managed to nod against his shirt, which elicited a laugh from Trip. "Well, you did say my pace was slow as a five year old's. Thought I'd pick it up a bit. If it's too much, Grady can walk us back to the barn for the dessert I promised you."

K.D. mumbled in his shirt. "Walk. Yes, a walk would be great."

Trip turned Grady with a touch of the reigns. K.D. managed to peel herself off him, but not before one last inhale of his cologne.

Back at the barn, Trip eased off the horse first, catching K.D. before she tumbled to the ground. "Why are my legs so wobbly when all I did was ride, Trip?"

"Horse riding is great exercise. You don't realize it, but you're squeezing your thigh muscles to stay on. Back in the day, when cowboys would ride all day, they'd literally fall off their horses when they returned to camp. It's hard work being a cowboy." He turned and walked off toward the barn, holding the reigns. "Give me a sec to rub Grady down and give him some water and oats."

"Want some help?"

Trip looked back at her in surprise. "Sure. I thought maybe I'd turned you off horses for good after that ride."

K.D. laughed, an honest to goodness genuine laugh. It felt good. Her body tingled, tired and exhausted, but alive. It was the same feeling she had riding on the river with Shelly Anne. Free.

"No, in fact just the opposite. I can see why you love it so much. I'll help." She followed Trip into the barn, who switched on a light before they put up the tackle. He threw a brush to her, which she dropped, but then followed his motions as they rubbed Grady down. After filling the feed bowl with oats and water, the two washed their hands with a hose and exited the barn.

Trip gestured for her to wait while he jogged over to the car. He returned with a giant picnic basket. "Let me spread out this blanket, and we'll eat. Even after the supper I ate earlier, I'm starving. You probably haven't eaten at all."

He unloaded a few Tupperware bowls and a giant bottle of water with plastic champagne flutes. The containers held fresh fruit and a vanilla-looking dessert.

Trip caught her stare. "Tiramisu. I hope you like Italian, although it's not authentic. I used pudding mix, but don't tell anybody. My aunt helped me fix it."

Pudding. A picnic. K.D.'s mind flew back to childhood, sitting beside the creek with her daddy. Back when life held order, security. Bills were paid, and food lined the pantry.

Her dad had sat there so handsome, tousled blond hair, work shirt dirty from the mill. "The trick, honey, is to get all the pudding from the lid in one lick. Like this." He'd lifted the silver foil to his long tongue and swiped off all the pudding. K.D. had tried, but her mouth was too small, leaving half the chocolate around the corner of her lips. He had laughed and laughed at her.

"What's wrong?" Trip's brow furrowed in concern. "You don't like Tiramisu?"

K.D.'s heart lurched around her chest. "It's not the Tiramisu. It's the pudding."

"You don't like pudding?"

"I love pudding. It's not the pudding."

"But you just said…"

"I know what I said!" K.D. stood and walked around in a circle, leaving a bewildered Trip to stare after her.

First, the guy made nice with her mom, complimented K.D. on her hair, and opened her side of the car. Then he drove to the family farm and introduced her to one of his greatest passions, sharing secrets about his upbringing. Quoting scripture. Then, oh boy, and then he opened up a homemade dessert, created by his own hand, reminding her of her father. The good one. The father who existed before he abandoned his family.

Why? What was the catch?

Come on, champagne glasses? Why not simple Dixie cups? The empty side of K.D.'s soul opened up, yawned across the earlier feelings of comfort and joy, filling her with wariness and distrust. Bring back Trip the study buddy. She could handle him. But this? Romantic Trip? No way.

"Why're you doing all this, Trip?" The words fell out before she could stop them.

He looked at her in confusion. "Why am I doing what?"

K.D. ran her fingers through her humidity-curled hair, and then threw out her hands. "This! All this! Why did you bring me here? Why did you make a dessert and think to bring a blanket and tell me you wanted to paint my hair?"

Trip looked at her as if she'd dropped her marbles, and she felt like she had. Then he laughed.

Heat climbed K.D.'s neck like it always did right before her temper unleashed. "This is funny? You think this is funny?"

He stood and stepped toward her, touched her arm and refused to let go when she tried to pull away. Instead, he urged her toward him, tucked hair behind her ear. "Why can't I do all this because I like you? Is that so hard for you to believe?"

Yes!! She wanted to scream. "You can like me at McDonald's, Trip, or in class. Why all this?"

A soft sigh escaped his perfect lips. "I had planned to get under your skin, K.D, when you weren't paying attention. To soften up that hard head of yours to the idea that maybe we could like each other outside of class. Be more than just study partners, but you're not giving me a chance if I have to disclose my whole game plan before I ever kick off."

"Stop with the athletic talk. You know it confuses me."

Trip took her hand and pulled her back onto the blanket, handing her a glass of water, which she drank in one gulp. "See that pond over there, K.D.?" He gestured toward the water, dark satin wrinkled by moonlight. "That pond is full of fish. Big catfish and bream swimming beneath the surface. Every once in a while one will jump out of the water. Why do you think it does that?"

"A breath of fresh air?"

Trip laughed. "Maybe. Or maybe it does it just because it can. Without thought. Acting on instinct."

K.D. thought of the turtle jumping into the river during her and Shelly Anne's clandestine mission last week.

"So?"

He leaned forward and brushed his knuckles softly along her jaw line. K.D. could see the moon in his brown eyes. "So, sometimes it's okay to jump without over analyzing things, to act on instinct. Ask your heart if it can like me as more than someone who cheats off your paper in class and steals your words so Professor Elliott thinks he's smarter than he really is. If it can, then let's act on that instinct without talking ourselves out of it. Don't over think this with that beautiful brain of yours. Let's jump."

K.D. leaned against his hand, the skin warm against hers. Her heart pumped *yes* through every vein in her body. A small breath escaped her lips, giving her answer before the word formed in her throat.

Trip scooted closer to her, their knees against each other's as he lowered his head toward hers. K.D. lost her breath in anticipation of the kiss, and closed her eyes.

A cell phone rang.

Trip jerked back with a nervous chuckle, checking his pocket. "I think it's yours."

K.D. released her breath and took her phone from her jeans. Seeing the illuminated home number, she held up a finger while answering.

Doomsday Doris cried from the other end of the line. "It's your mama, K.D. We're on our way to the hospital. Meet us there, quick!"

CHAPTER

14

"How's your madre, K.D.?" Maria looked up when K.D. entered the office.

"Why are you at my desk?"

"I told you, I won't stay in a room with man who is not mi esposo. I wait here for you. Hope you don't mind; I did answer the phone a few times. Mister Ingram yelled at me to do it. I don't like when he yells."

K.D. did not have the energy to argue. Fine, let Maria sit at her desk. She could have her job for all K.D. cared at the moment. The high-back chair caught her as she sunk into it. "Mom is fine. A few stitches on her forehead. She hadn't eaten in a few days, since she'd taken a cold. Got dizzy from the heat of the shower and fell. Luckily, our neighbor Doris had come by to visit and found her. No telling how long she'd been knocked out."

Trip had thrown everything into the car and broken all speed limits to the hospital. But as they pulled into the loop before the emergency room, he didn't get out of the car. "Do you mind if I don't come inside? I can come back and pick you up if you need me to. Or wait here." His tone had dropped; his eyes darted about. Definitely not the same Trip who had tried to kiss her less than an hour before. Maybe he had second thoughts about their evening.

"No, you go on. I can ride with the neighbor home." She hid

the disappointment from her voice, while conflicting emotions battled inside. On one hand, K.D. envisioned Trip beside her, comforting her from whatever waited on the other side of the automatic doors. But on the other more powerful hand, she felt relieved. She wasn't ready to air all the dirty laundry yet. He had called later to apologize and check on her mom. Even suggested a follow-up date.

Maria straightened some papers and stood. "Your madre has more than a cold, amiga."

K.D. sighed, not wanting to drag out details about her mother's condition and her financial inability to properly address it. "What's going on this morning?"

Maria questioned her with a look, but did not pursue. "I'm glad you're here. Mister Ingram is driving me loco. Keeps yelling, 'Where is she?' I say, 'I don't know!' And he say, 'Well get back here and do your job!' And I say, 'I won't come back there till K.D. is here!' And he say…"

K.D. held up a hand. "I get the picture. Come on. Let's both go do our jobs." She led Maria down the hall to confront Ingram's scowling face. "Don't start on me. I've had a long weekend, and I'm not even in the zip code of being prepared for tomorrow's class or hearing a lecture from you." She glanced around the room, papers strewn everywhere. "Tell me where we are in discovery."

Ingram must have picked up on the tone because he didn't press any issue. "I think we've gone through all the boxes and retrieved any paperwork relating to the morning of Bo's demise. I've tried to sort them according to priority." He gestured to his right. "Over here is what could be considered incidental material. Nurses' notes on cases prior to Bo's. I guess HIPPA doesn't apply to small-town hospitals because I believe they sent over every paper used that morning. Might be a good idea to glance through and get a feel for what was going on in the ER. This other pile is everything I found related to Bo's case. There seems to be some missing documents."

K.D. squared her hips. "Okay, what do you want me to tackle?"

"If you'll go through the incidental pile, I'll handle Bo's information. Should take us the entire morning for the first run through."

"Sounds good."

Maria cleared her throat. "What about me? I wanna work too."

K.D. started to speak, but Ingram interrupted. "Maria, would you mind sitting at the front desk and answer the phones or handle any walk-in traffic? We'll work more efficiently if K.D. doesn't have to race down the hall every time we hear the door open."

Maria straightened and offered a confident smile. "Yes sir I can. I will be your assistant. You can count on me, Mister Ingram. I need to go check on Lupe first. Will that be okay?"

Ingram nodded, and Maria left the office.

K.D. turned her head with a sly grin. "What gives? Y'all friends now or something?"

Ingram huffed. "I might have been wrong about Maria up there. She's a hard worker. I still can't understand her half the time, but you can't argue with her work ethics."

"Did you just say you were wrong?"

Ingram ignored the question. "Can we please get to work?"

K.D. obeyed, cleared some papers from a chair, and scooted it to a bare corner of the desk. She took out her multi-colored pen and clicked on pink. The documents seemed pretty standard. Doctor's progress notes. History of physical exams. Time of triage. Not much activity for the middle of the week in a small-town emergency room. One case of stitches. A fender bender in which one occupant complained of a neck injury, but a nurse noted a clean x-ray to forward to National Insurance Company of the South. K.D. made a table of the personnel, their shifts and the patients they treated.

During the changeover to the three-to-eleven shift, K.D. noticed a drop in nursing staff. The morning shift included three nurses for the eight-room ER, but only two nurses worked the afternoon. Two other patients came in about the same time as Bo.

One, a dehydrated child with a stomach virus, and the other, a diabetic with low blood sugar who had passed out while planting begonias in the 110 degree heat.

"Ingram, it says here only two nurses were on staff at the time Bo was brought in. Two other patients were already there so they had to have been short handed."

Ingram scribbled some notes before speaking. "Let's make sure to create a timeline of treatment for all the patients during Bo's time. Since the hospital is listed in the complaint, we might find dereliction of duties with some of the other cases. We can use that to support our argument."

K.D. shuffled through some papers. "One case involved a child who needed IV fluids due to a stomach virus. Seemed pretty cut and dry, no pun intended. But the other case involved a diabetic who passed out and hit his head on a rake or some other gardening instrument. Hey, this is interesting…"

"What?" Ingram shifted his bifocals on top of his head.

"I don't know what it says about Bo in your pile, but in this man's case he had to wait over an hour for a CAT scan. He ended up being fine, but if Bo had to wait that long…"

"It could have been the difference in life and death." Ingram finished her sentence while scribbling more notes. "We need to talk to the nursing supervisor and find the reason for the delay. Here's something else," Ingram pulled a paper from under his notebook. "Bo's temperature was 107 when he was brought into the emergency room. One hundred and seven. And the man treated him for a concussion. I can't wait to hear his reasoning for that. I don't even know how to get rid of an ingrown toenail, but even I know 107 degrees means a heck of a lot more than a bump on the head."

K.D. flipped some more pages, fingering through her notes. "I know the Murdocks don't want us to mess with the football coach, but look here." She passed Ingram a photo-copied newspaper clipping.

Ingram pulled down his bifocals, scanning the document. "Where'd you get this?"

"I looked some things up on the Internet at the library, came across the incident, and found the archived issue down at the paper. With everything going on, I had forgotten all about it." K.D. retrieved the article from Ingram, looked at the picture of Coach Mark Camp at a press conference.

Ingram grabbed an empty manila folder off his desk, jotting some notes on the outside. "So a bunch of mothers signed a petition against the coach, complained to the school board about his practice techniques, said they were dangerous. They go on to win state; petition is ignored. Maybe we should see if any other of his players had health conditions. Athletic directors tend to look the other way from harsh practices, especially when the coach consistently wins. How long has he been at the school?"

"Says here five years at the time of this article, and that was ten years ago. Guess he's in his sixteenth year by now. Want me to look into it?"

Ingram shook his hand, reclaimed the article, and filed it. "I'll do it. You wouldn't know your way around a hash mark."

"What's a hash mark?"

"Exactly."

Maria entered the office, holding a white board more than twice her size. "I took this from the restaurant. Lupe says he doesn't need it since we got the fancy menu now over the register. You use this. Write down things to keep in front of you, no?"

Ingram stood and took the white board from Maria. "This is perfect! K.D., we'll prop this against the wall like this." He leaned the white board on top of the credenza behind his desk. "That way, as things come up we can jot them down here. Keep a running list going. Good job, Maria."

The Hispanic woman grinned with pride. "I get back to my, uh I mean your desk now to answer phones."

"Maria, K.D. and I have to run to the library in order to type with a medical expert. Can you stay here at the office? If anyone needs us, we should be back in an hour."

K.D. gawked at the exchange, miles away from Ingram's earlier distrust of Maria's help.

"What's this type? Why you need to go to library to type?"

K.D. chuckled. "He means Skype. It's something you do on a computer or cell phone. A video chat with another person."

"Ah, si. I do it with my cousins in Mexico every Sunday. I love to Skype."

They both stared at Maria before Ingram glanced down at this watch. "We got twenty minutes to get to the library. Come on!"

On two tires, Ingram wheeled into the parking lot, and the two entered the building to a chorus of "Shhhhhs." K.D. ushered him to some cubicles in the back and showed the librarian her reservation card.

K.D. ushered him toward a small room, almost two phone booths in size. "Sit here, Ingram. You can put your notes on the table. See this camera?" She pointed to the top of the computer. "That camera films you. Your expert will come onto the screen here because he'll have a camera just like this one on his computer."

In tight quarters, Ingram shifted his shoulders to make room for K.D. and spread his notes onto the minimum amount of space offered. He handed her a card from which she typed in the web address. After a few seconds of transmission, a well-kept man's face appeared on the computer. Snow white hair. Trimmed brow. And only slight stubble to his chin. He appeared to be wearing a tie although he sat too close to the camera for K.D. to know for sure.

"Ezra Ingram I presume."

Ingram looked at K.D. who nudged him with her elbow. He leaned almost nose-to-nose to the monitor. "I am. Thank you, Dr.

Fellow, for meeting with us today."

"I'm sorry, I couldn't quite get that."

K.D. pulled Ingram back and addressed the camera. "Yes, Dr. Fellow. This is Ezra Ingram, and I'm his legal assistant, K.D. Jennings. Thank you for meeting with us." Her eyes cut to Ingram, and she spoke out of the side of her mouth, "You don't have to lean so close to the monitor."

"Please call me Jack. I'm assuming you received my credentials off my website."

Ingram cleared his throat and settled into the chair. "We did, Jack, but after reviewing the case, even I can see the doctor's incompetence is quite obvious."

"Why don't you let me advise you as to the obvious points? The fee for this initial consultation is minimal, so we'll hit the high level, but I'll warn you, many an attorney has failed clients by assuming incompetence is obvious when the defendant will prove the negligence did not result in injury. There's a big difference."

Oh, this guy was good. K.D. was already impressed with his cool demeanor.

"So, Ezra, why don't you tell me about the case, and we'll discuss whether you think my testimony is valuable following my initial assessment?"

Ingram tipped his head and gave the doctor an overview of the case.

"You see, Jack, we have a doctor from New York, here in the South all of two weeks, a patient who enters the ER with a temperature of 107, and the doctor treats him for a concussion because he arrives unconscious and his coach said another player hit him hard. The player died of a heat stroke before they received the CAT scan results. It's pretty obvious to me."

Jack stroked his chin, his movement causing the video to blur before settling again. "How was the temp taken?"

Ingram looked at K.D. who shuffled through the papers. "It says here ancillary temperature was 107."

"Well, there you go. Ancillary is when the temp is taken under the arm; a terrible way to gauge accurate temperature. There's your first mistake. You always take a rectal reading. Other things to consider would be whether or not you're dealing with tachycardia. How long it took between triage and time of death. Things of that nature."

Ingram straightened. "We don't have that information handy, but you see how obvious the incompetence was. Not just of the doctor, but the hospital in general. It's an open and shut case as far as I'm concerned."

"Mr. Ingram, you're forgetting the evidence has to be introduced in court. Sure you can introduce the nurses' notes or doctor transcriptions, but you need a medical expert on the stand to tell the jury exactly what this young man went through during the heat stroke while waiting on a useless and unnecessary CAT scan. Pieces of paper don't tell a story, Ezra. I do, and I can do it in a way to create a sympathetic jury. Compensatory damages are pretty straight forward, but you can really go for the jugular in punitive damages. Especially in Alabama. And we'll make sure the case is presented in such a way to minimize an opportunity to remit the award on appeal."

"You sound more like a lawyer than an ER doctor, Jack."

The doctor adjusted in his chair, blurring the screen for a second, before speaking. "Let's just say I've provided enough expert testimony to know what I'm talking about."

Ingram drummed his fingers against the desk top. "Jack, would you mind if Miss Jennings and I stepped out for a second?"

"Not at all."

K.D. opened the cubicle door, and Ingram followed her. "What do you think, Ingram?"

"I don't think we have any choice. Maybe we won't even have to go to trial. If we list Dr. Fellow in our witness disclosure, the plaintiff will know we mean business."

"But I thought you wanted to go to trial."

"Sure I do. But if we get a good enough settlement offer, and I mean at least in the millions, it's up to the Murdocks how they want to proceed. Now for the really painful part."

"What's that?"

"Hearing how much this is going to cost me. Come on."

Ingram squeezed back into his seat. "Thank you, Jack. You're right. A case this size demands all guns loaded. Let's negotiate your fee."

Jack laughed into the camera. "No negotiations, Ezra. My fee is standard. Today's consultation is fifteen hundred. Twenty-five thousand as a retainer, plus six hundred dollars a day for preparation and during the trial plus expenses. I'd ball park it around forty thousand to be on the safe side."

K.D. moved her head out of camera view before dropping her jaw. She didn't even look at Ingram, fully expecting him to conclude the call right then.

"Please have your assistant mail me the necessary papers. I'll return the contract to you with a check for your retainer and today's consultation," Ingram said.

K.D.'s eyes widened in disbelief as the conversation continued; Ingram did not miss a beat or provide any indication of surprise.

"Wonderful, Ezra. I believe, no, I'm confident I can help you win this case. I will forward you some information to collect as you cipher through your discovery, things for you to forward to me to help in my testimony. What's your email address?"

"I'm old-school, Jack. Please either fax me the information, or postal still works fine the last time I checked. Your secretary has my information."

The two signed off as K.D. remained dumbfounded in the chair. Ingram poked her. "Scoot before I pass out in this mouse hole."

K.D. started to talk as they walked toward the exit only to be shushed by more than one librarian. Walking through the door, she grabbed Ingram's arm before they stepped onto the parking lot.

"Please tell me where you've got forty thousand dollars laying around."

Ingram kept walking, stopping at his beloved Cadillac. Before entering the car, he patted the hood.

K.D.'s jaw remained ajar. "No…way. You're going to sell Hank Aaron?"

Ingram palmed his face and then massaged his temple. "I sure hope not. But I did pawn the title. It's the only way. I figured the expert would run anywhere between fifty and seventy-five thousand. That's why I didn't sit there like you did with your mouth hanging wide open for the flies to crawl in. The title company gave me enough to get us through the trial and pay the rent. I also paid off your credit card. Once the settlement comes in, I'll pay the title off and own him free and clear again."

"You paid my WHAT off?"

"You left your statement on your desk. I didn't go looking for it. Don't get all misty-eyed on me. You can pay me back when we settle the case."

K.D.'s heart tendered toward the weathered man in front of her. Times like this offered a glimpse into his solitary world. Divorced, no children. Far as she knew, no real friends. He was financially insolvent to the point he'd have to hock his own vehicle to stay in business, yet he still took the time to help someone in need. She'd give anything to return the favor, but a few rocks that looked like famous people were the only things of value in her possession. Mel Gibson in limestone couldn't finance a wrongful death suit. K.D. vowed in her heart to work hard for Ingram, to concentrate more on this case and limit other distractions. Except maybe Trip.

She sniffed, running a finger under her nose. "Thank you, Ingram."

The cell phone vibrated on her hip, displaying a new text message. She smiled when she read Trip's words, "Can't stop thinking about you. Glad your mom's okay." K.D. slid onto the seat, smiling as her heart soared. Ingram being nice. She having an *almost* boyfriend. Mom in a good place. Life swung into sunshine and butterflies.

Fingering the cell phone, she remembered the doctor walking around his darkened yard while talking on the phone. He had seemed agitated, raking a hand through his hair in frustration. The couple had no children, and Frances had remained in the kitchen while the doctor completed the phone call in privacy. The file said he had retired the call shortly after Bo's death so it shouldn't have been work related.

K.D. turned in her seat. "Hey, Ingram. Let's make sure we get the doctor's cell phone records. Can you subpoena the court for them?"

Ingram started the engine. "Sure. What's on your mind?"

"Nothing except an old saying that where someone spends his money the most is what he values the most. I'd even venture to say the person he called the most would indicate who he valued the most. Give us some insight into who he is as a person. You never know."

"I'll draw up the subpoena as soon as we get back. We might turn you into a plaintiff's attorney yet."

They drove in silence for a while, pulling into a parking space only to find Buck Murdock on the front steps of the office with a scowl across his face.

CHAPTER 15

K.D. wished Buck would stop pacing the room. The little man in the greasy mechanic's shirt seemed determined to cut a hole in the floor with his boots. "Can I get you something to drink, Buck? You look like you're about to explode."

"I AM! I mean, after all this, after everything we've been through, I finally get her to agree to the lawsuit. She attends one Bible study and BAM, suddenly it's not in the Lord's will for us to sue the doctor." He stopped, sat in the chair and dropped his head into his hands.

How in the world God figured into a lawsuit remained out of K.D.'s grasp, but she didn't want to scoff at the Murdock's belief system. After all, she believed in God too. Why wouldn't He want them to litigate? An eye for an eye and all that jazz.

Buck lifted his head and raked a hand through his hair. Ingram looked like he could use a stiff drink. K.D. fetched them both water instead.

"One minute she's all gung ho and the next minute we're going against God's holy plan and risking our salvation. All this from one hour at the fellowship hall this morning. Women with too much time on their hands is what I say. Nothing worse than a bunch of women gossiping and calling it Christianity."

K.D. bristled at the chauvinistic words and pushed off from the desk she leaned against, but Ingram held up a hand as he took a sip of water. "Okay, let's settle down. Nothing has to change right now. The trial date hasn't even been set. It can take up to a year to actually go to court on cases like this. Why don't we all simmer down, give y'all some time to work this out. Matter of fact, give it a few days without even bringing it up. She may come to her senses all by herself. If I've learned anything in my failed marriage it's when a woman's irritated, you better give her some space. Don't argue with her right away because you'll never win. You haven't heard anything else from Bart Cookson, have you?"

"Calls every day. I told him if he talked to Shelly Anne again, I'd get you to file a restraining order. Tries to sweet talk her, goes on and on about Bo and how he would follow his football games in the paper, knew what a talent he was. What a crock, but she clings to it, lets his fancy words make her feel better. Women."

K.D. felt outnumbered by the Neanderthals in front of her. "Why don't you let me talk to her? Shelly Anne seems pretty centered to me. Is she at home or at work?"

"She's at work now."

"I don't think she'd go off on some religious tantrum if she didn't feel she had a valid point. Plus it might help to have a woman's ears involved. You guys aren't coming across as the most sympathetic listeners." K.D. rolled her eyes.

Both men seemed relieved not to have to address the issue further, and K.D. left them to discuss the latest fantasy football numbers, whatever that meant. But instead of heading to the Waffle Iron, she had one pit stop to make.

K.D. found Trip in the library, the very place she should have been to prepare for the next class rather than running around trying to go up against someone's religious beliefs. Being as unskilled as she was in the argument ahead, K.D. figured she needed some ammunition.

She walked a wide berth around him in order to whisper in his ear. "Excuse me, Mr. Folsom. Could you please distinguish between the words *the* and *the* for me?"

She felt his smile before he ever turned his head. "K.D., I know you're not at the library to study. You probably read this case once and already have your case brief prepared. What in the world are you doing here?"

K.D. pulled out the seat beside him and plopped down. "I need your religious expertise."

Trip snorted. "My what?"

The exchange earned them a chorus of "Shhhhs" from various patrons. Trip closed his laptop and gestured for K.D. to follow him outside. They found a concrete bench under the generous shade of an oak tree, enough shelter to make the conversation barely tolerable in the heat.

Trip laid an arm across the back of the bench and fiddled with K.D.'s curls, raising goose bumps across her neck. "Now run that by me again?"

K.D. tried to focus on the task at hand rather than the dimple in his left cheek. "Okay, I probably shouldn't tell you this much, but you know I work for a local attorney."

Trip nodded.

"One of our clients has second guessed the suit. She feels like it's going against God's will for some reason, as if God wouldn't want her to sue somebody, and she's worried it would interfere with her walk with Him as a result. I personally think that's ludicrous, but before I meet with her, I thought I'd see what you thought."

"How did I suddenly become the expert?"

"You were the one quoting scripture the other night when we went horseback riding. I thought you could give me some insight and help me talk her out of it, or at least give me some scripture to counter the argument."

Trip retrieved his hand, leaned over to the ground, and picked up a twig in which he twirled with his fingers. He seemed to ponder her words, his brow knit together. Finally, after what seemed like forever in the sweltering wool of humidity, he looked up. "Maybe you shouldn't talk her out of it if it's her conviction."

Thoughts of Ingram losing his car collided against the beauty of the doctor's fancy kitchen in his ritzy house on the water, the Murdocks slugging away at the gas station and Waffle Iron. No way she'd advise Shelly Anne to drop the case. She shook her head. "I can't give you details, but I promise you this lawsuit needs to happen. There's clear neglect here. Someone needs to be held accountable."

"First tell me about your mom. Is she doing better?"

K.D. dismissed the question with a wave of her hand. "She's fine. Doomsday Doris took her to the hospital. It was a few stitches, but leave it to Doris to escalate it to something out of the book of Revelations."

"Who is Doomsday Doris?"

K.D. laughed. "The one who all but called the cops on you the other night. Remember? She's convinced the world is ending this November, and is cutting coupons to make sure she's stocked up on water bottles. I guess she doesn't buy into the Rapture and figures she'll be stuck on the ground for a while with a few hundred cans of Ravioli."

"That's right. I remember her now. She seemed a little direct."

"Understatement of the year, but she's a good friend to Mom. Seriously, Trip, I need your help. How do I win this argument with the client? It is absolutely in her best interest to pursue this case."

He chewed on the side of his mouth, then reached into his satchel and brought out a worn Bible. "My dad always taught me when in doubt, look it up. Let's see what the Word has to say."

"I thought you didn't put much credit in the Word these days."

"I never said that. I just said the words seemed hollower at a funeral rather than sitting around a Sunday dinner table." The tattered book opened easily in his hand, as if used often. Trip licked the tip of his fingers and scrolled through some pages, tracing down the paper before stopping.

"Okay, here it is. In the Old Testament, God gave the law to Moses for the people to follow."

"The Ten Commandments."

"Right, but the Israelites strayed from God's commandments, which forced Him to create Judges to rule over them."

"Eye for an eye, right?"

Trip shook his head. "Actually the eye for an eye quote is from Deuteronomy, which predates the book of Judges. The entire Old Testament is a cycle. Israel disobeys. God intervenes. Peace prevails until Israel disobeys again. He establishes the judicial system to bring order to a chaotic world. They disobey again."

K.D. smiled. "So I'm right! What was the scripture again? I want to write it down." She dug in her purse for a pen and paper.

Trip reached over and grabbed her hand. "Not so fast. We haven't gotten to the New Testament yet." He flipped through his Bible, stopping. "Here in Matthew, chapter five, Jesus says, 'Do not murder, and anyone who murders will be subject to judgment. But I tell you that anyone who is angry with his brother will be subject to judgment.'" Trip turned the page. "It goes on to say, 'Settle matters quickly with your adversary who is taking you to court. Do it while you are still with him on the way, or he may hand you over to the judge, and the judge may hand you over to the officer, and you may be thrown into prison. I tell you the truth; you will not get out until you have paid the last penny.'"

K.D. drew her eyebrows together. "What are you saying?"

"I'm not saying anything. I'm just reading the word."

K.D. leaned back, straightened her legs and crossed her ankles.

"Look, K.D. Forget judgment and making someone accountable. Forget making someone pay for whatever wrong has been perceived. I believe God is more concerned about broken relationships than broken laws."

She sat back as a tepid wind blew across them, rustling a few leaves. Why would God create judges if not to settle arguments among people? Are laws not necessary in order to keep order? From what Trip said, God Himself created laws and judges for that very purpose, yet Jesus chimed in commanding everyone to love their neighbor. How can you love someone and still sue them?

Trip reached over and brushed K.D.'s cheek with his knuckles. "You know, you're prettier when you smile."

Heat climbed her neck as she knocked his hand away. "Don't distract my philisolophical thinking."

"No such word as philisolophical."

"Far as you know." She drew up a knee onto the bench and faced Trip. "What does all this mean?"

"What do you think it means?"

Ugh! She wished he'd just answer the question instead of always offering another one. K.D. pondered a moment, rehashing the words in her mind before speaking. "I think He means for us to make relationships right, to not hold onto grudges, but if a law is broken, then accountability for the act is okay as long as it is done with a pure heart and not out of vindictiveness."

Trip smiled, deepening his dimple. "If more people bought into that, think of what a world we'd live in."

"If more people bought into that, we might not have a job when we graduate." They laughed together. K.D. took a deep breath and exhaled. "Okay, I think I got it. Thanks a lot for your help. I had no idea what I was going to say to the client. Still not entirely sure, but at least I'm not walking into this like a complete moron. Think you could write down some of that scripture?"

"Nobody could ever accuse you of being a moron. Except maybe in sports trivia." Trip took paper from his satchel and scribbled chapters and verses, bookmarked his Bible with it, and handed it to her.

K.D. shook her head. "No, no. I can't take your Bible." She tried to give it back, but he folded his arms across his chest.

"I don't want you to learn the scripture because you're trying to win an argument. You need to read it and then ask God to show you the meaning. Use the word to build the relationship we just talked about. Take the Bible, unless you have your own."

K.D. shook her head, somewhat embarrassed.

"I tell you what. Have dinner with me and my family. My aunt and uncle are dying to meet you. They've heard all about you, and you can return my Bible then."

She put her hand to her chest. "Moi? What in the world did you tell them?"

Trip took her hand and kissed it softly. "That you were smart and sweet and so beautiful it hurt my eyes."

"Why in the world would you lie like that?" K.D. snorted.

"Well, I only lied about the sweet part."

She punched him in the arm. "Are you serious? You sure you're ready for me to meet the folks?" K.D. gasped as she realized her guffaw. She'd never meet his folks.

Trip leaned over and kissed her cheek, lingering for a second as his breath tickled her skin before he whispered, "I'm sure. I've met your mom so it's only fair you meet my family. I only wish my parents could see you. You remind me a lot of my mother."

K.D.'s heart felt like it would burst, but for once she allowed herself to feel the moment instead of ending it in a puddle of unworthiness. Why shouldn't a guy like Trip care about a girl like her? She was smart, halfway attractive except for the back fat, somewhat sociable unless he wanted to talk sports, which she could learn in time. Trip wasn't exactly Mr. Jock himself. Maybe…

She eased back before he kissed her lips. So not ready for that move yet. "Well, if I remind you of your mom, she must have been spectacular."

A lazy, lopsided smile spread across his face. "She was."

They remained silent a moment. Trip's face held a peaceful expression; his brown eyes twinkled as if holding onto a secret, drawing her in to understand their mystery. She noticed for the first time that he was wearing jeans and a polo collared shirt, still too dressy for a study session at the library, but more casual than his normal khakis and button down. Could she possibly fit into this perfect man's world?

K.D. forced herself to pick up her purse from the ground and stand. "When do you want this big meeting to occur?"

Trip grabbed his satchel and joined her. "How about Saturday? I'll clear it with Big Daddy and let you know."

"Big Daddy?"

Trip took K.D.'s elbow, and they walked toward her car. "I always called my uncle Big Daddy. He's not really big so it's used kind of as a joke. You'll see. Let's plan on Saturday at six to give us time to visit before eating. He and my aunt have been so stressed lately it will be a welcome distraction. I'll pick you up."

"I don't know. My social calendar's been pretty full lately." They stopped at the car, and Trip leaned in to kiss her cheek. "I'll try to squeeze you in."

He laughed, and walked away, turning his head back to her. "Just so you'll know. I fully intend to kiss you properly Saturday night. I hope that's alright with you. Oh, and K.D.?"

She looked up from putting her key in the door and raised an eyebrow to his question. "Yes, oh wise one?"

"I also intend to ask you to be my girlfriend." He turned back on one heel and crossed the parking lot, leaving K.D. with her mouth hanging wide open while clutching his Bible, one hand on the door.

CHAPTER 16

The week limped on with K.D. mentally exhausted from her conversation with Shelly Anne, feeling inadequate and like a failure. Unable to tell Ingram of any progress, she could only report that she and Shelly Anne ended on good terms, leaving both of them with thoughts on which to chew. K.D. could see where Shelly Anne's argument originated. It did seem hypocritical to say she had forgiven the doctor and yet turn around and sue him. Yet the more K.D. perused Trip's Bible, the more she understood the potential to forgive and yet hold someone accountable to the law.

The free will of man mandated the existence of laws, and the subjectivity of a judge or jury mandated lawyers. If no one faced conviction for breaking the rules, what would become of the world? K.D. woke every day with a need to create order and battled the forces against her black and white existence – primarily her mother's bipolar condition. But she even had a plan for that once they received the settlement. Yet she did as Trip advised. She read his Bible daily, searching for the keys to open her heart toward the relationships Trip so easily made.

K.D. sighed as she opened the office door and called out to the silence. Ingram must be at lunch, and Maria wouldn't step foot in the office with no one there. K.D. dropped her purse by the desk, rolled up her sleeves and walked with determination to Ingram's office. Time to dive into the discovery landfill.

Instead, she turned the corner to the very definition of organization. Maria (Ingram could never manage this on his own) had divided different piles of paperwork and files into neat stacks with colored paper on top detailing the contents. They were grouped for different purposes: time, patient, treatment. K.D. picked up several pieces, realizing Maria had made multiple copies of documents if the information related to several different things.

She would kiss Maria on both cheeks next time she saw her. A woman after her own heart.

Even the white board Maria had brought from the restaurant held a wealth of information, all color coded which made K.D. smile. She walked over to analyze, taking out her notebook and pink pen. But a framed photo on Ingram's desk caught her eye.

A couple smiled from the front of a boat. Upon closer examination, K.D. recognized Ingram and his ex-wife from quite a few years ago as noted in the lack of Ingram's girth. A genuine smile spread across his face, an arm casually slung across Madeline's shoulders. K.D. had never seen this particular photo or any one for that matter as she'd entered Ingram's life post divorce. She thought of Ingram sitting alone in his office, lost in the memories of the picture, armoring himself with sarcasm and a rough exterior to mask the loneliness. She sighed, placing the photo where she found it, allowing him the privacy he rarely afforded her.

She turned to the white board, studying the scribbles, and then traced a particular set of words with one finger.

"Janice Parker." She said the name out loud, noticing the nurse's nighttime shift as eleven to seven, the last shift of the night. "Melanie Johnson was the nurse on duty when they brought in Bo around five." Why did the name Janice Parker ring a bell? K.D. flipped back through her notes, finding the name. Nurse Parker had completed the paperwork for another patient's x-ray who was treated the same shift as Bo was. Except Janice didn't come on until eleven, which meant she had finished someone else's paperwork, probably Melanie's, since she was the only nurse on that shift.

"Is that normal?" K.D. chewed on the end of her multi-colored pen.

"Is what normal?"

She turned at the sound of Ingram's voice. K.D. put down her notebook and gestured around the room. "Look at all the work Maria has done. Now argue with me about bringing her on the team."

Ingram laid the briefcase on the desk, eased the photograph into the lap drawer without acknowledging its presence, and sat down. "Can't. She has done a great job. So good in fact, I might get rid of you."

K.D. swatted at him, picked up her notebook, and took the chair across from him. "You can't do that. Her moral convictions won't allow her to be alone with you. Which, given your track record with women, probably isn't a bad thing."

Ingram ignored the comment. "What were you saying about not being normal?"

She flipped through some pages. "I noticed a nurse, Janice Parker, had finished up some paperwork from the shift before her, the shift in which they brought in Bo. I wondered if it was normal for one nurse to complete another's work. You'd make me stay until midnight to finish what I had started. Might not be anything, but I thought I'd check. I've got to go to the hospital anyway. Some of the nurses' notes are hard to read from the photo copies they sent so I asked them to pull the originals. They stonewalled me until I called your friend the administrator."

Ingram grinned. "Pays to flirt a little. Next time don't be so critical of me."

"Ha ha. She wasn't altogether excited to have me over, but I threw in how pretty you thought her new hairdo looked."

"I never said that!"

"You did now. Anyway, I've got an appointment with her

assistant to look over the originals." K.D. leaned over and picked up a file. "Which, thanks to Maria's superior organizational skills, I have the copies right at my finger tips. I'll try to catch a nurse in the hall, see how they operate with leftover work at shift change." She paused and peered at Ingram. Did his eyes seem more drawn? K.D. needed to pay him more attention. She knew what depression could do to a person.

"What? Why are you looking at me like that?"

"What do you mean? I'm not looking at you any way."

"You look like you're about to give me advice I don't want or need."

Was she that transparent? "Ingram, I wouldn't waste my breath giving you advice. Be like telling the Appalachians to scoot over."

The chair squeaked as Ingram moved to open his briefcase. He took out a clipped stack of papers and tossed them across the desk to K.D.

"What's this?"

"This was your great suggestion to subpoena the courts for the good doctor's phone records."

K.D. flipped through the pages, noticing the same number highlighted many times a few years back, dwindling over the past year. She also noticed a marking on the night she and Shelly Anne crouched behind pine trees, waiting on the doctor to conclude his phone call.

"So, whose number is it?"

"Nurse Janice Parker."

K.D.'s jaw dropped. "Are you sure?"

Ingram's smile spread from ear to ear. "Positive. What's even more, Miss Parker lives in an apartment owned by Dr. Thomas. The rent is six months in arrears, and he still hasn't evicted her. Sure wish my ex-wife was as lenient on me. What a kind man the doctor must be to a woman twenty years his junior who just got divorced at the origination of these phone calls." Ingram's voice dropped into sarcasm as he tapped a pen against the lip of the desk.

"What would this have to do with a malpractice case?"

"It paints a picture of what type of man the doctor is. If he's capable of running around on his wife of many years with a young hussy under his authority, then he's certainly capable of malpractice. Especially when he's thinking with his pants and not his brain."

"Gross, Ingram." K.D. compared the man Ingram described to the couple she had witnessed through the kitchen window. It didn't seem possible the two were the same. A thought nudged her. "I bet if Shelly Anne knew of the doctor's infidelity, she sure would change her tune."

"She already has. I rode out to their place this morning and talked to both of them. She says she had already changed her mind based on your conversation, so the type of man he is didn't sway her decision. Shelly Anne said something about how she'd forgiven him, but understood there needed to be accountability and felt peaceful about the decision rather than angry, blah blah blah."

Wow. K.D. could even successfully argue theology. She straightened in the seat a bit. "Good. Looks like we're back on track. We have a doctor who can't keep his britches zipped and a football coach who uses his player's puke to fertilize the field. Makes for quite a square dance, doesn't it?" She stood, collecting her things. "I'll head on over to the hospital, see what I can dig up. What's on your agenda?"

"I petitioned the court this morning to move up the trial date. Based on the expiration of my contract with the pawn company, this case needs to settle within the year, meaning we needed to be in court yesterday. If I wait, I could lose my car. Guess who now owns the title?"

"I thought you left it with a title company?"

Ingram shook his head. "Wouldn't give me enough money. Borrowed against it down at Shady's Pawn and Title. Little did I know, Shady sells the titles to a third party, who holds it."

"So, who's the third party?"

Ingram's beady eyes narrowed.

"Please don't say Bart Cookson."

He grimaced as if in pain. "Unfortunately yes, but there's no way I'll let that slime ball own Hank Aaron. We've got to move up the trial date. Plus, we have all the information we need, and Jack's on board for the expert testimony. Said he's never seen a more open and shut case. The insurance attorneys have already called, throwing out words like judicial process and mediation, but I think Judge Lucas will move it up. I mean, what else does Clear Point, Alabama have on the docket? Trespassing on hunting property again? Your coon dog bit my coon dog? Word is, Lucas is pretty fired up about the publicity of the trial so he's probably chomping at the bit to get started."

"You sure that's a good idea? We don't need to rush into this if we don't have to."

Ingram leaned back in the chair, his coat falling apart to show strained buttons across a wide girth. "That's just it. We really have to hurry up if we're going to get a settlement, avoid bankruptcy, and save Hank from Bart."

"Guess that's my cue to get to the hospital."

The automatic doors to the ER swooshed open. K.D. had a few minutes to spare before her appointment in the administrator's office so she decided to forgo the front entrance and mosey around the ER. One elderly man sat propped against the corner of the waiting room. She winced at the thought of all the germs crawling from the wall onto his head. A young man sat at a desk, seemingly a check-in location, so K.D. eased away from him to a table and picked up a magazine. She thumbed through several pages before realizing it was *Sport Illustrated*, but pretended to be enthralled until the guy stood and left his post. Glancing around, she moved over to the automatic doors, exiting the waiting room.

The empty halls screamed with the echo of each of her heeled footsteps, and K.D. fully expected the pimply clerk to come chasing after her. Instead, she rounded the corner and bumped headfirst into a nurse half her size. The poor thing about fell over with heel tracks across her forehead.

K.D. reached for her. "I'm so sorry. I wasn't even looking. Here, let me get your clipboard."

The name badge read Melanie, and the curly-haired brunette wearing it shot K.D. a look to melt steel. She reached for the papers scattered out of K.D.'s reach and snatched the clipboard out of her hand. "We're shorthanded enough around here without having to play traffic police." She straightened the papers and placed them under the clip. Blowing her bangs with a puff, the nurse seemed to collect herself. "Sorry. Days like today sit heavy on you, ya know?"

K.D. smiled. "Boy do I. At my office, it's only me. Answer the phone, do the paperwork, clean the coffee pot. Feel like a one-armed paper hanger in a gale wind."

"You too? Sometimes it's just me on a shift. At least now I got a new supervisor who halfway cares. My old boss could have given a rip." She stopped as if saying too much, her face relaxing into a girl talk kind of expression. "Is there something I can help you with?"

K.D. chewed her lip for a minute, unsure how to ask the question without being too obvious. "As a matter of fact, there is, Melanie. I was looking over a medical release recently on an ER visit, but noticed the nurse on shift was not the signature on the document." *Please don't ask me about the patient or why I'd want to know. Please. Please.*

A wary expression formed on the nurse's face. "How'd you know my name?"

K.D. pointed at her name badge.

Blushing, she gave a small laugh. "Oh. Sorry. There's been rumors some big lawsuit is being filed against the hospital. It's got us all a bit paranoid." She paused and looked K.D. up and down.

K.D. smiled and tilted her head in her best *trust me* look and mowed right over the comment. "I figured it was because y'all worked good together as a team, helped each other out. I bet you have to lean on each other a lot."

"We don't usually finish up each other's reports, but sometimes you can't help it. Take today, for example. I'm the only nurse here. Depending on who comes through those doors, I might not get to my reports until my shift ends. Well, I got a life, you know? My little girl's daycare don't care if Johnny comes in for stitches ten minutes before I'm due to pick her up. They're gonna charge me five dollars for every five minutes I'm late. I can't afford that. So sometimes we help each other out."

"It's not against regulations or anything?" As soon as the word regulations came out of her mouth, K.D. wished she could bite the legalistic word back.

Melanie clammed up. "No, we go strictly by regulations around here." Her brow knit together. "You sure you're only here on family business?"

I never said I was here on family business, so technically I didn't lie. But if you want to believe that to be my purpose, I'm not going to stop you. "Just curious is all. Thought it was kind of weird, but I guess we forget y'all are normal folks doing their job like the rest of us. Except you're dealing with life and death every day. Girl, I don't know how you do it. You must be superwoman."

Melanie laughed a little; attention diverted. "I wish. Sure would help on days like this. Is there anything else I can do for you? You really shouldn't be behind these doors unless you're with a patient."

"Oh, I'm sorry. I didn't know that. No one was out front, so I thought this was the way to the administrator's office. Might not even need to go now thanks to your help. Thank you, Melanie. I sure hope your day goes better."

K.D. waved off before the nurse asked any more questions and returned outside the building, walking around to the front. Replaying the conversation in her mind, she assuaged any guilt with the knowledge that she hadn't lied. She couldn't help what course

Melanie's assumptions took. And she said she *might* not have to go to the administrator's office, not that she wouldn't.

With her mind focused on the nurse's encounter, K.D. walked into the hospital lobby and right past Trip who reached out and grabbed her arm.

"Whoa, slow down, beautiful."

She halted and turned. What an unexpected surprise. "Well, hey there."

Trim waist poured into khaki pants. Shiny leather loafers. Good looking wouldn't be her choice of description for Trip, but rather neat, tidy, and controlled. Then the corners of his mouth lifted into a smile to transform his face straight off the pages of a magazine. Gorgeous emerged as her word of choice as soon as the dimples deepened. K.D. straightened her skirt.

"What are you doing here?" They both spoke at once and laughed together.

He nodded. "You first."

"Work errands. And you?"

"Same here. My uncle has me doing a few things here and there. Say, you're looking awfully spiffy today."

She felt spiffy. Ever since the library, where Trip had almost kissed her and promised to do so on their next date, K.D. felt the urge daily to spruce herself up a bit. Although the budget didn't allow new clothes, she took the time to mix and match colors, straightening her hair which she'd usually fluff with her fingers and be done. Her mom had even commented on her appearance, and the effect had rubbed off on her as well. Lydia had risen daily, showered, and had eaten breakfast with K.D. before she left for work. The sun shone brighter on the little trailer.

"Why, thank you. Thank you very much." K.D. gave her best Elvis impersonation. She looked at her watch, fearing the time. "I gotta scoot, Trip. I'm already late for my appointment. We still on for Saturday?"

He grinned. "You better believe it. My aunt is bringing out all the fixings. She's going through an Italian phase, and apparently four courses in Italy are a mere prequel to the main show. Bring your appetite because you're going to need it."

K.D.'s stomach growled on cue, and they both laughed again. "I don't think I'll have a problem with that. I'll see you at six, okay? What should I wear?"

"You could wear anything and be beautiful. But casual is fine. I'll probably wear blue jeans."

The thought tickled her. "You? In blue jeans? I think I've seen you in jeans once. But casual I can do. I'll see you then." She leaned in for the kiss on her cheek, common in their greetings and passings now. She felt beautiful, especially when reminded of it every time she spoke to him. His lips had begun to feel familiar, and yet her pulse still flipped.

With a full heart, she moved down the hall, but not before turning to find him still staring at her. Grinning, she floated into the elevator. A light feeling enveloped her, moving through pores to enter the flow of life, reaching the very core inside of her. Love? How would she know? But it sure felt like all the books and televisions shows. Whatever it was, K.D. hoped it would never go away.

She'd experienced flutters before, brushes with feelings greater than just liking someone. But her mother always seemed to gain her attention and time as if the thought of sharing or losing K.D. spiraled her down, to the point that any opportunity for love hid behind obligation. Until now.

Until Trip.

Stepping into the hall, K.D. read the directory to find the administrator's office, which sat right around the corner. Unsure of whether to knock or walk in, K.D. did both, easing her head around the door.

"Can I help you?" A stern-faced woman sat behind a massive desk, almost like a fortress protecting the door beside her. Bifocals pinched the end of her nose, which caused her to squint as if staring into sunlight.

"Good morning. I'm K.D. Jennings with the Ingram Law Firm. I have an appointment to look over the original files of copies the hospital delivered to our office."

The woman sighed as though the process of rising from her desk took the effort of the millennium. "I'll have you know I wasted my entire morning collecting these documents for you after having already re-filed them two weeks ago. Then I had to dig them back up. Took me half a day to copy them in the first place. There was not one thing wrong with the documents I sent you."

K.D. walked behind the hunched over woman who seemed angry at the world in general. She couldn't understand the rest of her mumbles, but didn't want to either. The woman gestured into a small conference room with several stacks of manila folders.

"Thank you, Miss…I'm sorry I didn't get your name."

"Angier. It's French so the g is soft." Ah, a little chink in the old bat's armor. Family pride.

"What a lovely name, Miss Angier." K.D. emphasized the soft g. "Thank you for your help."

K.D. swore the corners of the woman's mouth lifted, but the somewhat smile fled so fast, she wasn't sure. K.D. settled into the chair, pulled out her copies from the briefcase, and opened the first file, wondering if a few wasted hours lay ahead or if she'd uncover information to blow the case wide open.

CHAPTER

17

The steaming water poured out of the faucet, washing over K.D.'s head and over her shoulders. What she'd give for a bath, but the single-wide only housed one bathroom with a shower. No tub. The day sat in the small of her back, a growing ache stretching through every nerve ending. Bone-dead tired would be a conservative description considering the two hours of sleep the night before.

And this was the night to meet the aunt and uncle.

The time in the administrator's office had taken forever. K.D. found reports in different colored pens, creating the need to make color copies. Miss Angier with a soft g could not have put up more resistance, flat out refusing until she talked to her superior. K.D. called Ingram who in turn schmoozed the hospital administrator, telling her to send him the bill.

Hours she could have spent studying were instead spent watching the hag of an assistant move as if mired in cement shoes. This pushed class preparation to the day of, never a good idea, which shoved more work to the next day. On a bright note, K.D. heard from the doctor that her mother was approved for a clinical trial of a new bipolar medication, only insurance didn't cover it. But the proceeds from the trial would. She could charge the first round and at least get started on the program. Fingers crossed the court date would be moved up.

Stop! K.D. had to put the last few days behind her if a chance existed for her to enjoy the evening or at a minimum not have Trip's family think she was more than a robotic caricature of herself.

When the water cooled too soon, K.D. turned off the faucet and toweled off. Moving toward the bedroom, she faced a thin closet of unflattering clothes. She had resisted the urge to charge a new outfit on the credit card, knowing Ingram hadn't paid off the balance for her to hack it back up with frivolity. Wire hangers slid across the rod, the screech matching a sinking heart, longing for different circumstances.

"Why don't you wear this?"

K.D. turned at her mother's voice, finding her in the doorway. She held a silk blouse by a hanger, full in cut with a hippy kind of look. Old enough to look modern again.

"Where'd you get that?" K.D. took the blouse from her hands, holding it under her chin and turning to the mirror. The purple color, deep enough to be eggplant, stood in contrast to her pale skin and blonde hair. The fabric felt soft beneath her touch, a tad faded, but in a chic way.

Lydia smiled. "Funny thing about fashion. You hang onto something long enough, it comes back into style. I had this blouse in the 60s, back when I first met your dad. In fact, I might have even worn it on our first date. Like you, I always had more to love around my middle so the fashion worked to my advantage with the full shirts and tunics."

"First date with Dad? No thanks, I don't want it." K.D. returned the blouse to her.

Lydia laid it on the bed along with a pair of dark stretch pants. She turned to face K.D. with a frown. "Don't be ridiculous." She pointed a finger. "You have a big chip on your shoulder because of your dad. I get that. A lot of the way you feel is probably my fault. I never did a good job of telling you the good things about him. And there were good things."

K.D. offered a skeptical look.

"There were. One day I'm going to sit you down and tell you about the night we decided to have you, why he wanted to give you initials instead of a proper name. The way he cried when you were born." Her look softened in memory, her brow unfurled. "You can't drag grudges through life, K.D. All that does is give the person power over you."

"Isn't that what you do, Mom?" K.D. kept her tone soft, but the words strong.

Her mom paused, breathing in and out. "Yes. But I'm trying, K.D., fighting against what keeps me walking through life in a fog. But honey, your dad isn't my problem. I am. He's not yours either."

Lydia moved toward her, reaching out to twirl long strands of still wet hair. "Remember something, baby. Forgiving someone doesn't make what they do right. It simply sets you free."

"Hard to forgive someone who's not around to ask for forgiveness."

A knowing smile stretched across Lydia's face. "Didn't you tell me something you had read in your Bible the other day? Something about how Christ died to forgive us for our sins?"

"So?"

"Were you around to ask His forgiveness or did He do it anyway? In order to be forgiven, you have to receive it, but there's no prerequisite to forgiving someone else."

K.D. frowned at her mom in exaggeration, thinking of the very words she'd shared with Trip about his parents' demise. "What makes you the Bible expert all of a sudden?"

Lydia laughed and gathered K.D. into a hug. "Oh darlin', what your daddy did was wrong, but what you're doing to yourself is even more wrong. Forgive him, honey. And move on. Let this young man love you if that's what he wants to do. But more importantly, love yourself." Lydia walked over to the dresser, pulled open the small drawer on top, and searched the contents. She found what she looked for, closed the drawer and turned to K.D., palm out.

Inside lay the pendant K.D.'s dad had given her.

K.D. pulled back. "How'd you know I still had that?"

"I found it one day while putting away some laundry and put it in the jewelry drawer so it wouldn't get lost. No reason why you shouldn't wear it, K.D. There's good and bad in all of us. This here represents the good in your daddy."

Tears tickled her eyes. "I can't, Mama. I don't hate him anymore. At least there's that. But I can't pretend what happened didn't happen. That a grown man didn't walk out on his responsibilities."

Lydia sighed and reached over to K.D.'s neck. "Then take this chain off from around your neck. If you don't want to go back and address the past then at least move forward to a future." She removed the chain, clasping both in her fist. "It's okay to be a woman too. Even if you get hurt, at least you'll have loved. There's no greater feeling. It's worth it. You're worth it." She kissed K.D.'s cheek and left the room.

Could she? Really, truly, authentically love? Not just someone else, but herself? K.D. reached up to her unadorned neck, inhaled from her toes, so fast it stung her nose, and held her breath. The released air whispered, *Why not?*

K.D. heard the car door shut, and an adrenaline shot to her pulse. She turned to the full-length mirror, hardly recognizing the reflection. The dark stretchy pants minimized her problem areas, creating the allusion of almost thin. Then again, maybe they were. Stress seemed to eat away anything she consumed lately. The purple tunic hung mid-thigh, the embroidered edging dressing it up a bit. The v-neck fell appropriately while still showing milky-white skin, her collar bone a little more prominent due to the weight loss.

But her hair. Oh praise all things holy her hair straightened at first try, every piece razor-sharp and shiny, exposing the blonde with natural caramel highlights. The purple in the blouse created a violet hue to her eyes.

Was this reflection really her? She crossed her eyes and pushed up her nose like a pig. Yep, there she was. K.D. heard her mother greet Trip.

"Here goes nothing." She took her purse and walked down the hallway.

Trip sat on the couch with Lydia beside him. She held a crocheted pillow, describing the design as a granny square. "We had to start off with an easy pattern. Sewing never was K.D.'s thing. Never could get her inside, away from that creek and those rocks she collects."

K.D. cleared her throat from the doorway. "Do we have to go there, Mom?"

If only she could take a picture of their reactions. Mouths agape. Eyes enlarged. Instead she took a mental shot and stored it in her heart. Both Trip and her mother's face reflected the feedback given by her bedroom mirror.

K.D. walked over and waved a hand in front of Trip's face. "Hello?"

His eyes cleared, and he tried to speak. He cleared his throat. Dragging eyes off her, he nodded toward Lydia. "I guess we need to, um, you know, go." He looked as if he wanted to say more, but couldn't.

K.D.'s mother smiled at them both. She leaned to kiss K.D. on the cheek, whispering instead, "I knew you'd look like this. Remember what I said, honey. Give it a whirl."

Trip held open the trailer door, taking K.D.'s elbow as they walked down the steps. He navigated her over the rocky dirt parking pad to the car, opening the door and guiding her in.

She almost laughed at the fragile treatment. All because of some carefully applied makeup and a decades-old blouse.

Entering, Trip sank into the seat, but did not raise his hand to start the ignition. Finally, he turned to K.D. with an unreadable expression. "I don't get it."

She squirmed under the scrutiny. "Get what?"

"How can a brain as smart as yours exist behind something so beautiful? It's like God took everything good and wrapped it up as you."

Tears tickled the back of K.D.'s eyes. She opened her mouth to speak, but no words came out. She squeaked a thank you. Or maybe she didn't. Hard to tell over the lump in her throat. A fullness entered her to the point that she wanted to grab the hourglass and lay it on its side, to stop time. She wanted to stay right here in the car with Trip forever, a big ol' puddle of mush.

He leaned over, took her chin between his thumb and knuckle and moved her face toward his. The world condensed to just the two of them as his lips touched hers; hesitant, questioning. K.D. moved toward him, pressing into his gentle force, returning the kiss as soft as a sigh.

The earth slid to a gentle stop. No sounds. No movement except for the beat of her heart and an escaped breath. Trip and K.D. joined as one, clinging to the end of a kiss.

Too soon, he pulled back, and K.D. opened her eyes to his smile. "K.D., can I do that again later?"

She rubbed her lips together. "Yep."

He turned on the ignition. "Good. Because we're going to be late if we don't get a move on it." He reversed out of the parking spot and drove down the road.

The gentle jazz and soft purr of the luxury car pulled K.D. into sleep, as any other time she'd ridden in Trip's car, like swaying on clouds. She fought it, jerking her head up when it would loll against the seat.

Trip laughed and placed his hand on hers. "Reach down beside you. There's a button to lean your seat back. The drive isn't long, but I know you're exhausted. Your mom told me the kind of hours you've been keeping. Relax."

"I can't sleep on a date. How rude is that?" But her other hand found its way to the switch and she reclined the seat a bit.

"K.D., one day you'll get it through your thick head I like being with you. Period. I like looking over and seeing you beside me. Even with a line of drool at the corner of your mouth like at the library that one time."

Soft words eased her eyes shut, but she managed to flick him in the arm. Seconds seemed to pass before she felt his hand on her shoulder. The car had stopped in front of an elaborate home, lit up like an amusement park.

"Yowza." K.D. blinked hard and whistled as she exited the car. Spotlights illuminated a wide front porch, not the walk-up kind found on a Southern plantation, but more the deep kind, with the same Corinthian columns. The parking garage stood at a right angle to the house, joined by a covered walk way. The rubbed stucco gave the home a Spanish feel, especially with the climbing ivy.

"It's stunning, Trip. I mean, I know you said your aunt and uncle had money, but I've never seen a house like this, or even knew that one existed in Clear Point. Are you sure I'm dressed appropriately? I feel like you should be in a tux." She smoothed down her faded blouse, which didn't seem quite as pretty anymore, reaching to fiddle the chain no longer around her neck.

He walked to her, slipped his hand into hers, and brushed those perfect lips across her cheek. "You're perfect. I promise."

K.D. wanted to dive into his brown eyes and stay there. The tingling remained on her skin from the kiss, each heart beat now consumed with the look on his face. Trip had somehow worked into her marrow, filling all the hollow spots with something unfamiliar, but beautiful. Her feet seemed to levitate.

A little white dog ran around the corner, yipping with joy at the sight of Trip, who bent to pick it up. Familiarity tickled K.D.'s brain, but she couldn't coagulate the moment of déjà vu, her mind still webbed with sleep and the giddy hum in her brain.

"Come here you little fish bait." Trip scratched the dog behind the ears and gave it a kiss. "K.D., meet Sissy. Sissy, this is K.D."

"Well, aren't you cuter than a freckled baby? Hey there, Sissy." When she came face to face with the little dog, she froze. Sissy looked exactly the same as the dog who ripped her scarf in two during her night of adventure with Shelly Anne.

Wait. One. Minute.

Sissy?

Nuh uh, no way. Her heart caught, but then skipped back into rhythm. More than one tiny white dog existed in America. Pure coincidence they'd both have the same name.

It was possible.

K.D. slowly scratched its ears, straightened, and looked around. Her heart thudded again when she recognized the wrought-iron fence line through the covered walkway, the boxwood around the house.

Trip had said fish bait. Exactly what Shelly Anne called the white dog the other night.

"Come on. I can't wait for you to meet Big Daddy." Trip took her arm, but looked back when she didn't budge. "What's wrong?"

"Um, Trip, what subdivision did you say your family lived in?" Please don't say Riverwind. Please don't say Riverwind.

"I guess you really were asleep. I thought you were just resting your eyes." They walked a few steps onto the porch and moved toward the front door, K.D. moving through the sludge of fear. "This is Riverwind. Big Daddy has one of the biggest lots, right there on the river since he was an original investor. I wish the moon was out. We could take a ride on the pontoon boat."

Every miniscule amount of air left K.D.'s body. Her heart felt like a fire hydrant had been released to blast blood to her brain, roaring through her ears. Dizzy, she touched the door frame to steady herself. As Trip took out his keys to open the door, it flew open to reveal a small man with a shock of white hair. The exact man she had seen walking through the yard while she and Shelly

Anne crouched behind the bushes.

"Trip! Your Aunt Frances was beginning to worry about you all. You must be K.D." He pulled her into a hug. K.D.'s arms hung limply by her side.

Trip laughed. "Sorry about that. K.D., I forgot to warn you how physically affectionate my family can be. K.D., I'd like you to meet Big Daddy. Big Daddy, this is K.D."

Big Daddy looked at Trip with mock consternation. "Now, boy, don't be using that silly nickname around our guest. Frances would have a fit."

Trip smiled. "Sorry, you're right." He turned to K.D. "Allow me to introduce my uncle, Dr. Jackson Thomas. Dr. Thomas, please meet my girlfriend, K.D."

K.D. wondered if they heard the same "thud" she did, as if the earth had just shuddered on its axis. An acidic taste entered her mouth, the dull roar almost drowning out the word girlfriend.

"Please call me Jack."

The man K.D. vowed to pay for Bo's death, the one who appeared to have had an affair with his nurse and who deserved to be held accountable for all his bad choices, bowed before her as if she were a queen.

"My dear, Frances and I couldn't be more pleased to welcome you into our home. Won't you come in?"

CHAPTER

18

Despite the fevered prayers coursing through her mind, the ground did not open up and swallow K.D. whole. Her feet moved of their own accord, with no signal from a muted brain, and followed Trip over the threshold.

She'd heard near-death experiences were like this. Someone would exit the body and hover above the room, witnessing the scene below. She floated into the hall, ignoring the full-length gilded mirror, scared of the pale face sure to reflect from it.

The marble-tiled entry room centered the doorways to several rooms as well as a long hall which seemed to empty into the back of the house. A wrought-iron staircase curved to a walkway around the second floor. Everything shined and glowed as if dusted several times a day. A huge, life-sized elk stood in the back of the massive gathering room.

Trip must have picked up on her expression of surprise at the animal. "He guards Big Daddy's office. Aunt Frances made him put all his animals in there, but Bullwinkle wouldn't fit through the doorway. She calls it the Norman Bates room."

Dr. Thomas grimaced. "A fine day when a man brings home trophy mounts and can't even have them available for anyone to see." He nudged K.D. with his elbow. "I'll take you in there later and show you around. I got a beauty of a black bear that will terrorize your dreams."

"Sounds, er, lovely." K.D. allowed the doctor to take her by the elbow with Trip on the other side. They looked nothing alike. Trip stood tall and thin shouldered while the doctor was stooped and stocky. Then she remembered the blood relationship was through his aunt, not his uncle. "You have a beautiful home, Dr. Thomas." Further words escaped her, leaving only mundane responses. She should leave. Make up an excuse. Every ethical bone in her body screamed she should not be in this house. And yet she kept walking, unable to tear away from Trip's presence and cause him hurt. He had been through so much. The look of pain which had clawed across his face the night at the creek came to mind. K.D. had eased his tragic memories, brought him peace. For the first time she had felt wanted, not just needed. Why, oh why of all uncles and aunts did Trip's have to be the ones K.D. had to sue?

"I have to insist you call me Jack. Frances and I are pleased you're here."

As if on cue, Trip's aunt rounded the corner, holding a tissue in her hand. "Hi there, darling." She leaned up to kiss Trip's cheek, then turned. "You must be K.D. Please forgive me. Somebody forgot to let Sissy out, and she left a little surprise for us in the hall." She offered her husband a mock frown and stepped into a hall bathroom.

The toilet flushed and a faucet ran before Frances returned to the group. "How embarrassing, but that's us. Nothing like a little dog poop in the hall to keep you humble." Frances leaned in for a light kiss on K.D.'s cheek. "Thank you for joining us tonight. You're every bit as pretty as Trip said. Please, follow me to the study. We'll catch up over drinks and then venture to the dining room. I have a wonderful meal for all of us."

Catch up! What would she offer? *My firm is suing you because you don't know the difference between a concussion and a heat stroke, and because of your mistake, a young man died and a marriage is falling apart?*

"K.D., darling?" They had entered the study, and all three were looking at her as if she had stood in the middle of a play.

"I'm sorry. I was caught up in the beauty of your home. Did you ask me something?"

Jack stood, holding a wine decanter. "Would you care for a glass of wine? Or we have tea, lemon water?"

K.D. looked at Trip who poured himself a glass of water.

"I'll take water, please." The study was mahogany walled with a corner of floor-to-ceiling windows, with thick paneled curtains pulled to the side. Antique furnishings included love seats, high-back chairs, and portraits along the walls. It was truly unlike anything she'd seen. Frances excused herself to check on dinner, promising to return in a blink.

Trip took her elbow and leaned to her ear. "Are you okay? You look pale."

She whispered back. "I'm fine. I think the week's getting to me."

"Do you need to go home? Although I think Aunt Frances would cry if you did."

Jack cleared his throat, handing K.D. her water. "Indeed she would. Please sit. I know you young folks have a lot going on. We're not formal around here, although Frances enjoys decorating like we are. Let's all relax. Personally, I think every room would benefit from a wall hanger or two."

K.D. sat beside Trip on the love seat across from his uncle, a platter of antipasti on the table between them. "What's a wall hanger?"

"A waste of space." Frances joined them with a smile, accepting a wine glass from her husband. "How anyone could harm one of God's creatures is beyond me."

"The first death in the Bible came when an animal was used to clothe Adam and Eve. As long as you're responsible and the animal doesn't suffer, there's nothing wrong with hunting, Frances. I remember this one time…" Frances rolled her eyes as Jack launched into an African hunting escapade, complete with tales of jungle rituals and stalking antelope, only to be interrupted from time to time with gasps and outcries from his wife.

"But Aunt Frances, don't you own a fur coat?"

Jack laughed. "Touché, my boy. Keep the ol' gal honest."

Frances waved a finger at Trip. "Don't you go sassing me, darling. I only wear my mink to please Jack. He gave it to me on our thirtieth wedding anniversary. How could I not wear it?"

Jack leaned in to kiss her cheek, which caused his wife to smile. "And she looks like a million bucks in it."

Trip's arm found its way across K.D.'s shoulders, over the back of the loveseat. The domestic scene lulled K.D. into the evening. Why would she have to say anything right now? Her mama raised her better than that. You don't come into someone's home and create a ruckus. No, she'd have dinner, avoid a scene, and then take Trip somewhere private another day. Explain the dilemma and why she'd have to continue with the lawsuit. If she didn't, Ingram would lose the practice, she'd lose her job and future, and remain unable to afford her mother's new medication.

He'd understand.

A timer sounded somewhere down the hallway, and Frances jumped up. "Dinner's ready. Jack, darling, would you escort the young folks into the dining room then join me in the kitchen? We'll serve our guests."

"You go on, Big Daddy. I'll take K.D. to her seat." He took K.D.'s elbow and guided her from the room, down the hall, and into an expansive dining room with a massive stacked-stone fireplace. Three tear-drop chandeliers hung from a ceiling outlined in detailed molding, all mahogany. Trip held out her chair and then took the one beside her.

He leaned to whisper, "You sure you're okay? You're too quiet… too polite."

Was she that transparent? K.D. offered a mock frown. "I'm always nice to those nice to me, Folsom."

"Now that's more like it." His dimples deepened into a smile.

"Your aunt and uncle could charm a vampire off a meat truck." K.D. continued to look around at the landscape paintings. Sissy tip-tapped into the room and sniffed around K.D.'s feet, who leaned down and scratched behind her ears.

"They're such good people."

Oh, Trip, if you only knew. But she couldn't tell him. Not yet.

"Frances is my mother's sister. I think I told you that. Mama was the 'oops' of the family as Frances was about eleven years older than she. Mama told me Aunt Frances would dress her up like a baby doll, and they'd have tea together along with her stuffed animals."

The couple entered the room, carrying multiple dishes which they sat upon the table. Frances opened one to reveal a soup of vegetables. "I'm going through an Italian phase. Last month was German, but we never could acquire a proper taste for sauerkraut."

Jack grimaced, collecting their bowls for Frances to ladle the soup into. "Loved the sausage, but not much else. Frances is making her way around the world."

He placed the steaming soup in front of K.D as Frances described the meal. "It's minestrone. I hope you like it. We'll start with this and then move onto the third course, which is a fish."

Trip collected his napkin into his lap. "I must have missed the first course."

Frances jerked up. "Did you not try the antipasti? I thought I put it out into the study."

She seemed so eager to please, delighted to have their company that K.D. patted her hand. And to think her husband could cheat on her. "You did. Trip ate several bites."

Trip spooned some soup into his mouth, speaking after he swallowed. "Yes, yes I did, don't worry. I guess I didn't think of it as a course because we weren't at the table."

Frances sat upon Jack's insistence and accepted her bowl from him. "It's an appetizer. In Italy, meals typically take hours. Lots of wine consumed. Red, of course. Interestingly, they take their salads last. The oil helps with digestion. Trip's mama used to talk all the time about his sensitive stomach, how she'd have to stock up on..."

Trip coughed into his napkin. "I don't know if K.D.'s all that interested in the sensitive state of my digestive track."

K.D. joined in the laughter, especially when Frances said, "I sure wish someone had warned me of Jack's before we married."

The lighthearted conversation continued; the love shared among them evident. K.D. learned about Trip's childhood, tales of his tongue sticking to an outdoor pipe on a dare, and the scar on his forehead from a horse kick.

Frances spoke of how proud her sister was of Trip. "She told me the night he graduated college that she couldn't wait to see all the wonderful things he'd do with his life. She'd be so proud of you, honey." She paused with emphasis. "You know she would."

Trip drank a sip of water as Jack shushed his wife. She turned, red-faced toward K.D. "What, you don't know?"

"Don't know what?" K.D. looked at Trip who shook his head toward Frances.

Frances turned back to Trip. "Oh honey, I'm so sorry."

Jack stood. "I sure hope you saved room for dessert. It's my understanding Trip here made Tiramisu. Had some the other day. Deliciouso. How's that for Italian sounding? Or maybe it's Spanish. Anyway, Frances, let's take the kids' plates and bring out dessert."

K.D. sat dumbfounded and turned to Trip with a questioning look. He didn't answer the glance, diverting the conversation to a story about an in-school suspension related to his bringing a copperhead for school's show and tell. K.D., for once, took her cue and did not pry. She knew all about the need for privacy. But the abrupt end to the conversation about his parents and graduation night piqued her curiosity.

Trip held K.D.'s hand the entire ride home, the minimal streetlights adding to the sense of intimacy. His thumb stroked her skin. She felt his eyes turn to her at a red light.

"Thank you for coming tonight. It meant a lot to me." The huskiness of his voice warmed her face.

"The food was delicious. I don't think I'll eat for days."

The light turned green, and Trip eased the car forward. "I know you're probably wondering about what Aunt Frances said about my parents. I don't want us to have secrets between each other. I want you to know everything about me, but…" He paused as if searching for the right words, squeezing her hand to anchor them into the moment. "I don't want you to think I'm keeping something from you. There are things about me you need to know, and you will, I promise." He brought her hand to his lips, kissing it gently. The car moved toward K.D.'s trailer, and Trip pulled to a stop along the street.

She adjusted in her seat and turned to him, retrieving her hand. "Every life has secrets, Trip. Personally, I don't see anything wrong with a little mystery." K.D. tried to keep her tone light, not wanting to ruin this perfect night with reality, especially her ever-intruding conscience.

Trip rubbed his knuckles along her jaw line. "Everything about you is a mystery. One I can't wait to solve, but there's a difference in peeling off the layers of someone's life and deliberately withholding something from the other. I don't want to do that. One day, soon, I'll share with you about the night my parents died. I've never talked about it to anyone, but I'd like to with you. I want you to know I…"

"Shhhh. It's been a great night, Trip. Let's not ruin it with false declarations fueled by Italian sausage endorphins." She gave a nervous laugh.

Trip grinned. "You and your fancy words." He stared at her intently, the grin softening into a tender expression. "I love you, K.D."

The words hung in the air like a promise. K.D. had no memory of the declaration from a man's mouth. Not a man she believed anyway. And she wanted to believe Trip...desperately.

"I must have the first time you ran into class late and couldn't find the seating chart because the professor had already put it up. There were only a few empty seats, and I remember praying that your spot was beside me."

"You did?"

"Yep." He reached over and twirled her hair. "You and your mop of blonde curls flying everywhere. You had a brown stain on your white shirt."

"I can certainly see why you'd be attracted by the spilled coffee."

Trip laughed. "Then when the professor tried to embarrass you, and you quoted some case about time zones and relevance to the hours of prosecution or something like that. I don't even remember except you shut him up quick. I wanted to wrap you in a hug right then."

"He probably would have let you to get me to shut up."

Trip leaned toward her, bringing her lips to his in a sweet touch. "Thank you for being patient with me. When you hear it all, you'll understand."

K.D.'s mouth quivered as she said goodbye, hoping he would not see the tears clouding her vision as she exited the car. "Thanks for a great night, Trip. I mean it. One of the best I've ever had."

"It won't be as good as the next one, I promise. I hope every time we're together is better than the last. See you next week." He walked her to the front steps, kissed her again, her pulse jumping in her throat.

She waved him off and walked up the few steps to the trailer door, realizing she had not told him she loved him too. Did she? Yes. She knew she did. Maybe the words muted on purpose for as soon as Trip knew the truth about her job, he'd withdraw his love as sure as her own father did so many years ago, and she'd have to forget him too. She let herself into the trailer, the door creaking shut behind her.

CHAPTER

19

K.D. lifted her arms into the air and fell forward into what the instructor called a reverse swan dive, more like an unfortunate mallard on the opening day of duck season. She grunted, turning her head to Shelly Anne beside her. "Why again are we doing this?"

Shelly Anne, with perfect form and little exertion, lifted her arms and swooped down, stretching her hamstrings. "You need to relax. I need to be nicer to Buck. Yoga is a great way to accomplish both."

"How can I relax when I'm in such pain?" K.D.'s legs screamed with the stretch, and she groaned when the teacher instructed them to lower into the downward dog, moving into the plank position. What was it with all the animal names? K.D. sniffed her underarm positioned beside her nose. She sure smelled like one.

A sideways glance showed Delilah in spandex and a sports bra, bent in half over straight legs with no hint of belly fat or any fat for that matter. K.D. turned to Shelly Anne and whispered, "It's bad enough to have to sit behind her in law school. Why do I have to exercise with her?"

"With who?"

K.D. tossed her head toward Delilah. "Miss poster child for eating disorder."

Delilah turned her head as if she heard her name. K.D. forced a smile, dove back into the downward dog, trying to follow the instructions, and failed, landing on her face. Shelly Anne laughed beside her, causing her to scowl. "I'm glad you think this is funny, Shelly Anne."

"Are you okay, K.D.?" Delilah whispered concern from several folks down. Or maybe she really did care. Nobody could fake a bubbly personality 24/7.

"I'm fine. Just lost my balance trying to down the dog."

"Downward dog." Delilah giggled. What grown woman giggled? "You're funny, K.D." Several other class members snickered.

Shelly Anne stifled a laugh when K.D. turned to her and mouthed, "Save me!"

The class rolled into a sitting position. Shelly Anne pulled her ankles onto her crossed legs and whispered, "I don't know why you think that girl's got anything on you. You're way prettier."

K.D. snorted and stayed Indian style, closing her eyes. She tried to let her mind go, eliminate the sight of Delilah's perky boobs, and allow the teacher's soft murmurs to ease the stress from her brain, but the impending court date illuminated the backs of her lids, broadcasting the fact that in less than two weeks they'd be presenting the case before a jury.

She'd yet to tell Trip a thing, although months had passed since the dinner at his uncle's.

The two women stood and collected the mats, sliding their feet into flip flops. K.D. gulped from a water bottle and avoided Delilah's wave when she skipped out of class.

"Wanna hit the steam room?" Shelly Anne asked.

K.D. grimaced. "I don't have the strength to hit anything."

Shelly Anne tilted her head incredulously.

"Might as well. My blood pressure is already sky high. I'm sure a room full of 110 degree steam could only help."

They exited the room and made their way down the hall and into the dressing room. Shelly Anne stopped and looked around. "Hmmm. I thought I remembered the lady telling me it was off the dressing room. Oh, here's the door."

The heat of the vacant room blasted K.D., stealing her breath. The vein behind her ear pulsed under the wool of humidity. She fell onto the teak-wood bench, dabbing her face with a towel. "Have I told you lately how glad I am that you included me in on this free trial membership?"

Shelly Anne must not have picked up on the sarcastic tone. "You're welcome. It's about time Clear Pointe got a gym. I just wish we could afford the monthly dues."

K.D. leaned back and breathed deeply. As much as she fought the relaxation, the heat kneaded her screaming muscles, and the sweat running down her back took some of her mind's worry with it.

Thoughts of Trip broke through the lull, tugging a smile from her lips. His soft kisses, sweet texts, the way he brought her mother wildflowers he had picked. Even when they had argued over Professor Elliott's case assignments, so much she had slammed the door in his face and didn't answer his call for days, he still managed to burrow under her skin, finding a resting spot in her heart. Every time they were together, she vowed to disclose everything, especially when he hinted at the escalating stress in his home. When she'd almost be there, when the words made it onto her tongue, she'd smart off to him instead, even instigating an argument or two. Despite her feelings, the secret kept him at arm's length.

Shelly Anne broke the silence after a few moments. "I was really hoping we could settle this case before the trial. I can't believe Mr. Ingram got the court to set the date so quickly."

"We were hoping for a settlement too. But for some reason, the insurance company has dug in its heels, told Ingram they were going to make an example out of our firm. Stupid decision on their part, but what can you do?"

"You think you're ready? I mean, it hasn't been *that* long since Buck first came to your office. Isn't that unusual to move so quickly?"

K.D. inhaled through her nose and exhaled through her mouth like the yoga instructor said. "It sure is, but leave it to a small-town judge to consider publicity over precedent. We're ready, though. I'm telling you, the attorneys for the insurance company are idiots. Our medical expert says there's no way we won't win."

A rotund woman opened the door, wrapped in too small a towel, stepped over the threshold and looked around. "Lord have mercy, it's hotter than earthworms on July asphalt." She left as quickly.

Shelly Anne and K.D. burst out laughing.

K.D. wiped the tears from her eyes and the sweat that was running down a cheek. "Ingram says we'll have opening statements a week from Monday and then we present our case first as the plaintiff. I believe the medical expert will start things off, then we'll call the nurses. Normally we'd call one of you first, but Ingram thinks this course of testimony would have more impact. Did you know the defendant's team disclosed they'll call the football coach as a witness?"

Shelly Anne blew out a breath. "Do I ever. He about blessed us out after church Sunday. Buck's pretty fired up about it too. He said Ingram promised he wouldn't involve the coach. Men and their worship of football. I swear, Buck seems more concerned about back-to-back state championships than his own son's court case. Says calling Mark to testify would be too much of a distraction from practice and ball games." Shelly Anne blew out a breath and rolled her eyes.

"Coach Mark'll be in contempt if he doesn't show up. Remind your husband we're not the ones who involved Mr. Savior of the World Coach. The defense did. But I'm not worried. I think once we present our case, the defense will change its mind and try to settle. We'll make them pay for waiting so long. It'll work to our advantage because they'll be more likely to add some zeros once they see our loaded guns. We've got some personal information I can promise the defense does not want to see the light of day."

K.D. fell silent, thinking of the phone calls between Dr. Thomas and his nurse. K.D. had not seen Trip's uncle since the night of the dinner. Not out of fear of revelation, but more that nobody's schedule permitted a break. Somehow the picture of the loving looks he exchanged with his wife did not add up with the evidence of an affair. Ingram warned her things weren't always as they seemed, but he didn't know she had a first-hand account.

"Tell me about this new boyfriend." Shelly Anne knocked her in the side with an elbow. "Don't bother telling me you ain't got one. Maria's already spilled the beans. Every time your eyes glaze over, like they're doing right now, I know you're thinking about him."

"My eyes are glazing over because I can't breathe. You about ready to go?" K.D. stood, pulling up her hair from the back of her neck, thankful they had brought a change of clothes.

"Ah, I see how you're going to play it. Maria said she knows you have a fella, but you won't tell anyone who it is. I can't believe in a town this small someone can actually keep a secret."

"Maria doesn't know everything like she thinks she does."

"So? Who is it?"

K.D. opened the door, almost weeping at the cool air of the dressing room. A few young women scattered around in small talk, paying them no attention, and thankfully Delilah was nowhere to be seen. K.D. remained silent, washing her face and escaping to the small dressing room, trying to think of a way to appease Shelly Anne's snooping without telling everything.

After collecting their personal items, the two exited the building and walked onto the parking lot. Shelly Anne prodded her again. "I'm not letting you off the hook, K.D. Spill it. Tell me about this guy."

Knowing she had to offer something, K.D. turned to Shelly Anne. "Look, he's someone from law school. We spend a lot of time studying together. That's all."

"And you like him." Shelly Anne raised her eyebrows up and down.

"And I like him, but it doesn't matter because we're just friends." K.D. paused, taking a sip of water. Almost as an afterthought, she said, "He's good for my mom. I've never seen her more settled. Ever since meeting him, she rises and moves with purpose through the day. Can you believe I caught her looking through the classifieds? Said she might get a job."

"That's great!" Shelly Anne touched her arm. "You know, I'm glad you told me about your mom's condition. That's a tough burden to have to carry all by yourself. I wish I could help, but I've kept her in my prayers. Sounds like they're working. You ever hear anything else from that clinical trial?"

K.D. shook her head. "Yeah, she started the medication a few weeks ago. I can already tell a difference, so I'd bet my last chicken she didn't get the placebo."

"What's so great about the medication?"

"Overseas trials show a more moderate leveler to the depression episodes than daily pills. In other words, the highs seem less high and the lows less low. At some point, it all meets in the middle. It's an injection she takes once a week that works with some part of her brain to redirect signals which normally would cause her to either hide under the porch for a few days or weeks, or steal my credit card and buy a hundred protein shakes at Wal-Mart."

"What's the medicine called?"

K.D. shrugged her shoulders. "It's got some long, fancy name. Mom's doctor seems pretty optimistic. I wish it wasn't so darn expensive. Insurance won't touch it because it's only in a trial stage. I'm expecting the bill any day which is why I'm glad we were able to move up the trial date."

K.D. stopped a minute and looked at Shelly Anne with a smile. "You know, I'm kinda digging this girlfriend thing. Having someone to talk to. I mean, don't get me wrong, Maria is a great friend, but she stays busy with her family and the restaurant. And Ingram? Well, let's just say he'd never win any objectivity or impartiality awards."

"If I'm such a great girlfriend, why won't you tell me your fella's name?"

K.D. twisted her pinched fingers in front of her mouth as if locking her lips.

"You're seriously not going to tell me?"

K.D. walked over to her car as Shelly Anne moved toward hers. "Nope. No reason to. I have a feeling it won't ever be more than a good friendship anyway." Probably not even a passing acquaintance once Trip realized the truth. "I'd kinda like to enjoy him all to myself. That should be enough information for you and Miss Nosy Maria."

Shelly Anne waved her off. "I'll leave you alone for now. Let me know if you need me or Buck this week to help with anything. I got my best Sunday dress all ironed and cleaned. Made Buck try on his Easter suit. We'll be there with bells on come next week. Maybe for once we can put this all behind us." She got into the car, but not before K.D. noticed the downturn of her eyes, the draw of her mouth.

Shelly Anne had shared with K.D. the strains on her marriage the past two years. How Buck spent hours each week cleaning Bo's truck, waxing the exterior, refusing to sell or even drive it even though it reduced them to one vehicle. "He thinks this trial's gonna take away all his grief," Shelly Anne had told her over lunch one day at the Waffle Iron. "I think all it's gonna do is make him realize the problem is in his spirit. He's gotta find a way to forgive that doctor. Or even bigger, forgive God. Buck's got too much anger in his heart to move on. I'm afraid it's gonna tear our marriage apart."

K.D. remembered similar words from her mother and Trip, advising her to forgive her dad. Maybe forgiveness hadn't shown up yet, but a certain softening had started. At the very least, she didn't feel like she'd swallowed acid every time she thought of her father's desertion. Tender memories slipped through, especially during her quiet morning meditations. Walks by the water. Her daddy throwing her in the air when he returned from work. Teaching her to tie her shoes. A sweet peace and acceptance easing over the bitterness.

She lifted a prayer for the Murdocks, much in the same way she had for her and Trip ever since she started reading the Bible again. He had refused to take it back, telling her to keep it until she found one she liked.

Her daily readings also convicted her. K.D. knew she should talk to Trip. No way existed for them to be a real couple until she did. Every time she prayed, a small voice whispered, "Tell him."

K.D. always answered, "I will," but never did. Maybe she should start to limit their time together. He had planned to come over for dinner tonight, but she should probably beg off. The less interaction between them the better, she thought, although the idea sank in her gut like a dead weight.

The Chevette chugged along the streets of Clear Point, devoid of kids during the school-time hours. She didn't recognize a lot of the adult faces, but then again growing up in the county didn't introduce her to small-town society. Although her mother was raised along these streets, K.D. kept to the creek bank and trailer park, made friendly with the neighbors' animals, but not with the kids. Instead she played with her rock faces. Always easiest that way. Fewer questions about her absentee parents.

Her phone chimed with a text. A quick glance showed the number as Trip's. K.D. pulled into the municipal lot across from the office building before reading the message.

"Talked to your mom. Am bringing dinner. C u at 7."

K.D. sighed. So much for disentangling herself from tonight. Maybe it was for the best- an opportunity to come clean face to face. They could say goodbye down by the creek where she first felt her heart move toward Trip. Full circle and all that.

With heavy limbs, she locked the door and walked toward the

street, waiting for a car to pass before crossing. As it slowed in front of her, K.D. recognized her boss's vintage Cadillac and raised her hand in hello, but Ingram was not behind the wheel. Instead, K.D.'s eyes widened as Bart Cookson offered a gummy smile, accelerating the car down the street.

She ran across the asphalt, yanked open the front door to the building and hurried toward the office.

"K.D., wait!" Maria called down the hall.

"I can't right now. I gotta find Ingram."

"Mister Ingram not there. He and this hombre extrano start yelling, somebody throws something then the hombre leaves. Mister Ingram says something about his car and then he goes. I don't know what to do! Lupe gone. Mister Ingram gone. Just me in the building and I don't…"

K.D. walked over, putting her hands on Maria's arms to keep them in the sockets. "Okay, okay. Calm down. Tell me again what happened."

Maria inhaled, performed the sign of the cross in front of her chest then kissed her fist. "I was at your desk, waiting on the phone to ring because that's what Mister Ingram said to do. De repente, un hombre extraño entre."

K.D. held up a hand. "Hang on. I can't follow your Spanish when you speak that fast. English please."

"Sorry. This strange man comes in, grande man." Maria held her arms apart in exaggeration. "Said he was here to get Mister Ingram's car since he owned it. I told him he could not have his car. Mister Ingram loves his car! Then Mister Ingram comes down the hall, yelling at this Mister Crook to leave the office. Mister Crook says he owns the car and had something from the court, a title or something. They yell for a hundred years, K.D.!"

K.D. chewed the inside of her cheek, her heart breaking to know Bart Cookson took Ingram's car. "What happened then?"

"Mister Ingram goes back to his office, comes back with a piece of paper and the man snatches it from him along with a key. Then he leaves."

"Where's Ingram?"

"Mister Ingram says he was going to the courthouse and will be back. I was scared to stay so I run back to the restaurant." Maria began to wring her hands together. "K.D., is Mister Ingram in trouble? Am I going to lose my new job?"

The building door opened behind them as they spoke. "Nobody's losing any job, Maria. I'm sorry you had to see all that." Ingram looked like he had aged twenty years, stress lines raked across his already wrinkled brow. "Let's all go back in the office and act like we're acquainted with civility."

Maria locked the restaurant door, and the three made their way into Ingram's law office. K.D. entered first and turned for a closer inspection of him before he noticed her perusal. His tie hung lopsided around his neck, loosened as if yanked on for breath. A slight sheen brightened his brow before he pulled out a handkerchief. His shoulders sagged, and a frown pulled down his already sinking jowls.

"Ingram, you okay?"

Ingram pulled in a breath and released it. "I will be. Cookson's appearance certainly thwarted my amiable demeanor."

Maria stood mute in the corner as if the shouting scene scared the voice out of her. Ironic considering K.D. could often hear her and Lupe's tirades down the hall, even through closed doors.

"Did he really take Hank?" K.D. held her breath, scared of the answer.

Ingram nodded. "He did. I can't believe it, but I let the note mature. I guess that's what he counted on. Me being too busy to remember. I could have knocked the smirk off his face when he showed me the paperwork and threatened to bring the police if I didn't surrender the keys." He shrugged his shoulders in defeat. "I had no choice."

"You can borrow my car if you need to, Mister Ingram." Maria stood off to the side, biting a cuticle.

K.D.'s heart tendered at the new friendship. When she first joined the firm, Maria would make the sign of the cross whenever Ingram passed by. Now she offered to carpool.

Ingram actually smiled. "Thank you, Maria, but I have another vehicle, an old truck that runs on an egg beater, but it should get me to the office and back."

K.D. plopped down into a chair, the air both whooshing out of her and the cushion. "So that's it? No more Hank Aaron?"

"Maybe. Maybe not. I checked the law, and there is actually a clause which allows thirty days' restitution. I called Bart and reminded him of that, told him I'd have the note paid off within the month. Ticked him off. I guess he forgot I'm not roadkill waiting on the buzzard."

Ingram ran a hand across his chin, skin scratching stubble. "K.D., we need to buckle down, make sure we're prepared for next week. If we don't get the insurance company to settle before the end of the month, I lose my car and another month's rent will be due. Everything hinges on the opening statement, the first few witnesses. I can't afford to drag the case out." Ingram plopped down at this desk and began rifling through papers.

At that moment, K.D. knew what she had to do. Ingram was family. Family stayed with family, sure as Trip would align with his uncle during the trial. She didn't blame him for it. Hopefully he wouldn't blame her. If K.D. walked from Ingram now, if she left the firm in order to save her relationship with Trip, Ingram would surely go under, losing everything. No way she'd ever let that happen.

Tonight she'd have to tell Trip about the lawsuit and cut her ties.

CHAPTER

20

"No, no, no. Come on! Stupid car!"

K.D.'s neck lurched forward as the Chevette's accelerator lost tension and the engine died. She coasted to the side of the road, already late for home, although Trip and her mother would not have minded her tardiness. The thought irritated rather than warmed her. Things would be a lot easier if her mother disapproved of Trip.

Initially, the fact that her mom adored Trip gave her hope for the relationship. Now, the thought depressed her, worried about the other's reaction when she broke things off. Would Trip hate her? Would her mom spiral back down into a pit of bi-polar blackness? Anxiety tangled up inside her stomach. Worry spread across her forehead in true migraine form. K.D. dropped back against the headrest.

The entire situation could have been dealt with easier if Mama had disliked Trip on sight instead of thinking he was Cary Grant incarnate.

K.D. straightened and turned the ignition, only to have a puff of black smoke erupt from under the hood. Exiting the car, she lifted the top and waved a hand in front of her face in order to breathe.

Once cleared, she looked over the engine as if she had an inkling about what to do. K.D. could change a tire and the oil if money were tight, spark plugs if desperate, but plumes of carcinogenic smoke lay outside her realm of auto-mechanic skills. Glancing around, the length of cross-tie fence reminded her of the distance from home, from any house for that matter. A cow brayed in the pasture as if to mock her predicament.

Her cell phone stared darkly back at her. Out of power. Great. The ribbon of asphalt curled into the night with little moon to illuminate the long walk to the next house. High heels pinched her toes together as she left the door to the Chevette wide open, an encouragement to would-be thieves, and set out along the road, each step eliciting further aggravation.

"This is super. I have to break up with the only boyfriend I've ever really liked. The one who knows I like two packs of sugar with my coffee, three strips of bacon on my BLT, how I count to twelve and a half when I need to calm down, that I keep a rock in my pocket that looks like Ronald Reagan and make bad jokes when I'm nervous. He even laughs at them! And he still doesn't put me on leproscopic level."

K.D. could hear Trip laugh. "Leproscopic? As in you have leprosy? That's not even a word."

"It is now." She spoke to a shadowed oak tree, jumping at the sound of an owl. Something moved in the pasture, probably another herd of cows, but she half jogged to the middle of the road just the same, kicking some loose rocks.

"Only I could fall in love with someone I can't have, even though he's perfect for me. He's not like the date with perpetual sinus issues or the other guy who seemed to sprout extra arms whenever he'd walk me to the door, or any of the other dating disasters that defined my love life."

K.D. kicked another rock and continued arguing with the darkness. "I can't back off from this lawsuit. If we don't proceed, Ingram loses everything. I can't finance Mom's new medicine or finish law school. I've got too much invested in this. It's the only way out of the cess pool that is my life!"

K.D. shook a fist at the wind. "Ugh! It's not fair!" She reached down and picked up a larger rock. Raring back, she hurled it into the night, wishing her bad temper would leave with it. She longed for peace, for a modicum of tranquility to permeate her chaotic mind. To stop being so responsible and for once jump out of the water like Trip's fish or into the water like Shelly Anne's turtle.

My grace is sufficient for you, for my power is made perfect in weakness.

K.D. stopped in the middle of the road while darkness cloaked her. Twisting her head from side to side, she looked for who said the words, her heart beating wildly. It was met by silence except for the moo of cows.

Wait a minute. Hold on.

K.D. laughed out loud. Now she really felt the insanity take over. Hearing voices while walking a deserted road? She had read the scripture that morning. God really showed off when she was at her weakest because then He received the credit and not her. There were no voices in the night, just her memory.

"So I'm just supposed to give it to you?" K.D. kept walking, toeing the asphalt along the way. "How will I know what to do if I don't call the shots or make decisions?"

Therefore do not worry about tomorrow, for tomorrow will worry about itself. Each day has enough trouble of its own.

Words taped to her mother's bathroom mirror. K.D. had read the verse a few days ago and smiled at her mother's optimism, now applicable to herself. She sighed and threw up her hands.

"Okay, you win. I'll keep my worries to tonight. Like how my car is broken down on the side of the road. Or how in the world I'm going to make it in heels all the way home. Or how I break it to Trip that I'm suing his only living family for negligence." The worries knotted in K.D.'s mind until she stopped. Inhale. Exhale. "Okay, God. They're yours. You somehow work this out. I'll follow your lead." An owl hooted his concurrence with the decision, but the silent night following felt eerie. Dark shadows across the pastures moved, the wind shuffling the branches. The moon shifted behind some clouds, shrouding her in darkness and goose bumps. K.D. picked up her pace, her heartbeat quickening.

As she crested the hill, two headlights blinded her, almost running her over. She sidestepped, but the shoulder dropped into a ditch, causing her to fall. K.D. rolled down the damp grass until she braced against the dirt, stopping the momentum. Tires squealed against asphalt as if the driver stomped on the brakes, sliding before coming to a rest on the roadside. The door opened and a male voice called out, "Hey!"

She didn't recognize the voice, but she heard Doomsday Doris in her head telling her to run, something about a kidnapping in the thirties and a child being murdered or one of the million other stories that ended in Doris mayhem. K.D. jumped to her feet and took off running, scampering more like it, due to her high-heeled constriction. She kicked off her shoes, feeling her hose rip as a rock tore into her foot. She hopped forward, fighting not-so-nice words.

Footsteps caught up with her. Hands grabbed her arms from behind so she whirled with a fist, connecting with his jaw. Adrenaline kicked in, and K.D. fought with everything she had. She pushed against him, freeing herself for enough room to wrench away. K.D. made it as far as the split-rail fence, one foot lifted in a vain attempt to scale the height before the would-be-robber-attacker-rapist caught up with her.

"K.D., will you stop!?"

"No, I won't! Don't tell me to stop! Why would I stop and let you..." K.D. did halt her progress, slowly turning her head to the shadowed figure on the roadside. "Trip?" She looked closer at the car, recognizing the outline of the Audi.

Trip approached her as the moon shifted from behind a cloud, illuminating him as he rubbed his jaw. "Man oh man, do you have a mean right hook. We have *got* to do something about that temper of yours."

K.D. lowered herself off the fence, hung her head as she walked toward him, her heart collecting into a normal rhythm. "I'm sorry. Did I hurt you?"

Trip laughed, and then winced. "My pride says no, but wow. You sure you don't lift weights or something?"

"Well, I have been going to yoga." She reached his side, touched his arm. "I'm so sorry. My car broke down, and I was walking home. All the night noises already had me spooked. I guess you pushed me over the edge."

"K.D., you jumped off the edge some time ago. It's what I love the most about you."

There goes that word again. Oh how she wished he'd quit saying he loved her, yet her Judas heart leaped.

"What are you doing here, Trip? I figured you'd already be at the house."

"I was. But your mom got worried. She called your office, and your boss said you had left a while back. I volunteered to come find you, although I'm now regretting my decision." Trip continued to rub his jaw.

K.D.'s face heated at the mention of Ingram. Did her mom use Ingram's name? Tell Trip where she worked? She'd given her strict instructions not to, but this was the first time they'd been alone, K.D. unable to monitor their conversation. Yet his tone sounded the same even level.

Trip reached out and patted down her hair, sure to be flying all over her head due to the flight of the panic a few minutes ago. "What in the world is going around that brain of yours? Your face is scrunched up like you ate a raw lemon."

K.D. frowned. "Well, thanks." She paused and collected herself. "Nothing. Nothing's wrong."

"In that case, come on and get in the car. I'll call a tow truck when we get back to your house, see if someone can get it tonight. If not, I'll come take a look at it tomorrow."

The two walked in silence, Trip holding her elbow along the broken-up asphalt, avoiding the pot holes. K.D. retrieved her shoes, but left them off her feet. When he went to open the car door, she paused.

"Trip, can we stay here for a minute? I'd really like to talk to you about something." The moment of truth arrived and sat right down on K.D.'s chest, constricting her breathing. It was all she could do to hold back the tears. Oh how she didn't want to release Trip, to let him go, but she knew she had to, for both of their sakes. Either that or run away. She glanced toward the fence.

Trip took his hand off the door handle. "Sure, but why don't we head home? We can talk on the way or go down by the creek at your house. To be honest with you, I need to talk to you too."

We can't go home because I need neutral ground. The earth already feels unstable, as if straddling a fault line. I can't have the memory of you leaving be somewhere I'll see every day. "If you don't mind, I'd rather stay here and talk."

He looked at her with a knitted brow, but in typical Trip fashion, acquiesced. "Okay, but only if I get to go first." He opened the trunk, retrieving the same picnic blanket they had laid on a few months prior. He took her hand, and they walked over to the fence where he helped her climb. Joining her on the other side, Trip spread out the blanket.

He leaned toward her and kissed her softly, like a whisper. His cologne lingered in the space between them.

"What's that for?"

Trip smiled. "Because I have a feeling you are about to break up with me. I'm trying to make it harder."

K.D.'s eyes widened. "What makes you think that?"

He shifted, reached over and pulled out a blade of grass from her hair and twisted it around his finger, again and again. "I don't know, you've been so weird lately, more ornery than normal."

She punched him in the arm, eliciting a chuckle which quickly faded.

"It's like you're pushing me away. Picking fights where none exist. I've been through this before, can recognize the signs. The difference is, this time I don't want the relationship to end. I didn't care about the others. They weren't worth the fight. You are." He paused, smiled at her enough to deepen a dimple, and then the look faded. "But I know we can't move forward until we talk about the secrets between us. It's important for the truth to be known."

So he knew. Her mother must have let Ingram's or Shelly Anne's name slip, mentioning some connection to the lawsuit.

"Trip, I can explain."

He held up a hand and drew in his breath, then slowly exhaled. "No, I'm the one who needs to explain." Trip paused as if collecting his thoughts. He reached over and took K.D.'s hand, rubbing a thumb across her skin. Without looking up, he spoke in a voice she would not have recognized if she didn't know it came from his mouth. "I need to tell you how I killed my parents."

CHAPTER 21

"Wanna run that by me again?" His guilt-ridden tone clogged the air in K.D.'s throat. She stared at Trip, wide-eyed. A chill ran down her spine, causing her to shake.

"You're freezing. Hold on, I'll be right back."

K.D. lifted a hand to stop him, but dropped it back to her lap as Trip bolted toward the car.

Killed his parents? Surely K.D. didn't hear him right. What sounded like kill? Maybe billed his parents? For school? Or thrilled his parents? That sounded more like it. Who wouldn't be thrilled to have a son like Trip? But a dark foreboding climbed through her limbs, weighing her down.

Trip returned, carrying a jacket, and wrapped it around her shoulders.

"Thanks." K.D. wanted to pull it over her head and dive beneath the smell of Trip. "I thought your parents were killed by a drunk driver."

Trip stared off in the distance, his eyes cloudy in the now present moonlight. Ten eternities seemed to pass before he spoke, but when he did, he looked her right in the eyes. "They were. I was the driver."

The agony in his voice made K.D. want to wrap him in her arms and never let go. Pain emanated from Trip, as tangible as if it sat right there on the blanket with them. Words scrambled in her brain, bumping against each other in beehive fashion.

"Oh."

That's it? That's all she could come up with?

Trip cleared his throat. "Yeah." Cleared his throat again. "This is harder than I thought."

K.D. reached over and took his hand, waiting for him to speak. She silently searched for the words to erase the hurt in his voice. "How can I make this easier?"

A small smile eased across his mouth. "Being with you makes it easier. I only hope you'll want to stay once you know the truth. You see, when I realized I loved you, I knew I had to let you know what happened that night. I couldn't let you believe I was some poor orphan who had to live without his parents because a jerk decided to drink and drive. Especially since I was that jerk."

Trip retrieved his hand and ran it through his dark hair. A car drove by without stopping. "It was the night of my college graduation. I had been invited to a party before I was to pick up my parents for a late dinner. They broke out a keg, and I had a few beers. I didn't think a few beers would hurt. Didn't seem to affect my driving when I drove to my parent's hotel. We had a great time at dinner. My parents were pretty proud of me. My dad…" Trip's words trailed off into tears. He tried several times to start, but the grief suffocated the sound. He shook his head, breathed deeply, and clenched his jaw, grasping for control.

"Take your time, Trip. We have all night."

He nodded, silent until his cell phone rang. He frowned while looking at the number. "It's a text from your mom. We forgot to let her know you're okay."

"Here, I'll shoot her a message." K.D. punched out a text to her mom, asking her not to reply back, but they were fine and eating somewhere else. She returned the phone to Trip. "Go on with the story."

Trip wiped his eyes, trying to collect himself through stifled breaths. "My dad was such a good man, K.D., and my mama too. They were simple people, reserved like most folks from upstate. Not like Aunt Frances and Big Daddy. They worked the ground and gave thanks in even the roughest seasons."

K.D. frowned. "I don't understand. You said you only had a couple of beers and then ate a full meal. Seems like enough time would have passed for that not to be a factor."

"I did too. I never would have driven if I felt the slightest bit intoxicated. I never drove when I drank – ever. I didn't feel it when I picked them up and sure as heck didn't feel it after that big meal. I mean, I had a salad, rib eye, huge baked potato with the works. I was stuffed when we headed back to the hotel."

"What happened then?"

"We approached a crazy, busy intersection. It was raining. I thought I could make the light, but didn't. I swerved to miss a car, but when I did, I put us directly in the path of a utility truck. Insurance adjuster figured his speed was at least ten miles over the limit. But the way I turned, the truck hit the passenger's side dead on, which is where my parents sat. Neither of them wore a seat belt. I found out later the impact threw my mom out of the rear window of the car, and my dad…" Grief raged war across his face, battling composure and winning. Sobs drowned any other words, echoing through the silent evening.

K.D. inched forward, leaning toward Trip until he fell into her like a drowning man clawing through water for air. She held him, realizing she was crying too. Not the deep cavernous sobs he experienced, but silent, aching tears. She'd never seen a man cry, had no idea what to do. Time inched on before Trip pulled back, embarrassed, and palmed his face. He withdrew a handkerchief from his pocket and blew his nose while K.D. ran the back of her hand under his.

He looked up. "Sorry about that." He looked away, unable to meet her eyes.

"For what? Needing a friend? You don't ever have to apologize to me, Trip. I still find it hard to believe you were drunk, though. I mean, we all make mistakes in driving, get too aggressive trying to beat lights. I do it on a daily basis."

"I blew just under .08. Not enough to be issued a DUI, but the cops were quick to let me know even a small indicator like that could impair my driving. They made it pretty clear who was at fault."

"What happened to the other driver?"

"A few bumps and scratches. Nothing major, but his insurance company sued us because I ran a red light. Ours settled, but not without some financial implications on the estate. Another reason I couldn't start law school right away."

K.D. remembered Trip drinking water at his uncle's, forgoing the wine. "That's why you don't drink."

Trip nodded. A pregnant silence followed, heavy with an air of solemnity. K.D. waited him out, the hair raised on the back of her neck. Intuition prepared her for more disclosure.

He picked a blade of grass, fiddled with it as almost a buffer against what came out of his mouth next. "I'm an alcoholic, K.D."

K.D. looked at this man she had put on a pedestal. Not that he ever asked to be there, but she needed him to be, yearned for him to be something she wouldn't have to worry about, a man unlike her own parents. While his flawless character intimidated her, she also longed for the security it provided. K.D. drew to his light in the knowledge she would not have to mop up his suicide attempt or hide petty cash or even worry about the fact he might one day abandon her. Not perfect Trip. Those worries didn't exist with the Trip who had wormed his way into her heart.

Tarnish now spread across his armor, chinks and imperfections rose to the surface. Yet instead of seeing something ugly, something she should run from, K.D. thought he never looked more beautiful…more accessible. "How long have you been sober?"

"My longest time was two years, three months and sixteen days after the wreck, but I fell off the wagon right before starting law school. Nerves, I guess. I went on a bender that lasted an entire weekend. My uncle found me outside his house, laying in my own vomit. He never said a word, just carried me inside and cleaned me up. I woke to a note beside my pillow where he wrote the number to the local Alcoholics Anonymous. I've been going ever since and have not had a drop to drink. I know I can do this, but it's going to be harder than I thought."

The tightness in her chest relaxed a bit at his confident tone. K.D. thought of her mother. Lydia couldn't help her binges either. Depression and alcoholism were societal diseases in which blame did no good, but the person had to take control of his life in order to be healthy. Nobody could do it for him. She leaned toward Trip. "I don't know anything about alcoholism, but I know everything you'd want to know about manic depression. It's a battle you have to fight every minute. I'm proud of you."

Trip shook his head. "Don't be proud of me. My parents are dead because of my addiction. The guilt over that has almost killed me a thousand times over."

Chewing the inside of her lip, K.D. wrinkled her brow in thought. "Trip, I'm no legal expert yet. I mean, we haven't even read or discussed cases involving drunk driving, but if you didn't register as drunk in the breathalyzer, and you had just eaten a big meal and your last drink was hours before, as your attorney it wouldn't take me long to convince a jury this accident was nowhere related to drinking."

Trip shook his head. "I ran the red light, K.D. It was my fault."

"I didn't say you weren't at fault. But fault can be defined two ways. Intentionally or negligently. You ran a red light. Fact. Did you run a red light with the intent to kill your parents? Did you stand to benefit from their death? Did you in any way premeditate the event?"

"I think you know the answer to all of those questions."

"I rest my case then. What happened was a terrible, horrible accident. Stop for just a second. Do you think your parents would want you to spend one second of your precious life- the life they gave you- feeling guilty for an accident? Something you would take back in a second if you could?" K.D. snapped her fingers. "Do you think they would stand before you right now and blame you?"

Trip sighed, grabbed a handful of grass, and began picking apart the blades.

"Well, do you?"

"No."

"Okay then."

"I appreciate what you're trying to do, but it doesn't help. The fact remains my parents are dead because of me. It's not as simple as you're making it out to be." Trip's jaw clenched on the condemnation.

"Why can't it be that simple? Look, I can't lift the burden off you, Trip. You're the only one who can do that. But what I don't understand is this: if you love and respect your parents as much as you say, why in the world would you disrespect them in death?"

Trip sat back as if struck. "What's that supposed to mean? I've never disrespected my parents!" Anger clamped down on his tone.

Good. Let him be angry. K.D. could deal with that better than sobs. "You said your parents would never place any blame on you for the accident. So if you continue to carry something around that you've already been forgiven for, isn't that disrespectful to the ones who forgave you?"

A thought nudged K.D.'s heart. "Even better, aren't you the one who always told me Jesus came to this earth to forgive us for our sins? For our mistakes? To take away the burden of guilt so we're not straddled with anything to prevent a free and pure relationship with Him? I believed you when you told me that, about letting go of my anger toward my dad, but now I guess I was wrong to have done so."

"Don't turn this around on me, K.D."

"Why? Is it that hard to admit when you're wrong? Stubborn's not the relative to keep at the table, Trip."

"You're one to tell me about stubborn? You got a lot of nerve." Trip stood, glared at her and then stormed off. K.D. let him go. She drew her knees up Indian-style, resting her elbows. He circled a massive tree trunk several times, reaching out to snatch off bits of bark. Stopping, he rested his back with one leg bent, a foot flat to the oak. Wrestling with words inside his head, he dropped and lowered both elbows on his knees, putting his head into his hands. Then he fell to the ground, prostrate as if in prayer for what seemed like ten eternities.

Should she join him? K.D. stayed put, not wanting to interfere with the sacred moment. Crickets chirped and owls hooted. Cattle sounded in the distance while Trip stayed pressed to the grass. Finally, he stood, hesitated, and then palmed his face and returned to the blanket, holding out a hand.

K.D.'s lips slid into a smile. "There wasn't any cow poop over there, was there?"

"I made sure to grab a handful just for you." He shook his hand toward her again. K.D. took it and stood with him. Trip gathered her in his arms. Her cheek nestled right under his left clavicle where his heart beat into her ear. She swayed with him a minute, moving to their hearts' rhythm as the nighttime air dampened their skin.

"Thank you." Two words whispered into K.D.'s hair. There was still pain, but less agony. The moment lightened somewhat.

She spoke against his chest. "You're not mad at me? Sometimes I overstep a few lines here and there."

He laughed over her head. "You wouldn't see a line if it were drawn down your eyeballs. But regardless, I'm grateful."

"You're welcome. I don't know for what, but you're welcome."

He held her out, tucking a curl behind an ear. "For holding me accountable. I don't want to feel this way anymore, K.D. I want to be free of this burden." Moonlight bounced off the tears in his eyes.

K.D. reached up and wiped one clinging to his chin. "You will be. When is up to you, but you told me yourself God forgave our sins long before we ever committed them. But you can't honor His forgiveness until you receive it for yourself. Weren't those your words?"

He took her hand and kissed it, then gathered up the blanket and tucked it under one arm. He threw the other across K.D.'s shoulders as they walked toward his car. "You learn well, little grasshopper."

They stopped at the fence, and she turned to him. "I have a good teacher."

He leaned over and kissed her nose. "I think this might take some time, though, but I'm willing to try. I'm thankful I have you to help me."

K.D. smiled as they walked across the asphalt. She eased into the Audi before realizing she had not spoken a word about the upcoming trial against Trip's uncle. She'd have to tell him tomorrow, the next day at the latest, but there was no way could she burden him tonight.

Trip entered the driver's side and turned the ignition. Before accelerating, he took her hand. "Thank you for not breaking up with me. I want you to know, I'm here for you too, in whatever circumstance. I mean it, K.D. I hope you know that."

K.D. bit her lip as they drove off.

CHAPTER 22

Two high school boys lined up helmet to helmet, feet planted yet poised for launch, three fingers in the dirt. At the whistle blow, the football players locked together, the sound of the collision mimicking that of a car wreck as pads crashed against pads. K.D. winced when one fell down hard, and the other player left cleat tracks across his chest.

Coach Mark lifted the boy off the ground by a fistful of shirt. "You call that a block? What's wrong with you, Pansy? My eighty-year-old grandmother could have held him up longer than that." He pushed the boy away. "Give me three laps, Michael, and don't line up again on my field until you're ready to play with men and not Barbies!"

K.D. felt sorry for the boy as he trotted off, wading through the record-high heat. Her breaths were shallow just sitting on the bleachers, much less actually exerting aerobic effort in the humidity. Yesterday's rain marinated the small town in today's soupy feel.

Coach turned to the cluster of players watching the interaction, seemingly unfazed at their peer's humiliation. "Okay, fellas. That's it for today. We got the finals coming up. Let's keep our eyes on one game at a time. Billy? You got the break."

A mountain of a boy, his bulging forearms dripping sweat,

huddled up the team. "Tigers on three. One, two, three..." And the group chorused "Tigers!" with a clap, and then scattered toward the building behind them. K.D. felt like she was watching some sacred tribal ritual as poor Michael completed his punishment, but stopped to catch his breath, folded over his legs, before entering the gymnasium.

What in the world was she doing here? K.D. should have listened to Ingram and avoided Coach Mark altogether. "He's their witness, K.D. He could file a harassment charge if you start provoking him outside his deposition or the actual trial." Ingram had fumed at her.

"I'm not going to harass him. I'm simply going to ask him if he remembered anything else. You'd think you'd be a little more supportive that I'm going above and beyond my pay grade here." Ingram had hmmmphed at her and left the room.

She could not, would not, proceed with this trial and lose Trip without knowing, beyond a shadow of a doubt, that Dr. Thomas was negligent in his treatment of Bo. All arrows pointed in that direction, but still, K.D. couldn't let Ingram know her true motivation. Besides maybe she would find something out that would help their case, like she had told him.

K.D. walked from the bottom bleacher where she had sweltered the last half hour, along with what looked like some of the boys' daddies, waiting on the man to stop barking at his players. The backs of her knees felt mushy with sweat. She held back as the men circled the coach, offering advice and suggestions.

"Mark, I was thinking that if we..." One man held up a notebook pad, showing Coach Camp a rudimentary drawing of Xs and Os. K.D. hid a grin at the coach's feigned interest. She had watched Ingram through many a meeting with clients to recognize that his expression really meant, "Please shut up so I can go home."

A few players slapped the coach on the back and the impromptu critique wagon broke up. K.D. hurried to him. "Um, excuse me, Mr. Camp?"

Coach Camp looked up from his clipboard, pen in hand. His face was bloated and red with sweat-plastered hair peeking from beneath a filthy baseball cap. "You can pick your son up in front of the school. Moms aren't allowed on the practice field."

Well, now that was downright insulting. A babysitter, maybe, but there was no way she could have been a mom to a teenager unless she gave birth as a teenager herself. Plus, no wonder he didn't allow moms anywhere near his practice. They're the ones who filed a petition to have him fired.

"No, I'm not a mother. I actually need to speak with you. My name is K.D. Jennings." She offered her hand. Coach Camp took it in his wet, meaty palm. K.D. refrained from wiping it against her skirt.

"What can I do for you?"

"I'm a legal assistant in the law firm Ingram and Associates. We're suing Dr. Jackson Thomas for the wrongful death of Bo Murdock. You're listed as a witness for the defense, but I had a few questions I wanted to ask you."

Coach Camp's face scrunched into a frown to the point his eyes disappeared under his brows. "I don't have anything else to say. I can't believe y'all are dragging me into this thing. I had to cancel practice for that dadgum deposition thing. I told you everything I know then. Y'all need to leave me alone and let me do my job."

He started to walk off, but K.D. grabbed his arm. "I know you did, and we appreciate your time. I just have a few more questions, please."

He shrugged her off and continued walking.

"Coach Camp, a kid is dead, and we're trying to hold the person accountable who might have killed him. I would think that's worth a few minutes of your time." Sometimes she wished she would watch her tone, but his condescending treatment made her want to strangle him with his own whistle.

He stopped and slowly turned. Stomping back to K.D., he put a sausage finger in her face. "Don't you dare come on *my* football field and lecture me about *my* players. I take them away from their mommies and turn them into men. I love these kids like they're my own."

You'd have your own kids puking in 110 degree heat because they let someone twice their size run over them? His breath blew in her face, but she didn't back down. "I understand that, Coach Camp. But I need to make sure I do my job. That if someone was negligent in Bo's care, they be held accountable. I know your impact on these kids is immeasurable. You're highly esteemed in the community and those state championships aren't anything to scoff at. That's why you're vital to this case. You were there with Bo. You saw it all. You're more than just a coach here. You actually stand for justice."

Good grief, could she pour it on any thicker? Her admonitions seemed to work as the muscles in the coach's face relaxed and his expression softened.

"I told you I already gave all the information I know during the deposition. What other questions could you possibly have?"

K.D. stopped short of patting herself on the back when he adopted an informal stance, like a military person at ease, clipboard behind him.

"You did a great job in your deposition. I'm just wondering if there's anything that might have come to you later on. You said Bo had run a play where he ran out into the field and another player hit him…"

"A slant route."

"I beg your pardon?"

"I said he ran a slant route."

"What's that mean?"

Coach tilted his head and squinted at her. "Not much a football fan, huh?"

K.D. shrugged her shoulders in apology.

"A slant route is when a receiver runs at a forty-five-degree angle to find the hole between the linebacker and linemen. We had us a heckofa quarterback so we're able to run the play cause he can thread a needle."

K.D. tried to stay focused, scribbling notes, but didn't understand much of anything the coach said.

"Bo ran the route perfectly. Problem was, we also had a heckofa safety who popped Bo as soon as he grabbed the ball."

"Which direction did he hit Bo?"

"From behind. A safety keeps the receivers in front, especially if they sniff out a slant route. Why?"

K.D. frowned. "I'm just wondering why the doctor would ever consider a concussion if he knew the safety hit him from behind and not helmet to helmet."

The coach shrugged. "He did hit the ground pretty hard. Sometimes the snap of the neck on a hit can rock the brain some. He passed out for a few seconds and woke up puking. I knew then I had to get him to the hospital."

A teenager ran from the gymnasium, garnering the coach's attention. He excused himself from K.D. and joined in a whispered conversation, giving her time to think as she waved away a pesky gnat.

If the player hit Bo from behind, he surely would have braced his fall with his hands, protecting his body. Anyone would do that on instinct. So if the doctor knew he was hit from behind, coupled with the fact Bo had a temperature of 107, then why in the world would he have a preliminary diagnosis of concussion? Come on, Dr. Thomas. K.D. was running out of rocks to turn over in order to find Trip's uncle not liable for breach of the standard care. Guilt tweaked her a bit at her line of thinking. Shouldn't she work to prove him liable instead of slaving to find evidence of his competence? Which side did she work for anyway?

Coach Camp concluded his conversation and rejoined K.D. "What were you saying?"

K.D. scribbled some notes and then looked at the coach. "I guess I'm wondering why in the world Dr. Thomas would treat Bo for a concussion. You said yourself he wasn't hit helmet to helmet.

I highly doubt he hit the ground in such a way it would lead the doctor to conclude an automatic concussion rather than consider heat stroke. Add that to the fact his temperature was 107 when he entered the hospital, and even I would think he suffered from the heat and not a head injury. It seems so cut and dry that I feel I must be missing something. Is there anything else you can think to tell me? Anything at all?"

Coach Camp looked at his watch, glanced behind him at a few boys waiting outside the gymnasium, holding their football pads, their expressions drooping in the heat. "Look, Bo was one of the best athletes I've ever seen, but more importantly, a great kid." Coach choked up a second and cleared his throat. "Did we do all we could to save him? I go to bed every night with that question. If you think for one second I'd hold back any information that could bring justice for Bo, you have lost your mind. Now, if you'll excuse me, I gotta get these boys home so they can do their homework. Some don't have daddies, and their mamas work all day. Leaves me to be both parents at times." He turned to go and walked toward his players.

K.D. hollered after him. "I appreciate your time. I'll be in touch."

The coach waved behind him as the boys fell in line, walking toward a beat up truck and hopping in the truck bed. Coach pulled one boy aside, and K.D. recognized him as Michael whom coach had made run laps till he about lost his breath. They now stood head to head with Coach Camp's hands on the young man's shoulders, talking quietly together. Michael nodded, and Coach embraced him, patting him on the back as he climbed into the truck bed with the others.

K.D. guessed the relationship with players and their coaches mirrored hers and her mother's dog, Sophia. She could scold her one minute for urinating on the carpet, but then the little dog would lather her with kisses seconds later. For the number of mothers who protested Coach Camp's practice techniques, five times the number of players had stood in his defense. The very ones who had to endure the heat and brutal tactics. K.D. shook her head and walked toward her car, stopping when Coach Camp pulled up beside her with his window rolled down.

"Miss Jennings, did you say Bo's temperature was 107 when he came to the hospital?"

K.D. nodded. "According to the nurse's report."

Coach Camp frowned. "I find that hard to believe. I didn't check it with any thermometer or anything, but there's no way his temperature was that high. I'da felt that with my hand."

K.D.'s mouth hung open as the coach drove off. She closed it before the dust of the natural parking lot entered. Could a temperature spike to 107 in the short ride to the hospital? If not, how did the 107 number find its way into the nurse's notes? K.D. entered her car and took a right out of the school, heading toward the library. It was time to become an expert in heat exhaustion and its effect on a body's temperature.

CHAPTER 23

The pile of books stacked higher than K.D.'s head as she perused through the medical journals. All the computers were occupied, and she hadn't the time to wait on availability. Besides, the fact that Ingram didn't have Internet access at the office made her a pro at hard-copy research.

She looked at the column on her note pad. The headline read *facts*. Underneath, she had written, 1) Bo became incapacitated during the slant route play. 2) Bo did not have a high fever when he left the ball field, according to Coach Camp. 3) The temperature was not taken at the hospital in the proper context, ancillary versus rectal. 4) Hospital understaffed during Bo's visit. 5) Had to wait over an hour for CAT scan. 6) Dr. Thomas's professional history showed he never treated anyone for heat exhaustion. Entire career was spent in upstate New York where oppressive heat is unusual. 7) Nurses did not note any head trauma or anything about the play that injured him.

K.D. began to write her lingering questions beneath her notes. How did Bo's temperature spike so quickly? The nurse's notes clearly indicated a 107 degree temperature less than an hour after the play in which he was injured, according to the time in Camp's deposition. Why would the nurse not draw immediate attention to a patient with such a high temperature? Coach Camp said he described the incident to the nurses, pointing out that Bo always protected the ball whenever tackled, which could have caused the head trauma because he guarded the ball and did not break his fall.

Everything pointed back to the temperature. To K.D., it was the needle pressing into her side. Even with the concussion diagnosis, any medical professional, nurse or doctor, should have reacted differently to such a high fever. At that level, K.D. had read, enzymes began to deform and break down, and damage to the brain was highly likely. Why in the world would the hospital staff allow Bo to cook in his own body while not only waiting for the doctor, but then the subsequent testing?

The answer had to exist, but K.D. could not figure out where it lay. At first glance, she tended to believe the hospital staff was more negligent than the doctor. But then again, according to her research, the doctor could have saved Bo's life even if his fever had been 107 prior to the doctor beginning his examination. Brain damage might have occurred, but death would have been prevented if the doctor had only addressed the fever the minute he reviewed Bo's vitals.

K.D. leaned back her head, popping her neck from side to side. The passing shadows reminded her of the dwindling afternoon. She started carrying her book pile to the return station, in no hurry. Trip had texted earlier to say he had to work late with his uncle, causing her to cringe when he'd typed, "Working...mand K.iss u" She had yet to say those words back, knowing they'd be thrown in her face once he realized the truth. K.D. had tried her best to find a way to excuse the doctor, to find him not liable for Bo's death, or maybe even somewhere else to point the finger.

But the evidence did not support any of it. The chart read a temperature of 107 when Bo was admitted, written in the blue pen of the nurse on duty, clear enough for Dr. Thomas to have noticed the spike, and yet he still ordered a CAT scan rather than address the burning blood which eventually killed Bo Murdock.

With the last book returned, K.D. sighed and collected loose papers on top of her notepad. With her mother acting like a normal person lately, maybe K.D. could talk her into making chicken pot pie from scratch, like she used to. K.D. hadn't requested it in years because it was her father's favorite, but her stomach now growled at the thought. Stupid. Why should she punish herself just because he couldn't hack it as a parent?

Lost in a memory of flaky pie crust and creamy vegetables, K.D. walked out the library door and straight into someone, papers flying everywhere.

"Oh, I'm so sorry. I wasn't paying attention." K.D. stooped to grab her papers, but only succeeded in knocking heads with a man. She straightened, eyes shut against the blinding pain for a second before opening them.

"You are trying your best to bruise every inch of my head and face, aren't you?" Trip stood before her, holding a hand against the growing knot on his forehead, but wearing a smile. Seeing a few papers light off across the lawn, he hurried after them and returned to hand them to K.D. "I mean, the bruise has barely gone away from the last time you cold-cocked me."

She snatched them before he could see. The public library was not where she had planned to disclose everything to Trip. K.D. bent and collected the rest of her things. "You do have a habit of running into my fists and other hard objects." Straightening, she smiled. "What are you doing here?"

He frowned, glancing at his watch. "Did you forget we were supposed to study?"

Heat climbed K.D.'s neck as she shifted the stack of books to another arm. "Yes. I can't even come up with a good enough lie. I thought you were at your uncle's farm anyway?"

"I was, but we finished sooner than we thought. I'm working with my uncle on a court case so I came here early to look some things up before we were supposed to meet." Immediately, his face fell, and he clamped a hand over his mouth. "I can't believe I said that. Forget I did. I had promised him I wouldn't talk publicly about this, and until now have kept the promise. Please don't say anything or ask any questions."

The poor thing really looked horrified. If he only knew.

"Your secret is safe with me, Trip. No worries, but I can't stay. I'm sorry. I know I need to read over next week's case for class, but honestly, I don't have the energy to read a cereal box right now." K.D. talked fast while she walked sideways toward her car, garnering a honk from someone backing up, causing her to jump out of the way. "I plan to go home, put on my flannel jammies with the hole in the knee and call it a night. I'll make it up to you. I promise!" Her voice grew louder the farther away she walked.

Trip looked confused, but then again between her bad jokes and sarcasm, he often did when trying to decipher K.D.'s moods. "Okay, well, I guess I'll talk to you later." He cupped a hand around his mouth to be heard.

"Sure thing!" K.D. eased into the seat, blowing out her breath. That was closer than a freckle on a frog. With opening arguments slated to start next week, K.D. knew her time was running out to either find Dr. Thomas not liable or to tell Trip the truth.

CHAPTER

24

The fountain outside the courthouse misted her face as she waited for Ingram to finish in the office. The day rained sunshine, falling temperatures elbowing a little humidity out of the way. Too pretty to stay inside and tap her foot while Ingram argued with his ex-wife over the tardy rent. Lucky for her, the office sat a few buildings down from the courthouse, and she could enjoy the beautiful day while she waited and watched for his exit. Her stomach grumbled at the late lunch hour, the thought of last night's chicken pot pie entering her mind.

"Come on, I'm starving." K.D. leaned back on her hands and stuck her legs out straight, grimacing at the hem loosened at the bottom of her pants. She couldn't wait to pass the bar and buy nicer clothes. A couple sizes smaller, too, since she'd lost some weight. K.D. had added an extra hole on the belt that morning, smiling while doing so. It had been a long time since she'd had to take in the waistline. Might even give Delilah a run for her money soon as the skinniest girl in law school.

K.D. snorted, scattering the pigeons at her feet when her phone vibrated in her pocket, Trip's number on Caller I.D.

"Hey Folsom. What do you do if you're stranded on an island with two bullets, Adolf Hitler, Attila the Hun and a lawyer?"

"Shoot the lawyer twice."

K.D. frowned into the phone. "How'd you know the answer?"

"I've been doing my homework. I have a whole book of jokes I've been reading. You're not the only one with a sense of humor. Hey listen, where are you right now? You dropped something outside the library yesterday, and I've been trying to remember to call you. Looks like some sort of research you might need for work because I don't recall The Case of the Unencumbered Employee being anything about the body effects of high temperature."

The words snatched K.D.'s breath for a second, her mind scrambling. Which paper? She had copied several, taken notes on others, but none of them needed be with Trip. She had to get that paper out of Trip's possession, but Ingram would be joining her any minute. "I'm actually sitting outside the courthouse waiting on a colleague to go to lunch. Can I call you when we're done? I can swing by wherever you are." Please don't let it be the paper with her notes. She reached for her satchel only to remember she had left it in the office.

"You're outside the courthouse? I'm a few blocks over. I was heading to lunch myself, but I can swing by there. See ya in a few."

The phone silenced before K.D. could protest. Hopefully Ingram's plea for rent extension fell on Madeline's deaf ears, giving K.D. some time while they duked it out. Come on, Trip, hurry. Eyes darted from the office to the courthouse doors, back and forth as if looking for a getaway car. Thankfully, Trip wasn't kidding when he said he was only a few blocks away. K.D. watched him turn the corner toward her.

He wore a business suit and royal-blue tie, his white starched shirt peeking out. Her heart sighed. His brown curls danced in the fountain mist when he dropped beside her, holding out a piece of paper as he leaned over to kiss her cheek. "I didn't know you were going to be here today. We could have ridden together or something, gone to lunch." Trip pulled sunglasses up to his eyes from where they rested around his neck.

K.D. waved him off, trying to read his body language. It remained typical of Trip, friendly and accessible, glad to see her. She shoved the folded paper into her pocket without looking at it. "No, no, that's okay. I already have plans. Thanks for bringing it." She stood, glancing back at the office, and fidgeted with her purse.

He stood with her. "Are you in a hurry? I didn't recognize the paper as being mine, but it looked like your handwriting and I remembered how your stuff scattered when you barreled over me at the library. That's not for school is it?"

"No. Something I'm doing for work, but I do need to…"

"Whew. I got nervous. I knew if tomorrow's case had anything to do with temperature regulation, I was as out of luck as a rooster in a duck pond."

K.D. snickered, forgetting Ingram for a second. "If that's your idea of catching up to my sense of humor, Trip, you got two flat tires and a blown engine standing in the way of the finish line."

He laughed out loud and for a second, K.D. lost herself inside its bubble. A few nights ago, they'd laughed themselves to the point of crying over a card game of UNO with her mom. The two had ganged up on K.D., slamming her right and left with Reverses and Draw Twos until K.D. had to hold her stack with two hands. She finally picked up on the sign language. An ear pull for a Draw Four, a nose scratch for a Skip. K.D. stood, threw down her cards, yelling, "Cheaters! I'm surrounded by cheaters!" Trip had charged for her, and they both landed in a heap on the couch with Sophia the dog yipping beside them. Lydia had waddled from the room, saying she thought she'd wet her pants, spewing the same laughter Trip now rained down on her.

A pigeon danced close to her sandaled feet, calling attention to the reality of Ingram's looming presence as well as the sad state of her toenail polish. Her laughter faded. "Seriously though, Trip. I gotta scoot. Where are you parked?"

"I'm out back." He cocked his head, looking at her sideways almost as they stood.

"What?"

"I don't know. It's hard to keep up with your mood swings lately. One minute you're laughing, and the next it's like you can't wait to get rid of me."

K.D. inched backward to encourage his forward momentum. "I'm busy is all. I told you I had plans. Sorry if I'm not all Perky Pattie, but I've got a lot on my mind right now."

"Hey." He pulled at her hand, stopping her progress. Reaching down, he smoothed the hair away from her face. "I know you've got a lot on your plate. What can I do to help? You don't have to do it all, you know."

Yes, she did. She had to do all she was doing in order to make a better life for herself and help her mother stay healthy, even if it meant losing Trip. K.D.'s shoulders sagged, and she had to lean away from him to keep from dropping her head on his shoulder. How wonderful it would be in different circumstances, to truly be able to let go and let him help, to have someone carry the load when her side drooped a bit. But not now. Not here.

He pulled on her again and before she could resist, he held her in his arms, rubbing a strong hand over the back of her head. K.D. breathed him in, musky cologne and all, and wondered if she could stay right there forever. And she did, until he pulled back.

K.D. forced a smile. "Sorry, Trip. We do need to talk, but I've been putting it off. When you hear what it is, you'll understand why I've been so impossible lately, but I'd rather not do it here. I'd rather talk to you privately. Do you have plans later?" Over his shoulder, K.D. spied Ingram exiting the office door. He turned and waved to someone in the parking lot across the street. The Murdocks walked toward him and returned the greeting.

K.D. looked at Trip hastily. "I really gotta go. What do you say about us getting together later? Want to meet somewhere?" Her sentences ran in one linear blurb. She walked quickly toward the side of the building, speeding up with an increased heartbeat.

He half-jogged a few steps to catch up with her. "Sure, I guess.

Let me check on things at home and call you later. But I wanted to ask your conclusion after reading next class's case about the unencumbered employee. Do you think she would violate the non-compete from Massachusetts if she accepts the job in California? I mean, after all, it's different industries although the new employer would benefit from her prior knowledge."

"Let's don't talk school right now. We'll go over it tonight. Call me later."

Ingram's voice stopped their process. "K.D.! Hang on a second!"

Trip pulled up, but she tugged on his arm. He looked down at her with a furrowed brow. "K.D., that man is trying to get your attention."

K.D. stopped. Her heart dropped to the bottom of her feet. When it had nowhere else to go, it quit beating all together as Ingram and the Murdocks caught up with them. A grin split Ingram's face while his teeth clamped down on a cigar. "Who do we have here?" Ingram glanced from K.D. to Trip and must have picked up on the embarrassment intent on burning through her skin. He stuck out a hand to Trip. "You must be K.D.'s young fella. Ezra Ingram, her employer."

"Trip Folsom. Pleasure to meet you." The two shook hands.

Please don't let the name register. K.D. grabbed Trip's arm again, turning him toward his car. "I'll be right back, ya'll. As a matter of fact, why don't ya'll go onto lunch? Call me on my cell and let me know where you end up. The meat-and-three down at Minnie's is supposed to be amazing. I'll see ya'll in a few." She and Trip started walking away, but not before she caught Shelly Anne's eyebrows shoot up and down suggestively.

Trip then stopped up so fast K.D. stumbled over the upper lip of a sidewalk break. She hated to look, but forced her eyes on his. His face was unreadable, but his brow slowly folded. He turned and walked back to Ingram and the Murdocks before K.D. could stop him.

"Did you say your name was Ezra Ingram?"

Ingram rocked back on his heels as if pleased with the recognition. "I did."

"As in Ingram and Associates law firm?"

"One and the same, although the associate part's singular at the moment. Miss Jennings here's the only associate."

K.D. tried for Trip's arm again. He jerked it free, glaring at her. He glanced at the Murdocks as if putting the pieces to a puzzle together. "I don't think I introduced myself to you. Trip Folsom." This time with no smile, he extended his hand, which Buck took. Shelly Anne stared as if sensing more than simple introductions.

"Buck Murdock. This is my wife, Shelly Anne."

Trip's face darkened. He looked around the group again and then narrowed his eyes at K.D., who stood on the shoreline bracing against the Tsunami, every muscle in her body clenched, no air found.

Trip put his hands in his pockets. "I know who you are. You're the couple suing my uncle, Dr. Jackson Thomas. The one whose trial starts in a few days." He turned to K.D. with an expression begging her to deny the accusation.

She fought the tears burning her lids. "Trip, let's talk about this somewhere else." Her words traveled over the gravel in her throat.

He turned to Ingram. "Am I right? K.D. works for you, and your firm is suing my uncle."

Ingram removed the cigar from his lips. "K.D.? This is the guy you've been talking about?"

"You're dating the defendant's nephew?" Shelly Anne's voice broke from betrayal, her blue eyes darkening. Buck took his wife's arm, pulled her into his side. Everyone stared at K.D. who wished the big oak swaying with the fall breeze would lift its roots and plop down on her head.

Ingram intervened. "I think this conversation is over. Young man, we're not going to answer your questions now. We'll answer them in the courtroom." He turned his attention to K.D. "You need to come with us. I believe you have some explaining to do.

The two of you can work out whatever you need to work out at another time."

Trip turned a dark face to K.D., almost unrecognizable as the same one that was filled with laughter a few minutes before. "We don't have anything to work out. I spill my guts to you, tell you every secret I have. What do you do with that trust? Lie to me? Eat at my uncle's table? No, we don't have another word to say to each other outside of the courtroom, but I will leave you with this," he pointed at Shelly Anne and Buck. "You're trying to ruin the second-best man I've ever known in my life. I'll die before I let you do that."

Trip turned and walked away. K.D. wanted to run after him, beg him to understand, but anger and betrayal threw a wall before her, impassable even if she had tried. The other three glared at her as her shoulders sagged in defeat.

Ingram took her elbow. "Come on. Let's all go back to the office. We'll get Maria to bring us down some lunch while you explain how you came to date a member of the opposing side of our lawsuit."

Shelly Anne had already turned toward the office, marching off. K.D. could almost inhale the trail of steam she left behind. Buck followed, eyes steady on the concrete.

CHAPTER

25

"I never lied to anybody." K.D. stood her ground, tired of the accusations, the hard stares. "I never violated attorney/client privilege. I never disclosed anything related to the case. As you could see from Trip's reaction, he had no idea I even worked for Ingram. The only thing I did wrong was pretend I could straddle two limbs with one butt."

Across the room, Shelly Anne continued her attempts to laser through K.D. with her eyes while Buck tapped the wall with his heel. The sound ground into K.D.'s ear. Ingram gnawed on the end of an unlit cigar, deep in thought, until he finally shoved off the corner of the desk. "Shelly Anne, Buck, we're two days outside the trial. We're ready to walk in there and make that doctor pay for not settling this lawsuit before now and wasting all our time. But I need K.D. with me. There's no reason to take her off the case. She's telling the truth, here. I'll stake my reputation on it."

Shelly Anne snorted. "I've seen more truth from television evangelists on Saturday night, flashing numbers on the screens so grannies around the world can pledge half their retirement on preacher man's vacation home. Yes sir, I've seen more truth outta them than I'm seeing here."

K.D. palmed the wall with a slap and started forward, but Ingram reached out to stop her. "Now hang on right there." He moved across the room toward Shelly Anne. Buck joined his wife, hands on her shoulders. "I'll admit K.D. didn't exercise the best judgment when withholding full disclosure, but she's an honest person. If she says she didn't violate attorney/client privilege, then she didn't. And that's that. I'll not have you question her character again. If you think you can walk out of here and get better representation somewhere else, then that's exactly what you need to do. Otherwise, I'm sure you'd like to know what to expect the first few days of the trial, what will be expected of you. Now, we can sit around here squawking about whether or not K.D.'s personal life is our business, or we can order some Chinese food, go back to my office, and get to work. Now, what's it going to be?"

K.D.'s heart swelled for Ingram in that moment. He had every reason to toss her on her ever-shrinking fanny, but he didn't. Instead, he stood up for her, willing to lose everything. She relaxed back against the wall.

Shelly Anne snatched her purse off the couch and shoved it under her arm. "I'll tell you what it's going to be. I'm going home and paying that Bart Cookson a call. I'll bet he's got more professionalism in his pinky finger than I've seen in this entire office." She started for the door, but stopped when she noticed her husband did not follow her. "Buck!" The little man jumped, tucked his chin and walked behind her out the door.

Silence fell in their wake, the scattered ticking of Ingram's broken cuckoo clock the only sound to mar the quiet. Words danced around K.D.'s mind, with none forming into coherent thoughts except for three words. "I'm sorry, Ingram."

He shoved the cigar back between his teeth and inhaled deeply through the nose, his large girth rising and falling. "I know you are."

"Did I lose us the case?"

Ingram remained silent, chewing on the faithful stogie, and sank deep into his thoughts. K.D. knew the look and respected the quiet by keeping her mouth shut for once. Ingram walked over to the tattered couch and gestured for her to take the seat across from him. K.D. obeyed with no sound.

"Did I ever tell you about the time Uncle Pop Pop bagged himself a trophy buck down in Louisiana?"

K.D. twirled through the story rolodex in her mind, ranging from backwoods stock-car racing to his grandmother's stint in jail from blackening the principal's eye with her purse. Ingram mentored K.D. much like Jesus did the disciples, with words and parables, lessons found in the morals of the stories. Uncle Pop Pop didn't ring a bell so she shook her head.

Ingram twirled the cigar in his finger. "Well, you see, Pop Pop was my granddaddy Fish's brother. Both of 'em raised in the Louisiana swamps." Ingram said Louisiana like Loozanna, his dialect falling into the story.

"Does any of your family have real names?"

"You gonna listen to me or not?"

K.D. motioned an apology with her hand, locking her lips with pinched fingers and pantomimed as if she threw away the key.

"Pop Pop was about fourteen at the time and had been scouting this bad boy for days, checking scrapes, looking for where it bed down. A few of its kin had ventured out, pretty deer too, but Pop Pop knew Monster Man was somewhere close. Said he could smell 'em. Sitting in the stand one day, with the sun fat on the water, out he comes. Boldly too, like that fella knew who ruled the woods. Pop Pop raised the gun to his shoulder, but Monster Man took one sniff and took off." Ingram clapped his hands together, causing K.D. to jump.

"So there goes Pop Pop, dragging his pride and gun behind him, back home for G-Daddy Fish to make all kind of fun at him. Their daddy caught him at the pass, asked him what was wrong. Pop Pop said he couldn't understand why the day ended like it did. He'd done everything right, followed all the rules, and he still didn't have the deer."

K.D. sat up in her chair like she always did when Ingram reached the climax of the story.

"His daddy took his wrist and held it up in the moonlight. Pop Pop still didn't understand the point until his daddy told him to smell his arm. 'Son, I've taught both you boys never to wear a leather watch band when hunting. You can cover yourself in mud, stick wet leaves down your britches, spray yourself with any deer urine you can buy, but a leather band'll give your scent away every time. The devil's in the details, son.' Pop Pop said he coulda thrown up right then and there, knowing he was right. His dad said, 'When you stay focused on the end, on the prize, instead of being mindful of the steps to get there, on those small details, you take a chance of messing the whole thing up.'"

"What'd they call Pop Pop's daddy?" K.D. asked, distracted for a moment by the story's characters.

"Larry."

K.D. fought the laughter. Of course his name was Larry. Why wouldn't it be with children called Fish and Pop Pop? She nodded her head, getting back on track. "I see your point. On both sides, all I could think of was myself instead of doing the right thing. I didn't want to lose Trip, so I kept the truth from him. Shelly Anne and I had gotten to be friends, so I didn't want her mad at me. Plus the fact you and I both need the settlement from this case. I didn't watch my steps, and I guess I ended up losing the buck in the process, just like Pop Pop."

"Pop Pop didn't lose Monster Man."

"How so?"

"He started all over. First, by taking off his watch. Second, he scouted him all over again, nose to ground on every snake trail he could find for evidence of that deer. Finally, Monster Man edged out from behind a massive oak about a week into the chase, head high and full of bravado. Pop Pop dropped him in one shot, right in the lungs. My cousin Stump hung him in his office the day of Pop Pop's funeral. Still there today." Ingram rocked back and forth, until his bum knee took his weight, and heaved out of the couch. He squeezed her shoulder as he walked by. "You can make this right, K.D., by starting over, taking the proper steps, and don't get ahead of yourself. We do need this case, but like anything in life, it's not worth it if it's not done right. Remember what G-Daddy Larry said. The devil's in the details."

After Ingram left the room, K.D. stayed seated, rolling through her thoughts. She had to make things right with Shelly Anne, not only as a client, but as a friend. She could feel the woman's hurt from across the room, knowing Shelly Anne had asked repeatedly about K.D.'s new love. Not because she was a busy body, but because she was her friend and genuinely cared. K.D. kept the information from her for all the wrong reasons, and her heart now beat with the need to make it right even if they decided to take the case to Bart Crookson. She sighed, picked her purse off the floor, and walked out the door, hoping amends waited at end of the Murdock's dusty driveway.

K.D. roadblocked thoughts of Trip. She couldn't go there when his angry face blared at the end of her thoughts.

The drive across town took mere minutes, and K.D. slowed to a stop and waited on a flatbed truck heavy with vegetables to pass before turning off the main road toward the Murdocks. A group of sketchy, denim clad young adults congregated on the corner, four guys and a girl who looked at her, a cigarette dangling from her teeth, trying to appear tough. K.D. locked eyes with her as the others remained bent under the hood of a rusted pick up.

Thin and tall as a corn stalk, the girl shifted her weight on one hip, hand resting on a knobby bone protruding over the low-waisted shorts. Her body never moved, but her head followed K.D. as she inched the Chevy onto the dirt road. At closer glance, the girl appeared younger, closer to the age of a teenager than a woman, aged by the copious amount of makeup clinging to her upper lids and a shirt too short for her torso. The girl flicked the cigarette toward K.D. in an Old West kind of way, except the wind blew it back against her bare stomach, causing her to jump in pain. K.D. depressed the accelerator as the guys straightened, laughing at the poor girl's flailing.

K.D. wanted to turn around, take the young girl home where she belonged, and scrub the years off her face. Then again, who was K.D. to say where the girl should be? K.D. didn't even know her own place, with a foot in one life and the other planted on the rotten steps of her trailer. Pretending to be a lawyer. Thinking she could be a girlfriend to someone who rode horses in clothes more expensive than her car, and her with initials for a name.

As K.D. approached Murdock's trailer, the anxiety tightened in her chest. Twice she slowed to an almost stop, wanting to turn around, but she kept on. K.D. might be a lot of things, a coward inching to the top of the list, but she was loyal. Ingram had stood up for her. Shelly Anne had been her friend. Ingram deserved for her to make this right. Shelly Anne deserved an apology. The thought of Trip nudged on her brain, but she slammed that door shut. Ingram had always told her to fix one broken window at a time.

K.D. exited the car, waved away the natural driveway's dust and made her way to the home. Buck opened the screen door and stepped out before she could come any further.

He waved his hands in front of his face, whispering like he tried to scream, but had to be quiet. "Shelly Anne's putting Gabby to sleep. You need to go, K.D. I ain't never seen her so mad. Ain't ever seen anything like it. Not even that time I bought her a weed eater for her birthday. I mean it. She needs time to settle down." Buck grabbed her arm to walk her back to the car.

K.D. shrugged loose. "I gotta explain things, Buck. I can handle mad."

He shook his head. "Not this kinda mad. I ain't ever seen anything like it." He kept repeating the same phrase, as if he were hoping K.D. had a vial of anti-anger serum in her pocket.

"Who drove up, Buck?"

Buck's head whirled around at the sound of Shelly Anne's voice from inside the house. "Nobody. Just somebody turning around. They're gone now." He gestured wildly for K.D. to leave. "Go on now, get."

Shelly Anne poked her head out, saw it was K.D., and slammed the door shut.

K.D. pushed around Buck and walked back to the house. "Shelly Anne! We gotta talk about this sometime!"

Buck evaporated.

"No we don't, K.D. I ain't got nothing to say to you."

K.D. stared at the closed door, feeling ridiculous talking to the vinyl siding. "You don't have to say anything, just listen. You can't be mad at me about dating Trip. At least not from a violation of attorney/client privilege. I didn't do anything wrong in regards to this case."

Shelly Anne snorted. "That's all you care about anyway. The case. Well you can leave now. Buck and I ain't firing Ingram. We're too close to opening statements. We might be country folks, but we ain't stupid. So go on. You'll get your settlement."

K.D. dropped down on the steps, hands hanging limply over her knees. After a few seconds of quiet, Shelly Anne eased open the door only to shut it back once she saw K.D. remained.

"I'm not going anywhere, Shelly Anne. This isn't about the case." K.D. waited on the door to open again, but continued talking when it stayed closed. "I'm sorry. I know I hurt our friendship by not sharing with you about Trip. I have my reasons, but no good excuse. I guess the simplest way to put it is I knew things wouldn't last as soon as I realized Dr. Thomas was Trip's uncle. I wanted to enjoy the sunshine awhile because I knew clouds were moving in. I tried to keep the worlds separated as long as possible because once the collision occurred, I wasn't sure of the collateral damage."

Buck eased through her peripheral vision, grabbing a drink from an outdoor refrigerator before vanishing into the shed. Two squirrels raced around an oak trunk, barking like an old married couple.

The door cracked. "What in the world are you jabbering about? Sunshine and clouds? World collision? Why can't you just say you're sorry without all those fancy words?"

K.D. turned. "I started the whole conversation with an apology. I *am* sorry, Shelly Anne. I should have told you."

Shelly Anne opened the door, leaning against the frame. She looked off into the distance, collecting her thoughts as the sky gathered clouds. She sighed a few times, clinging to an anger intent on easing off her face. "No, you shouldn't have."

K.D. stood, confused. "Huh?"

Shelly Anne shrugged her shoulders. "I would have done the exact same thing in your shoes. Because as soon as you had told me, I would have jumped on my soapbox and demanded you break up. I would have put my needs above yours. Probably why I got so mad because you held a mirror up to my own selfishness."

K.D. shifted her weight, shaking her head. "There's not a selfish bone in your body. I'm the one who did wrong, not you. I reached for a life I didn't deserve, pretended to belong somewhere I didn't. It's time to concentrate on what I do know and that's this case. Your boy didn't have to die. I want to prove it in a court of law."

"Why do you do that to yourself?"

"What?"

"Ever since I met you, K.D., it's like you're stumbling around some restaurant, looking for your blind date."

"What's that supposed to mean?" Shelly Anne was worse than Ingram with metaphors.

Shelly Anne gripped K.D.'s shoulders and turned her face-to-face. "It means you sit there waiting on a life you wouldn't even recognize if it passed you on the street. You say you don't belong here or there, as if you're having some sort of identity crisis. You need to take charge, K.D. Figure out who you are instead of waiting on it to introduce itself to you. Live your life on purpose instead of by accident."

K.D. toed the next step, chewing a cuticle before continuing the conversation. "Does your bossy tone mean we're friends again?" K.D. changed directions, not enjoying the path of conversation, feeling like she'd been doused by a bucket of truth with no towel to dry off.

Gabby sounded off down the hall, screaming for a Mr. Monkey. Shelly Anne rolled her eyes. "The darn thing's a turtle, but Gabby insists it's a monkey. God bless her kindergarten teacher who tries to tell the Gabster a turtle doesn't eat bananas." Shelly Anne opened the door wide and gestured for K.D. to enter. "Come on, friend. You can take her the monkey/turtle and be the hero for once."

K.D. snorted as she walked into the house. "Hero. Hah. That'd be a first."

Shelly Anne patted her on the back. "You gotta start somewhere."

CHAPTER

26

"Would you look at that, Maria." K.D. and Maria stood at the restaurant window, peering around the curtains at the media congregating outside the courthouse. "You'd think this was some murder case or something instead of wrongful death."

Maria shook her head and stepped away. "I feel bad for you, K.D. How are you and Mister Ingram going to get to the courthouse through all that? Looks like Dia de los muertos where I come from."

"What's that?"

"It's a time of celebration and honor of our loved ones who have died. We make ofrendas, or altars, in the home, decorate their graves and celebrate their lives. The bigger cities have crowds like that." She gestured outside.

"Celebrating the dead. More like feasting on his bones. I hate this." K.D. walked to a table where her briefcase lay open. She sat, fiddled with papers she knew by heart, glanced at depositions she could recite. Maria left the room, returning with two drinks she placed on the table, and took the seat across from K.D.

"You heard from your novio?"

K.D. never looked up, but her heart sank at the thought of Trip's silence. "Nope. And he's not my boyfriend."

"He was."

"For about as long as it takes roaches to scatter when the lights come on." K.D. stacked her papers against the tabletop, replaced them in the briefcase and sipped her soda, bolting her emotions down. "Look, Trip's gotta stick with his family. I don't fault him for that. I wronged him, Maria. I'm getting what I deserve." He only did what K.D. knew he'd do all along. He bailed. Not that she hadn't given him a reason to.

Maria's brow furrowed, and she shook a finger at K.D. "You act like this boy's Jesus or something. Nobody's that perfect, K.D. Deserve. What does that even mean? None of us deserve any good in this world, but we keep working hard, doing what we think is right, apologizing when we do wrong. If you ask me, I don't think this guy deserves *you*."

K.D. smiled when Maria flew into her Spanish monologue of scolding. The native tongue dominated her speech whenever passion laced her words. After a minute or two of K.D. listening to words she couldn't understand, she held up a hand. "Regardless, Maria, of who deserves whom, I lied to Trip. I took advantage of his family's hospitality. I've left him a dozen messages to say I was sorry with no response. He'll have to forgive me on his own time if he ever does." K.D. glanced at her watch, butterflies birthing in her stomach, as much from the thought of Trip as anything. "Meanwhile, I need to get Ingram because we're due in court for opening statements in twenty minutes. Hard to believe we were able to pick a jury so fast last week. Everything about this case seems to be in fast forward. Sure hope that works to our advantage."

On cue, the back door to the restaurant opened, and Ingram walked through, the epitome of a Southern lawyer in a blue seersucker suit and red bowtie with slicked-back hair, straight out of a John Grisham novel. He adjusted the belt around his girth and straightened his shoulders. "Let's go do this thing."

K.D. stood. "Where's Buck and Shelly Anne?"

Ingram waved at Maria as she told them good luck. He held open the door to the restaurant and followed her out of the building. "They're coming in the back way. Shelly Anne didn't want to fool with the crowds. Said enough folks know her business here without broadcasting it clear to Mobile."

The two walked with purpose down the sidewalk. With each step, K.D. cloaked herself in someone else, like a little girl playing dress up. Even if she didn't feel like a lawyer, even if the ground swayed a little with each step and her lips would not stop their nervous twitch, she had to fake it. For herself, her mom. And for the loss of Trip. She still leaned over and whispered to Ingram, "Why can't *we* go around back?"

He quieted her with a hand wave, and she fell behind him as he snaked through the reporters. One recognized him and called his name. "Mr. Ingram, how confident are you going into trial? How do you feel about going up against a bigger firm and clients like a hospital with such deep pockets?"

Ingram stopped on the top step so abruptly that K.D. ran up against his back. She stepped to the side, watching him control a rising temper before speaking. "The only thing small about Clear Point, Alabama, is the minds of those who look down on us because we wave at friends we pass on the street or send over supper when someone dies or has a baby. When you have the truth on your side, it doesn't matter if your law degree is from Harvard or the FAB College up the road or even the size of your bank account. Those big-shot malpractice attorneys wasted everyone's time by not settling this case. The general public will now see the citizens of Clear Point will not stand by and let one of our own be taken advantage of by anyone. Good day."

Ingram whirled and stomped off, but a grin tugged at his mouth. K.D. couldn't help smiling either, proud of the man she'd grown to love as a father. If this was a preview to the show yet to come, she couldn't wait to see Ingram in action. The reporters continued to shout questions, which Ingram ignored as he and

K.D. walked into the courthouse.

Ingram greeted all those he passed, from security to local citizens to fellow attorneys. The lack of Internet capability at the office made him almost a daily presence to the staff. He was a king in the castle, holding court and feeling like a winner already. K.D. couldn't help but pull the enthusiasm into her spirit.

Buck and Shelly Anne waited down the hall. Shelly Anne approached them, leaving her husband to hold up the wall. "Did you see all those people? What in the world could they want with our business? Why is this a big deal to anybody but us?" The frayed tissue twisted in her hands, bits falling to the floor. She looked on the verge of tears, fancy in her pretty Easter dress with her hair in lengthy waves.

Ingram held up a hand. "Calm down. I told you to expect this. This case is as salacious as any with all the markings of a Lifetime movie. Football hero. Worshipped by the community. A coach second only to God, and a doctor who's not only a philanderer, but a Yankee!"

Ingram said the last word as if a birthplace north of the Mason-Dixon anted up the pedophile, rapist or adulterer probability.

Buck joined them and put his arms around Shelly Anne while Ingram continued. "Honestly, I don't even think we'll get through presenting our case. I'll think they'll settle within a few weeks. The good news is, when dealing with a small court's anemic docket, we don't have to schedule around other trials. The judge scheduled this trial alone and put all the other piddly cases on the backburner. It'll be over before you know it." Ingram glanced at his watch. "Come on, now. Let's go take our seats."

The four moved into the crowded courtroom, filled with mostly local folks and a few members of the media, but there were no cameras at the judge's insistence. "We'll not turn my courtroom into a circus," he had said upon conclusion of his own well-publicized press conference.

K.D. felt as if her cheek pressed against a wall, preventing her from turning to look across the room because she knew Trip was there. She felt his presence the moment she walked in. It was bad enough he had already requested another seat in class, right beside Delilah, three rows and ten eternities away from her, but now she'd have to see him every day of the trial. That is, if she ever gathered the courage to look over.

Buck and Shelly Anne moved through the swinging gate on the rail which partitioned the room. Shelly Anne turned back when K.D. didn't follow. "Why aren't you sitting with us?"

K.D. sat in the front row. "I'm not allowed until I pass the bar. Only attorneys, their clients, and called witnesses are allowed, for security and all. The judge gave special permission to let Buck sit with you since you're the actual one suing on behalf of Bo's estate. Don't worry, I'm right here."

A loud clatter sounded from across the room, gathering everyone's attention as a woman stooped to collect the contents of a spilled bag. K.D. locked eyes with Trip before he glanced up to study the ceiling tile. Her heart flew to the pressure point below her ear then dropped to the pit of her stomach just as quickly. Heat climbed her neck, but she couldn't look away. He wore the same suit he had on outside the courthouse, the day that full disclosure took center stage and he realized her betrayal. Trip's face bore the same look of anger, but today his hair was mussed, his tie askew. The word *unkempt* came to mind. He was the same Trip, but there was a different air about him. Frances sat beside him, stoic in her pearls and yellow business suit, hair perfectly coiffed. She never glanced in K.D.'s direction. Dr. Thomas sat with his attorneys in whispered conversation. K.D. dropped her attention to an errant cuticle and didn't look up again until the bailiff announced the judge. The crowd rose on command.

The judge took his seat, adjusting his glasses and the microphone. "We're here today on the matter of Murdock versus Memorial Hospital and Dr. Jackson Thomas. Is the Plaintiff ready to proceed?"

Ingram stood. "We are, Your Honor."

The judge turned to opposing counsel. "Is the Defense ready to proceed?"

A lawyer beside Dr. Thomas half stood. "Yes, your Honor."

The judge cleared his throat. "I'm not aware of any housekeeping matters or last-minute motions." He looked above his bifocals at both sides, waiting half a beat for a correction to his statement. Receiving none, he continued. "Let's proceed. Bailiff, please bring in the jury."

Thirteen citizens of Clear Point filed into their seats, twelve jurors and one alternate who would remain anonymous until the end of the trial. Ingram had been satisfied with the selection, a good mix of working-class folks with a few college graduates thrown in for balance. Ingram had argued, but lost out on Steven Mellon, the all-state quarterback who now sold cars in Clear Point after blowing out his knee in the NFL; but, overall, Ingram felt good about the final jury.

The judge adjusted some papers and offered instructions to the jury, then turned his attention to Ingram. "The plaintiff may now proceed with opening statements."

K.D. drew in her breath as Ingram stood, trying not to consider everything riding on the trial from both of their perspectives. Bart Cookson held title to Ingram's beloved Cadillac, waiting on Ingram to default. The firm was pushed against bankruptcy with Ingram nearing retirement. Dwindling finances held her future hostage along with the ability to continue purchasing her mother's medication; the same medication which lifted her mom from a self-imposed tomb and into a functioning world. K.D.'s stomach knotted up, the butterflies raging at the confinement.

She thought back to the night on the side of the road, words whispering through her memory. Don't borrow tomorrow's troubles or something like that. She released her breath as Ingram approached the jury box.

"Good morning, y'all. I appreciate you taking the time to be here. I know that to a lot of y'all, if not all of y'all, time is precious. I'm pretty confident once you hear the strength of our case, we'll wrap this thing up pretty quickly and get on back to work and providing for our families."

K.D. fought a snicker over his exaggerated Southern drawl. It wasn't fake or anything, just heavier than she'd ever heard it. Come to think of it, she'd never heard him say *y'all*. Ever.

Ingram continued. "Let me talk to y'all a minute about why we think you should rule against the hospital and Dr. Thomas over there. I'll give you the details when we present our side, but right now I'll offer the *Reader's Digest* version of why an otherwise healthy sixteen year old died when he didn't have to."

Ingram paused for dramatic effect. He walked over in front of the plaintiff's table and gestured toward the Murdocks. "This is Buck and Shelly Anne Murdock. Folks like you and me. They get up every morning, go to work. Buck over at Harold's Tire and Auto, Shelly Anne at the Waffle Iron. Took care of their two kids, their oldest Bo and their baby Gabrielle. Two years ago, they did the same thing. Only that afternoon, they got a phone call from Coach Camp saying he had Bo in the ambulance on the way to the hospital."

Ingram returned to the jury box, leaning on the rail in front of a woman about Shelly Anne's age. "Let me tell you about Bo. Good looking kid. Straight As. Disciple leader in his youth group. Heckofa football player. Coach Camp said he would have gotten a full ride to college, and if he stayed healthy, would have gone pro first round, probably taking a Heisman trophy with him. Bo would have been the first one in his family to go to college, to be eligible to work for something more than minimum wage. Brightest future you can imagine.

"The nursing report will show his temperature had elevated to 107 degrees when he entered the hospital. One hundred and seven degrees, folks. We've got a medical expert who will describe what happens to the brain when the blood reaches that temperature. But I ask each of you with more than your share of common sense, what's the first thing you think of when you hear 107 degrees?"

One of the jurors mouthed, "heat stroke." Ingram acted as if he answered audibly. "That's right. Heat stroke. But what did the doctor do? He ordered a CAT scan for a concussion. He never ordered ice packs for his body. He didn't check another gauging of Bo's temperature. He signed off on the CAT scan and moved onto the next patient. By this time, Buck and Shelly Anne had reached the hospital. Shelly Anne's sitting beside her son, holding his fevered hand, when all of a sudden the alarms start going off, and they're rushed into the waiting room. Bo died, folks. Right there with his mama and daddy on the other side of the wall. Gone, just like that. Burned up by his own blood waiting on the results of a CAT scan." Ingram snapped his fingers. Sniffles sounded from the jury box while Shelly Anne openly cried into a fresh tissue. Buck cleared his throat, widening his eyes toward the ceiling. Ingram let the reactions continue for a few more seconds.

Ingram's stance relaxed a bit, and he held up his hands. "I'm sorry to have upset y'all. I'm upset myself. This is as tough a case to present emotionally as it is for you to hear. We have the evidence to show that young man did not have to die. He should have been iced down to lower his body temperature, gone home to rest on the couch while his mama fixed him some supper. He should have suited up for the state playoffs the next month.

"The evidence will show the hospital staff did not take his temperature properly, the hospital employed faulty equipment which caused a delay in the useless CAT scan, and a doctor who spent the majority of his career in upstate New York had never in forty-something years treated anyone for a heat stroke. Once we do, you'll have no choice but to find the defendants liable and make the proper statement with the damages awarded."

Ingram paused again, lowering his tone of voice, tempering the passion a bit. "You have the power to make sure something as simple as a heat stroke doesn't ever turn into another kid's death again." Ingram pointed a finger toward the jury and then smiled. "Listen, thank y'all again for your time. The Murdocks appreciate it more than you know. We'll all do the right thing here. I'm confident in you." Ingram nodded at the judge to communicate the conclusion and returned to his seat beside Shelly Anne.

The attorney for the defense rose and offered his opening statement. K.D. recognized him from a county over. They'd gone up against him a few years back on a much smaller matter, so small K.D. couldn't remember the case. When she'd recognized his name in the court filings, Ingram had said the hospital's firm was from out of town so it was common practice to hire a local attorney for "relate-ability."

Ingram had laughed when he saw the name. "Curt'll do as good a job as any. They'll probably use him for opening and closing statements, places in the trial which call for a lot of dialogue."

Curt offered the expected information about Bo's unfortunate death, emphasizing that the entire community continued to grieve with the Murdocks. But, he claimed, the hospital and Dr. Thomas acted appropriately and expeditiously given the circumstances, and the evidence would prove so. He described Dr. Thomas as a family man himself. Although unable to have children, he and his wife had a lifelong commitment to youth ministries, sponsoring several third-world charities, and were devastated at the loss of Bo.

Curt droned on a little too long in K.D.'s opinion, but it was hard not to walk away with a little respect for the doctor after Curt described his career and ultimate decision to retire in Alabama because of all the "good folks like you," referring to the jury. Opening statements wrapped up, and the judge dismissed the courtroom until after lunch.

Against her will, K.D. turned to glance at Trip. He stood, wobbled, and then straightened when Frances took his arm. He shrugged her off, stumbled against a chair, and halfway smiled at his aunt. It was a look unlike any she'd seen on his face. The word sardonic came to mind, as if his smile hid darkness. K.D. worried he was sick, and then a realization entered her thoughts. *He's drunk.* Guilt hammered K.D., knowing her betrayal would have triggered a relapse. *Oh no! Please don't let him be drunk.*

The family left the courtroom, but not before Dr. Thomas turned in her direction. K.D. straightened, preparing herself for a look of hatred, but instead received a small, genuine smile and nod. She tried to smile back, but couldn't find one to fit her face, wishing Trip's uncle had ignored her instead of compounding her heavy stomach with kindness.

She stepped aside as Ingram held open the swinging gate for the Murdocks to step through. As the group filed out of the courthouse, K.D. searched for Trip, aching to know if he was okay, but finding him nowhere. Maybe he wasn't drunk. Maybe he took some medication or something or was tired from school. But in her heart, K.D. knew what she saw. Not that her dad was a heavy drinker or anything, but she remembered him lumbering from the recliner after a few beers, exactly as Trip had a few minutes ago.

Her heart heavy, she followed Ingram and the Murdocks into Maria's restaurant for lunch and strategy. Their hired medical expert would take the stand that afternoon, provided he showed. K.D. had offered to put him up in a local B&B the previous night, but he'd refused and opted instead for the Marriott in Mobile, adding it to their bill. He was to drive up before noon, but K.D. had yet to hear from him. She punched in the numbers again, immediately receiving his voicemail. Don't borrow troubles, she chanted in her mind, and pasted a smile across her face before joining the others.

CHAPTER

27

Trip was nowhere to be seen after lunch; the chair remained empty beside his aunt. K.D. widened her eyes to stave off tears, not even relieved when Dr. Jack Fellow entered the courtroom just as Ingram stood to ask for a recess due to his absence. The numb feeling she had toward the trial began to grow, knowing how lives would be affected regardless of the verdict. How they had already been affected. K.D. could relate to Shelly Anne's earlier struggles about proceeding to trial. She felt a growing separation from her heart right then, distant from her conscience, focused only on facts and evidence. Was that the result of being a lawyer? The one thing she wanted so badly? Was she entering a career that was nothing more than a robotic pursuit of the truth with no consideration of relationships? K.D. sighed as Dr. Fellow took the stand as the first witness.

Upon Ingram's opening question, the doctor described the difference between ancillary and rectal temperature gauging, and why one was recommended by the American Medical Association over the other. Ingram entered into evidence the nursing report, showing the staff had performed an ancillary gauging rather than the preferred rectal reading.

"Dr. Fellow, what is the difference between rectal and ancillary? Why is it preferred?"

The doctor answered in a matter-of-fact manner. "Ancillary is an under-the-arm reading, but rectal is less influenced by external factors such as room temperature or recent liquid consumption." A few jurors adjusted in their seats at the description. K.D. did as well. He went on to explain the medical association's endorsement.

Ingram turned to the jury. "Folks, I need Dr. Fellow to describe what happens to the body during a heat stroke. I apologize. I know it's going to be tough to hear."

An attorney for the defense stood and said, "Objection! No question is being asked of the witness, Your Honor. Mr. Ingram is addressing the jury instead of the witness."

"Sustained. Mr. Ingram, please refer all statements to the witness."

"My apologies, Your Honor. Dr. Fellow, will you please describe to the jury what happens to a body as the temperature rises to 107 degrees?"

"Certainly. Enzymes begin to break down in the brain, causing the body to lose functions. Symptoms include loss of control over bowels and kidneys."

Ingram took a report off the plaintiff's table. "If it pleases the court, I'd like to admit the nursing report into evidence." The court accepted, and Ingram handed the paper to Dr. Fellow. "Would you please read to the court the nurse's notes on Bo's symptoms?"

Dr. Fellow put on his bifocals and scanned the paper he'd already reviewed several times. "The report here indicates Bo had begun to bleed through his nose and other orifices, defecating uncontrollably while throwing up. The doctor was called back to the stall, but by then it was too late."

Shelly Anne moaned from the plaintiff table. The judge asked, not unkindly, if she'd like to be excused. She shook her head as K.D. reached over the rail and squeezed her shoulder.

Ingram asked his final question. "Dr. Fellow, in your expert opinion, did the hospital and Dr. Thomas breach the standard of care of Bo Murdock on the day in question?"

Dr. Fellow shook his head. "According to the nursing reports and medical records, Bo Murdock should have immediately been diagnosed with a heat stroke. His temperature should have been addressed the moment he arrived. If it had, he would have lived. It is my expert opinion that the hospital and Dr. Thomas breached the standard of care in the case."

Ingram nodded. "Thank you. That's all I have, Your Honor."

Ingram sat down, turning the witness over to the defense. As expected, the Illinois attorney in his custom suit attacked Dr. Fellow's credentials, noting the fact that he made a living as a professional witness for medical malpractice cases. Upon questioning, Dr. Fellow calmly explained his hourly rate. "The fact I charge for my credible testimony doesn't make what I say any less true."

The attorney whirled to the judge. "Move to strike from the record."

The judge obliged and ordered the stenographer to erase the comment. He turned to Dr. Fellow. "The witness will only answer the questions posed."

Dr. Fellow nodded, and the attorney continued to pound him, hoping to cause a stumble. He failed. He excused the witness, and Ingram continued by calling the nurse Melanie McKnight to the stand, the one K.D. had encountered during her scouting mission in the ER. When their eyes met, Melanie widened hers in recognition. K.D. fought to maintain a neutral expression over the guilt.

The testimony felt stagnant, but necessary. Melanie described the hospital that day, testified to her reports, but couldn't recall Bo's temperature by memory so she had to rely on her notes. Ingram handed her the photo copy, and she agreed it was her handwriting. The defense had little questioning, and she was dismissed.

Ingram called his final witness for the day, Janice Parker, the nurse whose phone records indicated a relationship with the doctor outside of work. Ingram and K.D. had debated whether or not to save her for the next morning when the jury was fresh, but he felt it would be more powerful to close with her, giving them the entire night to consider whether Dr. Thomas was having an affair with one of his nurses.

Janice was a small-boned, not unattractive woman, eleven years younger than the doctor's wife according to the records. Ingram asked her to tell the jury her nursing credentials and work experience. She'd been with the hospital for twenty years, and had come on board right out of high school while attending college. Janice had worked her way up to shift supervisor.

Ingram leaned on the rail in front of the witness. "On the day in question, you were the nursing supervisor, correct?"

Janice fidgeted in her seat, tugging on a strand of shoulder-length brown hair. "Yes."

"Nurse McKnight testified earlier that you finished up her report. What does that exactly mean, 'finished up?'"

"Sometimes a nurse may have to leave before making sure her reports are in order. It falls on me to make sure they're properly documented. I believe Melanie had a sick child that day or something so she had to leave a little early. I looked over her report for her, but if I remember right, all was in order."

Ingram handed a photocopy of the report already admitted into evidence to Janice. "Is this your handwriting?"

Janice put on her bifocals with shaky hands and scanned the paper. "The only part I wrote on the report was the date. Melanie had forgotten to date the report. Other than that, it's all Melanie's handwriting."

"So Ms. McKnight noted a temperature of 107 degrees within five minutes of Bo's arrival, a fact your signature testifies to as the nursing supervisor, correct?"

"Yes, that's correct."

K.D. knew Ingram's strategy and prepared herself for the next line of questioning. He lulled the nurse with standard questions in an effort to send her brain down one track. K.D. knew he was about to land a one-two punch by entering Dr. Thomas's phone records into evidence, and her gut soured at the thought of Frances's reaction, so very glad for Trip's absence.

Ingram turned toward the jury, wiping his hand across his jaw as if stroking an imaginary beard before speaking. "Miss Parker, are you or have you ever had an inappropriate relationship with Dr. Jackson Thomas?"

"OBJECTION!"

K.D. thought the doctor's attorney would burst a window with his bellow, the sheer force of it causing the entire room to jump.

The judge held up a hand. "Will both attorneys approach the bench?"

K.D. couldn't hear a word, but opposing counsel mimed his fury while Ingram remained collected. After a heated discussion, Dr. Thomas's attorney returned to his seat, red faced and enraged. Frances's mouth hung open while Dr. Thomas appeared defeated.

The judge addressed Ingram. "I'm going to allow this line of questioning, but you'd better offer evidence to back it up. If not, I will hold you in contempt. Proceed."

Ingram stared at Janice, causing her to squirm. "I'll repeat the question. Did you ever have an inappropriate relationship with Dr. Thomas?"

She looked down at her lap. "What do you mean by inappropriate?"

"Did you have contact with the doctor outside the boundaries of a manager/employee relationship? Don't you in fact rent your apartment from Dr. Thomas?"

"I do. Why is that inappropriate? I needed a place to live, and Jackson was kind enough to let me rent one of his properties."

"Jackson? So you're on a first name basis with the doctor?"

"Objection! Relevance, Your Honor."

"Overruled. I'd like her to answer the question."

Ingram turned to Janice. "Miss Parker, are you on a first name basis with Dr. Thomas?"

She nodded without looking up. "I guess so. I mean, I've rented from him for several years so we know each other outside of the hospital. Jackson has always been a good friend, especially through my last divorce."

Ingram nodded, coaxing the witness with a sympathetic expression. "It's nice to have friends, but Miss Parker, I'm a little confused by something. According to Dr. Thomas's tax records, he shows a loss of income on the property you're renting from him." Ingram asked the court to enter the taxes into record. "So, according to his filings, either you've paid Dr. Thomas cash to which he didn't file as income, or you never paid your rent. Which leads me back to my original question, would you not consider the fact that you are staying, free of rent, at a property of your employer, an inappropriate relationship?"

"No sir, I wouldn't. I would consider it as kindness on the part of Jackson. He's a good man trying to help out a friend."

Ingram snorted. "I'll say. I rent from my ex-wife and trust me, as soon as the clock ticks past midnight for the second of the month, she starts howling for her money." A few members of the jury snickered.

Opposing counsel stood again. "Your Honor, I fail to see the relevance to this case as to whether or not Dr. Thomas charges Miss Parker rent. Mr. Ingram is wasting the court's time."

Ingram held up a hand. He walked back to the table and retrieved a stack of papers. K.D. held her breath, hating what was about to happen.

"Your honor, I'd like to enter into evidence the doctor's cell phone records." The judge noted the evidence and nodded at Ingram. "Let's land this plane, Mr. Ingram."

Ingram held up the paper to Miss Parker. "Please inform the jury if this is your cell phone number."

She perused the bill and nodded to Ingram. "It is."

"Miss Parker, please inform the jury how many times in the last two years you have called Dr. Thomas."

Janice squirmed. "I don't know. A lot I suppose."

"A lot? An average of ten times a day seems like more than a lot."

"If you say so."

Ingram chuckled. "I don't say so, Miss Parker. The cell phone records say so. Between your calls to Dr. Thomas and his to you, your number appears on average ten times a day for the past two years. Now, for the last time, I'd like you to answer whether or not you have had or are having an inappropriate relationship with Dr. Thomas."

"Objection again, Your Honor. Mr. Ingram has failed yet again to prove the relevance of Miss Parker and Dr. Thomas's relationship to the day in question."

Ingram retrieved the cell phone records from Nurse Parker. "On the contrary, your Honor. It's more than arguable if Nurse Parker and Dr. Thomas were having an inappropriate relationship, dare I say affair, it merely compounds the environment for error and further demonstrates the unprofessional medical staff these poor people entrusted their son to on the day in question."

The judge pondered for a moment before turning to the witness. "Miss Parker, answer the question."

The nurse raised her eyes to look directly into Ingram's. "I would not call what we had inappropriate because we were in love. I loved him then. I love him now. Nothing about our love is inappropriate." For the first time in the entire testimony, her voice held steady with authority.

The courtroom fell silent as Ingram allowed the last statement to hang in the air before announcing, "No more questions for the witness." He turned to the plaintiff table with a smile.

The judge banged the gavel even though no one spoke a word. "The witness may step down."

Dr. Thomas's attorney stood. "But Your Honor, I haven't had a chance to question the witness."

As Ingram had hoped, the judge dismissed court for the day.

"Cross examination will begin at eight o'clock tomorrow morning. The witness is instructed to return to court then. We're dismissed."

Ingram looked over at K.D. with a victorious smile, but she felt no joy from the strategy. She could not, would not, look over at Dr. Thomas or his wife. Even if he had cheated on Frances, K.D. felt sick to have to expose their personal business in court and at some point to the general public once the records were released. Ingram spoke with the Murdocks while K.D. collected her things and stood. She didn't turn toward the Thomases, scared the doctor's earlier look of kindness would be replaced with anger, or even worse, devastation.

As they filed out of the room, she sensed the other side had not adjourned. Turning her head, she noticed that the attorneys remained huddled with the couple, and in the corner, slouched with both elbows on knees, Trip stared at her through red-rimmed eyes.

CHAPTER 28

K.D. pulled to a stop in front of her trailer and turned off the ignition. She exhaled her breath deeply, pushing her head back against the seat. Her body felt as though it weighed two thousand pounds and refused to move. Instead, she watched clouds shaped like outstretched greyhounds wander across the full, blood-red moon.

"I see an elephant trunk holding a sword, Daddy." K.D. used to sit with her father down by the creek, watching the clouds through a filter of pines, fiddling with her necklace. They'd escape to the water, always to the water, when her mother's darkness choked any joy from the trailer. They'd find shapes in the clouds, faces in the rocks. Always looking up or around, but never at the home behind them.

K.D. wondered if her daddy ever glanced back that last day or thought about her sitting in elementary school, pondering a times table, while he drove away never to return. She sighed again, breath traveling over a dry throat with no more tears.

The screen door slamming next door at Doris's trailer caught K.D.'s attention. Doomsday Doris carried a box to the opened trunk of her Impala where more boxes had been placed. She stumbled over an oak root, causing the canned goods contents of the box to roll everywhere. K.D. jumped out to help her.

"Here, Doris, hang on. I got it." K.D. righted the box and collected the cans, chasing one as it rolled toward the trailer. Doris straightened with a wince as she laid a hand on her lower back.

K.D. took the can from her, picked up the box and placed it in the trunk filled with water bottles, canned food, and paper products. "Doris, what are you doing? You know you shouldn't be wandering around the yard this time of night. You shouldn't be carrying these boxes by yourself."

Doris looked off into nothing and then shuffled over to a rusted swing she had purchased at a yard sale eons ago for the grandchildren who never visited. She sat, juxtaposing the image of her old lady nightgown with the child pose she assumed on the swing. The chains squeaked as her small bones swayed a bit. K.D. walked over and sat in the swing beside her, sticking out a foot when the entire set wobbled.

"What's going on, Doris? I thought you were saving all your food, ready for the end of the world or something."

Doris sat defeated, shoulders hunched, head down. A souped-up Chevy droned by as the driver tossed out a beer can before gunning down the street. Doris sighed and lifted her head. "The end of the world passed by a couple of days ago. I watched a program tonight with that fella trying to tell me there was a miscalculation, that the world is gonna end next year. Course he said that three years ago too. And the year after, and the year after."

K.D. hurt for her neighbor, often the only coherent adult in the confusing years following her father's abandonment. Doomsday Doris would be the one thing standing between her and foster care, reassuring K.D. she'd assume guardianship if those "fools ever show up on our doorstep again, threatening to take you away from your mama. The very idea." Doris lived her life waiting on it to end, preparing for the day she'd walk out of the trailer and meet Armageddon face-to-face armed with canned ravioli and bottled water. Defeat cloaked her now with the acknowledgement that she had no control over one minute to the next, much less over mankind's extinction.

K.D. reached out and patted her gnarled up hand, crippled with arthritis. Her veins felt like the gummy worms her daddy would bring her after work. "I would say I'm sorry, Doris, but I guess I'm kind of glad to still be kicking. I know how hard you've worked to prepare yourself. It's disappointing to feel like you've wasted a lot of time on something that will never come to be." Trip entered K.D.'s thoughts, pressing down her shoulders more. She didn't feel that their time together was a waste, but she knew now it would never come to anything more than a bittersweet memory.

K.D. started to swing, but the set once again bucked so she stilled herself. "What are you going to do with all that food?"

Doris glanced over at the car. "I called the Food Pantry today. Figured there were folks hungrier than me somewhere. I'll never eat all that, and you don't stay home long enough to eat a bean. Your mama don't like canned food now that she's feeling better. So I figured I take it on down to the church, let them use it in the Food Pantry."

"Well, you see then? You didn't waste your time. Some mama gets to feed her babies thanks to you. If you hadn't been storing all this up, that mama would be starving tomorrow. Nothing's ever all bad, Doris."

K.D.'s words filtered through her own ears, lifting her heart. As much as she missed Trip, hating the hurt she caused him, some good came out of it. Worthiness had introduced itself to K.D. again, shook her hand and gave her confidence through the pages of Trip's Bible. Prayers became conversations, grudges morphed into forgiveness. Sweet memories of her daddy had been sneaking up on her, no longer painful. No, the time with Trip wasn't wasted, just too short.

"...with a different color pen." K.D. caught the last of Doris's words, lost in her own thoughts.

"I'm sorry, what did you say?"

Doris squeaked in her swing, her cotton gown hanging around her knees, bird-legs full of veins running into cowboy boots. K.D. hid a smile at the quirky neighbor.

"I said I got mixed up in my colored pens. Each week, I'd mark the cans with a different colored sharpie so's I'd know when I bought 'em, but when I was taking them out, I noticed I musta gotten the pens mixed up, cause this week's red and one can was marked black which was last week. Maybe I ain't cut out for the end of the world after all if I can't even keep my colors straight." She smiled at K.D., despite the fact that she'd left her bottom teeth inside.

K.D. smiled back, but a thought gnawed through her mind. Different color. Why did that bother her so much? Different color pen. She thought about the pens she used in law school, how she would depress different colors to vary the writing. K.D. had specific colors for different classes to keep her notes straight. No, that's not relevant. The line of thinking didn't quiet the thumping in her brain.

Wait one second.

K.D. shot up from the swing, causing the set to sway. She reached out to steady it and helped Doris to her feet. "I gotta run back to the office a second." K.D. glanced back at the trailer where a single light shone from the kitchen. "Have you heard from Mom tonight? She okay? I really need to go run an errand."

Doris waved her hand. "You go on. Lydia helped me fill up the car earlier, but took a break to get supper going for us. I'll let her know you'll be back later." Doris patted K.D.'s arm. "You're a good girl, K.D., for putting up with this ol' fool. I'm proud of you, honey."

K.D. smiled. "Takes a fool to know a fool. I'll be back directly." K.D. bolted toward her car, pumping the accelerator to encourage cooperation when she turned the ignition. After two cranks, the engine turned, and K.D. took off for town.

A different color pen.

Of course!

K.D. flew through the office, not surprised to find Ingram at his desk, tie shifted and bifocals on his forehead. He jerked up when she rounded the corner and threw a hand across his chest. "Good gracious, gal, you 'bout gave me a heart attack! I've already had one of those in my life. Not looking to add to it. What are you doing here?"

"I have a hunch about something, but I don't want to tell you what it is until I know for sure. Where are the nurse's reports from the day Bo died?"

Ingram waved a hand toward the love seat. "One of those boxes. Maria filed all copies of entered evidence over there. Why?"

K.D. held up a finger. "Not yet. Let me check something first." She plowed through the box, searching for Melanie's report on Bo. She found it with a smile, which disappeared as she read the diagnostics. "Shoot."

"What?"

She looked up into Ingram's tired face. The round plastic clock above his head read a time far too late for either one of them to be working.

"I was hoping the report would confirm my suspicion, but I'm not seeing what I thought I'd see."

Ingram frowned at her. "K.D. you are a one-legged duck swimming in circles right now. What in the world are you talking about?"

"I wanted to check the color pens the nurses used. I remember going through discovery and learning that the hospital required the nurses to use different color pens, but this report is all one color, black, the color assigned to Melanie."

Ingram leaned back in his chair, hands clasped behind his head. "You still trying to prove your boyfriend's uncle isn't liable?" His tone shifted to suspicion hovering over anger.

K.D. bristled. "I'm trying to find the truth, Ingram. I'm not going to stand by and let anyone be found liable of something unless I'm absolutely convinced myself. Now granted, all the evidence points that way. The Murdocks have every right to sue the doctor and the hospital. I believe that, but I owe it to myself, to my love of the law, to turn over every rock for the sake of justice, which is what I always want to uphold." She ran out of breath, her sentences fast and passionate. In all her struggles with right and wrong the past few weeks, K.D. realized her need to bring integrity to the law profession.

Ingram stroked his chin, palmed his eyes, and then ran his hands over a balding head. "You know you're looking at a black and white copy."

"What?"

"A photocopy. The paper in your hand is a black and white photocopy of the original report."

"Where's the color copies?"

"Entered into evidence."

K.D.'s heart sank, knowing the longest night stretched before her until court tomorrow. She returned the paper to the box in its original place, not wanting to face Maria's wrath for messing up her organization. She gathered her purse and turned to go. "Guess I'll have to wait for tomorrow then. I need for you to find a way for me to see that report, to see if what I feel happened really did." All the alarms and whistles in her brain screamed at the validity of her hunch, but she wouldn't articulate it without the evidence. K.D. walked toward the door.

"Hang on a second. You're always in such a hurry, K.D. Park it." Ingram tossed his head toward the chair. K.D. obeyed, too tired to argue against his bossy tone.

Ingram turned in his chair, sliding on the rollers toward the console which housed even more boxes of evidence. He dragged one onto his lap, perused the contents until finding what he looked for. He handed the paper to K.D.

"What's this, Ingram?"

He smiled. "I may come across as a pretty gruff fellow. Life has taken a sharp edge to me and left a few nicks, but it might surprise you to know I'm as interested in justice as you are. You're a smart lady, K.D. I trust your instinct."

She smiled with heated cheeks, embarrassed. "Well, thanks, Ingram." She glanced down at the paper and then looked up at her boss. "Is this what I think it is?"

"Yes ma'am. A color copy of Melanie McKnight's report of Bo. Now for all things holy, please tell me what is so important about who used what pen?"

K.D. glanced down again at the paper. She knew what she'd find, but goose bumps scattered across her arms when she actually saw it.

"Ingram, this right here is exactly what we need to provide justice for all." She scooted toward the desk and showed Ingram the document, wishing the night would hurry on the morning.

CHAPTER 29

The judge called court into session, but before opposing counsel could put on his glasses, Ingram stood. "Your Honor, I'd like to request to reopen direct examination of the witness, Janice Parker."

The other lawyer rolled his eyes. "Your Honor, Mr. Ingram's flair for the dramatics is a little tiresome. Yesterday's attempt to discredit my client was borderline slanderous I adamantly object to continuing this line of questioning."

Shelly Anne looked back at K.D. with a raised eyebrow. K.D. responded by holding up a hand in a "give us a minute, we got this" fashion.

The judge ordered both lawyers to the bench, and once again, Ingram won the argument. The judge turned to the bailiff. "Please bring in Miss Parker." He turned to point his bifocals at Ingram. "Sir, I will not tolerate salacious testimony if it's not relevant to this case. You're walking a fine line. I suggest you stay on the right side of it."

"Of course, Your Honor." Ingram stood when Miss Parker entered the courtroom and nodded when the judge reminded the court she remained under oath. The opposing counsel took his seat while K.D. chanced a perusal of the courtroom. The usual suspects clustered at the defense table with Frances Thomas behind them, this time in a royal blue business suit and customary pearls around her neck. Her eyes appeared drawn; the trial seemed to be picking at her hairdo like a bird collecting straw for a nest. She hardly resembled the perfect hostess K.D. had experienced over dinner a few months back.

Trip was again nowhere to be found. K.D. turned her head both ways, searched the entire courtroom, but the room contained only a few members of the media, security, plaintiffs, and defendants. She sighed and turned back around when Ingram began his questioning and prayed everything played out the way she and Ingram hoped.

"Miss Parker, I'd like us to revisit Miss McKnight's report, the one you said you finished for her. According to yesterday's testimony, you said the only place you wrote on her report was the date. Is that correct?"

A fresh night of sleep slipped a little steel into Janice's spine as she straightened and glared at Ingram. "That's what I said."

"So the only place on the report in your handwriting is the date."

"Objection, Your Honor. Miss Parker has answered the question. There's no need for Mr. Ingram to harass the witness."

"Sustained. Mr. Ingram, move on. The witness has answered that the only place on the report in her handwriting is the date."

Ingram held up a hand. "Sorry, Your Honor. It's just I'm confused by something. Here, let me show the court." He handed a piece of paper to the judge and the defense. "This report has already been entered into evidence. This is a color-copy of Miss McKnight's report. Because we had been primarily looking at black and white copies, we found something last night we had overlooked."

Ingram walked over to the witness and handed her the report. "Miss Parker, isn't it true the hospital requires each nurse to complete their reports in different color pens, so as to distinguish among them?"

Heat bloomed across Janice's face as she scanned the report. Her hand began to tremble as she placed the paper on the edge of the witness stand and lowered her face to study her lap.

"Miss Parker, will you please answer the question? Does the hospital require nurses to use different color pens?"

Janice mumbled something inaudible to the courtroom. The judge leaned over. "Miss Parker, you're instructed to answer the question out loud."

"Yes. The hospital requires the staff to write in different color pens," Janice said.

Ingram stroked his chin, the other arm across his girth in a pose of deep thought. "I see. As the supervisor, can you tell me what color was assigned to Miss McKnight?"

Once again, Janice whispered in such a hushed tone that even the stenographer leaned toward her. Ingram put his hand to an ear. "I'm sorry, I didn't quite get that. What did you say?"

"I said her pen was black."

"What color are you assigned, Miss Parker?"

Opposing counsel started to rise. "Objection! Your Honor, I don't…" His voice trailed as his eyes stayed on the report, a look of surprise spreading across his face. "I'm sorry. I withdraw the objection, Your Honor."

The judge looked at Janice. "Answer the question."

"I am assigned blue."

"I see. Miss Parker, will you please look closely at the temperature written on the report. Miss McKnight noted the temperature as 107. But if you would, please look particularly at the number seven. Will you tell me what colors are shown in the number seven?"

Waves of whispers fell over the courtroom, rising in volume until the judge lowered the gavel. "We'll have order, or I'll clear the courtroom. The witness will answer the question."

Janice veiled her face with contempt. "Blue and black."

Ingram nodded. "Blue and black. Why would your color pen have modified Nurse McKnight's initial notation of a temperature of 101 degrees?"

Silence stretched across the courtroom, marred only by a car horn blaring outside the window. Janice continued picking at something in her lap, blocked by the witness box, but K.D. assumed she was ripping at her cuticles like pulled pork. Shelly Anne's back sat rigid in the wooden seat in front of K.D. while Buck slid his chair back a bit, leaning forward on the table with his hands clasped. Time stood still while everyone waited on Janice to testify as to why she would have adjusted Bo's temperature on the initial nursing reports.

Ingram spoke again. "Miss Parker?"

The judge leaned over. "Miss Parker, you're instructed to answer the question."

Janice raised her head with narrowed eyes. "I don't know what you people want from me."

Ingram raised an eyebrow. "I beg your pardon?"

"Nurses like me are the reason lives are saved," Janice said. "You think it's a doctor? You think with their big salaries and hoity toity wives and expensive cars that they do anything?" She looked around the courtroom, projecting her voice. "I can promise you, the reason you're all here today is because, at some point and time in your lives, a nurse did her job to get you healthy. And now you want to point some kind of finger at me?" Janice jabbed herself with a finger to the chest, heaving with angry breath, her composure unraveling.

Ingram held up two hands. "Whoa whoa, Miss Parker. All I want to know is why you modified Miss McKnight's temperature notation. I'm not asking you to extol the virtues of your profession."

When Janice still didn't answer, Ingram turned to the judge. "Your Honor?"

The judge lost his patience. "Miss Parker, if you continue to waste the court's time with your refusal to answer the questions, I'll have no choice but to hold you in…"

"HIM!!!" Janice screamed, pointing a finger and a scowl of hatred toward Dr. Thomas. "He deserved to be punished. He should be up here, not me! I loved him. I would have done anything for him, but no matter how hard I tried, no matter what I did, I was never good enough." Janice began pulling at her hair, her voice rising in mad decibels. "Jackson belonged with me, but he wouldn't leave his wife. He let me stay at his apartment for free so we could have a place to meet. I know that's why he did it. He never said it out loud, but I could tell. Well, I had had enough." Janice gave a sardonic laugh. "When Bo came in that hospital and Jackson ordered the CAT scan, I changed Melanie's report so everyone could see the kind of man I knew he was all along!"

No one said a word, not even the scratch of a pen or a cough to be heard. A few members of the jury adjusted in their seats. K.D.'s heart hammered when the truth flew from Janice's mouth. She had suspected it as soon as Doris had uttered the words *different color pen*, but chill bumps now ran across her arm. She glanced over at Frances who glared at the witness stand. Dr. Thomas lowered his face and shook his head.

Ingram walked over beside the jury. "Let me get this straight. Because Dr. Thomas thwarted your advances and refused an inappropriate relationship with you, you decided for yourself to falsify Bo's records in order to punish Dr. Thomas. Does that about sum it up?"

Janice looked over at the Murdocks. "What I did didn't kill Bo. His body was shutting down as soon as he got to the hospital. Wasn't anything could be done for your boy."

Ingram addressed the judge. "Move to strike from the record."

The judge nodded at the court reporter. "Sustained. Witness will answer only the question."

Ingram approached the witness with authority in his countenance. "Did you, or did you not, falsify Bo's records in order to punish Dr. Thomas for not having an affair with you?"

Janice sunk into her seat, her body folding in on her as if in protection. She nodded her head. "Yes."

K.D. released the breath she didn't realize she had been holding. Even though all evidence had pointed to Dr. Thomas's negligence attributing to Bo's death, K.D. knew of his innocence in her heart. Her father had branded her spirit to recognize a man's potential for abandonment, but in no way did she see that quality in Dr. Thomas. Not from her personal view, not from her times with Trip listening to family stories, not from anything she had read related to the court case. K.D. knew that deep down Dr. Thomas was a good man, and she could no more have rested until that was proven than she could sing the national anthem on Super Bowl Sunday.

Opposing counsel stood at the table. "Your Honor, in light of this disclosure, we'd like to move for a recess to discuss strategy."

The judge lowered the gavel. "Court is in recess until 8 a.m. tomorrow morning, giving both sides time to review these new events and propose to the court any changes in how they'd like to proceed." The judge turned to the court reporter. "Let's go off record a second."

The stenographer relaxed in her seat and lowered her hands to her lap. The judge turned to Janice. "Before I dismiss you as a witness, Miss Parker, I would advise you to seek counsel. Please do not leave town as I'm sure there will be some folks from the hospital or possibly members of the police force who'd like to question you." He nodded back at the stenographer. "Court is adjourned. You're all dismissed."

Janice turned to the side door, avoiding the Thomases all together. Dr. Thomas took Frances into his arms, she lowered her head onto his shoulder, and they swayed together for a few seconds. K.D. wished Trip had been in court today. As she and Ingram had discussed with the medical expert the previous night, it would be impossible to prove negligence on the part of Dr. Thomas since Bo had entered the hospital with a temperature of 101 degrees, coming off hard head-to-ground contact and exhibiting symptoms of concussion. They fully expected opposing counsel to request Dr. Thomas be dropped from the suit.

Shelly Anne erupted from her seat and turned to K.D. as Ingram joined the group. "What in the world? That woman just admitted to killing my boy and now they're letting her walk?"

Ingram took her arm and guided them all to a corner of the courtroom. They sat down, huddling together as the room cleared.

Ingram leaned on his knees. "She didn't admit to killing Bo, but I would imagine someone will have more questions for her. She won't be going far, I can promise you that." As if he sensed Shelly Anne's blood boiling, he reached over to squeeze her clasped hands. "Trust me, Shelly Anne. That nurse won't get away with what she did."

Shelly Anne inhaled deeply and nodded.

"As far as everything else that happened, you can credit K.D. here for finding the truth. Why don't you tell them, K.D.?"

K.D. sat tall. "I know y'all got mad at me for dating Trip, but the night I had dinner at his uncle's, well, let's just say my spirit would not believe him capable of having an affair. That didn't mean I believed he wasn't liable for Bo's death, but something didn't smell right. I kept looking and looking, and I couldn't find anything to prove otherwise. As you saw from Ingram's questioning, the nursing records backed it up, the phone records with Nurse Parker backed it up, his own medical history backed it up since he'd never treated a heat stroke before. Still, something wasn't right."

K.D. described her conversation with Doris. "When the different color pen comment clicked in my brain, I realized I had been working off black and white copies all along. Ingram and I looked at the color copies and realized Nurse Parker had modified the temperature, just like she said. Furthermore, after we reviewed Dr. Thomas's phone records, every single phone call was her calling him, with only a minute charged against the record, meaning either she left a voicemail or he hung up." K.D. paused, and then grinned. "Now, I'll take credit for discovering the information, but that's about as useful as a box of money buried in the backyard. Ingram here had to get her to admit to everything, which he did, brilliantly."

K.D. and Ingram exchanged visual pats on the backs and smiles.

Buck adjusted in his seat. "So, what does all this mean?"

Ingram spoke. "My guess is they will move to have Dr. Thomas removed from the suit, which I would advise us to do. K.D. and I talked last night with the medical expert who said that given the fact Bo's temperature was actually 101 degrees, not 107, coupled with a hard blow to the head and concussion-like symptoms, we'd be hard-pressed to prove Dr. Thomas acted negligently."

"So we lose?" Shelly Anne's voice sounded small. "All of this was for nothing? We revisited everything, I went against my Bible study, all of it for nothing?"

Ingram held up a hand. "No, no. The hospital should offer a settlement. They're the ones with the deep pockets any way. My guess is that not only will they request Dr. Thomas be removed, they will offer you money to avoid the bad publicity. Might not be as much as we originally hoped, but enough you can send Gabby to college several times over."

Shelly Anne chewed her lip before speaking. "What about Nurse Parker? Even if her messing with the records didn't kill Bo, there should still be consequences for her actions."

Ingram nodded. "I agree. I suspect the hospital will file criminal charges against her. At the very least, her license will be revoked, and she'll never work in a medical profession again."

The four stared at each other for a moment. K.D. felt like she'd just stormed Normandy and was now waiting for the muscles to unknot. Buck spoke first. "What now?"

"We wait," Ingram said as his cell phone vibrated. He removed it from his pocket and smiled. "It's the defense attorney. I knew we wouldn't have to wait long."

K.D. reached over to take Shelly Anne's hand as they watched Ingram's face split into a grin.

CHAPTER

30

K.D. left the group and walked down the courthouse steps, anxious to be alone. The creek called to her, the place of refuge when life beat down in droves. Today, however, she didn't need to hide; she yearned for the quiet to consider how to approach Trip and strategize how to win him back. K.D. knew once he considered how hard she'd worked to exonerate his uncle, he would forgive her and offer a fresh start to the relationship. She skipped down the last step, her feet light and airy. She *would* win him back.

"Excuse me, Miss Jennings? K.D.?"

K.D. turned at her name, surprised to see the Thomases approaching her. She stopped, her heartbeat skipping in preparation of a confrontation.

Instead, Frances walked up and kissed her cheek. Dr. Thomas shook her hand and said, "We wanted to thank you for all you did. We know it was you that found the evidence to end this nightmare for us. We're very grateful."

"How did you know?"

Frances smiled. "We just received a phone call from an older gentleman who told us you wouldn't rest the entire time until you could prove Jackson wasn't liable. The caller wouldn't give his name, but I would imagine doing so had to have cost you some trouble with your clients. It truly shows the character we knew you had all along. I'll admit I was deeply hurt that you were involved in the lawsuit, as was Trip, but I hoped it would all work out in every way. It did, thanks to you."

Heat ran up K.D.'s neck from the praise. "Thank you, Mrs. Thomas. I sure wasn't winning any popularity contests the last two weeks, but I'm thankful it all came out the way it did."

"We heard from our attorney that the hospital offered a nice settlement to the Murdocks," Dr. Thomas said.

K.D. nodded. "There's a confidentiality disclaimer so I can't say how much. Not as much as we would have received from a jury, but the Murdocks are happy. It wasn't about the money for them."

"We've never been allowed to reach out to them following Bo's death. The hospital would have fired me," Dr. Thomas said. "I've always wanted to help them if I could. Now that I'm retired and no longer obligated to the hospital, I hope you'll let me know if they need anything."

K.D. smiled. "Thank you. I'll let them know that." She hesitated, looked off a second in thought, and then spoke. "You think I could speak to Trip? I gave up for a while on him because he wouldn't return my phone calls, but now that everything's over, I'm hoping we can be friends again." *Or more.*

Frances' eyes glistened with tears as she touched her husband's arm. She shook her head. "I'm afraid not, dear. Trip has voluntarily entered an undisclosed, in-patient rehabilitation clinic. The stress of law school coupled with the trial pushed him too far, but he's going to be fine. Trip is a strong, smart young man who knows when he needs help. He knew he couldn't do it on his own anymore so he left."

Dr. Thomas pulled an envelope from his pocket and handed it to K.D. "He wanted me to give you this when the trial was over."

K.D. put the envelope in her purse, her heart heavy. The excitement of exonerating Dr. Thomas plummeted, leaving emptiness from Trip's absence and a knot in her throat.

"Thank you. I guess ... I don't know..." K.D. widened her eyes to stave off tears. "I guess I was hoping for a different outcome."

Frances reached over and squeezed K.D.'s hands. "Don't give up on Trip, honey. I know that boy loves you, and I suspect you love him too. If you can, wait for him. He's worth it."

The couple embraced K.D. once more before walking away. K.D. turned to the parking lot, needing her creek now for a totally different reason.

The afternoon sun sprinkled light through oak leaves and pine needles, giving enough warmth to ward off the hint of a winter chill. K.D. sat on her rock, the one she had shared with Trip, folding herself where he had rested. Hard to believe she might not see him again when she could still feel his kisses on her cheek.

She looked down at the opened letter, reading his words again.

K.D.,

Now you know where I am, but I want you to know why. I'm an alcoholic. It's something I will battle my entire life, and no one can fight it for me. It snuck up on me this last time. I really thought I had control, but I forgot control is only an illusion. Before I completely fall over the cliff, I am checking myself into rehab.

K.D., I am not here because of you. Sure I was hurt that you didn't tell me everything as soon as you knew, but I did the same thing to you by not telling you of my drinking problem from the very beginning. I guess that's what people do in a fallen world. We hurt each other, ask forgiveness and receive grace. I want you to know I forgive you, and you are not the reason I fell off the wagon. I drink because I find it hard to accept imperfection in myself and others. It's the truth, plain and simple. Take that burden off your shoulders if you think for one second you had anything to do with it.

I also want you to know I love you. If you're the cause of anything, it's to motivate me to get healthy. I won't ask you to wait for me, but I do promise I'll be back as soon as I'm strong enough to be the man you deserve.

Please pray for me. I'll feel it, and it will help me heal. Keep my Bible. It will help me stay close to you and hopefully keep you close to God.

All my love,
Trip

K.D. turned to the sound of footsteps, surprised when her mother pushed aside some hanging kudzu. "Hey, Mom. What are you doing out here?" K.D. folded the letter and placed it in her pocket. She patted the rock beside her, and her mother sat down.

"Doris said you might be at the creek. She told me how the trial ended. I'm so proud of you, K.D. She said they didn't say on TV how much the settlement was, but I'm sure it was a lot or Ezra wouldn't have agreed to it."

K.D. nodded. "It was."

Lydia looked at her with a puzzled expression. "You don't sound too happy about it. What's wrong? I thought you'd be celebrating by now."

K.D. shook her head, wanting to cry and break something all at the same time. The unfairness of life overwhelmed her. "I don't know, Mama, I thought everything was going to be okay. You know, like in the books? Where everybody lives happily ever after? Why can't I ever have the happy ending?" She told her mother about Trip, his drinking, his absence. The future she had imagined with him was now blank.

Lydia stared off, considering her words. "I guess it feels like everybody's always leaving you, doesn't it honey?"

K.D. nodded, watching a small limb meander down the water, wishing she could grab hold and travel with it.

"What if it wasn't about you?"

K.D. turned her head toward Lydia with a frown. "What do you mean?"

"I mean, what if the end of all this wasn't about you at all? What if it were about Trip? Or his aunt and uncle? What if it was about the Murdocks? Or maybe, it wasn't about you falling in love or living happily ever after. Maybe it was about sTriping everything away so you could finally see the real problem."

K.D. looked sideways at her mom, raising an eyebrow.

Lydia reached over, stroking K.D.'s cheek. "I never did tell you the story of your name, did I?"

K.D. sat straighter. "No."

Lydia smiled and brushed a stray hair from K.D.'s face. "It wasn't my idea. It was your father's."

K.D. bristled.

Lydia held up a hand. "No, hear me out. I wanted to name you something glamorous like Marilyn or Lillian Rose. From the way you wailed in that nurse's arms, I felt certain you'd be a singer or something. But he wouldn't hear of it. Said he wanted to name you K.D. I said, 'Katie? Whose name is Katie? We don't know anybody by that name.' He told me not Katie, but K.D. Then I said the same thing you did. I mean, really, who *does* name her child with initials?"

Lydia elbowed K.D. in the ribs, eliciting a smile.

"But the way he explained it made perfect sense. He said he didn't want anybody putting labels on his daughter. Not him. Not your friends. Certainly not some boy. He wanted you to search your heart for your own identity, to see what you wanted in the world rather than somebody creating it for you."

"So I don't mean anything? My name means nothing?" Fitting end to the day. Why should she mean something when she felt so empty?

"No, just the opposite. Your name can mean anything, everything. Listen, your daddy wasn't a religious man, so I don't think he had God in mind when he thought of this, but I've spent a lot of time reading that Bible you brought home, watching programs at night when I can't sleep. I'm no expert, so take this with a grain of salt. I feel like our foundation, the very thing we know for sure about ourselves, has to be formed from God in order to have peace in our hearts. Doesn't mean everything always works out, but it means we'll be stronger to face whatever comes at us. Everything – our jobs, our identity, relationships – everything has to spring from Him. He has to be the source which everything flows from."

Lydia picked up a stick, rolling it around her fingers. "I don't know, darling, it just seems like you're running away from something all the time instead of running to something. You can't find a future for yourself until you deal with the past. If you do that, then you take away what's standing between you and the person God created you to be. Be deliberate about what you want in life, be purposeful. Live life on purpose. You can't do that holding onto grudges, refusing to forgive. Gets in the way of all your relationships, especially the one with God." She paused for a minute, scrutinizing K.D.'s reaction. "What do you think?"

Life on purpose. K.D. remembered Shelly Anne saying the same thing, when she had accused K.D. of treating life like a blind date, waiting on it to introduce itself to her. Trip's words returned to her. How God cared more about a relationship with her than anything else. How it all started there.

"Wow, Mom. You've become quite the scholar." K.D. smiled at her mom.

"I gotta have something to do all those nights I can't sleep." She patted K.D.'s hand. "It's up to you. You love the law, don't you? I see it every time you talk about it. Run after that dream, honey, if you feel in your heart that's what God designed you to do. If Trip is supposed to come back, he will, or maybe someone else is waiting for you. Who knows? But in the meantime, know who you are. Be strong in what you believe. Only then can you stand when people fail you or when you fail others."

K.D. unfurled her legs and put a bare toe into the running

water, her calves brushing against the silky moss. The chill shocked her, but she stayed still, enjoying the contrast with the warm rock on her legs.

Life on purpose.

Made sense.

She did love Trip. K.D. knew that in the far corners of her heart. He didn't abandon her. He left to take care of himself. She could be grateful for that. She wanted healing for him. Enough time had also passed that she should stop defining herself by her mother's illness, her father's abandonment.

There was one thing she saw with as much clarity as the crystal water before her. Her mother was right. K.D. was a lawyer. She felt it in every corner of her being. The case against Trip's uncle reinforced the belief that if she worked hard with integrity, she'd always do her best to provide justice for all those she served. That was enough for now.

K.D. felt her mother nudge her and turned to find Lydia holding out a necklace, the butterfly charm on the end, the last present from her father.

"I think you should wear it, K.D. It's a wonderful symbol of rebirth, of a creature born into this world one way, but refusing to accept anything except who it was created to be. You're just like this butterfly, K.D., waiting to emerge from your cocoon."

A tear slid down K.D.'s face as she took the necklace and looked at it. Oh how she loved its gold trim and pale pink eyes, the blue colors of the wings. Something beautiful shoved to the back of a drawer because of her own anger. The words her father had said didn't stick in her mind, but she could see his smile as if he stood before her now. She raised the chain and fastened it around her neck.

It no longer burned into her skin, nor did it weigh down her heart. K.D. looked into the sky and felt the very presence of God at that moment, losing the last shred of anger toward her father, life, Trip's disease. She forgave even her mother. Sweet, blessed release swept over her as she rubbed the butterfly charm between her two fingers. K.D. inhaled deeply, exhaled, and watched the darkness float away.

Free. She felt free for the first time in forever. A clean page washed off the ugly she'd dragged with her through the years. Time to write a new story. Time to talk things over with God and become the woman He created her to be.

K.D. stood, almost shot up, no longer burdened. She turned to her mom and held out a hand. "Come on. I bet Doomsday Doris has some canned Ravioli we can heat up for a late lunch." Lydia smiled, joining her daughter, and the two left the creek behind and moved forward toward home.

The End

ACKNOWLEDGEMENTS

All books are a shaken box of puzzle pieces shaped and formed through many eyes, brains, touches, etc. Some do not even know their influence – maybe unusual dialects picked up in the exhausting DMV line or the relative's story of childhood whose ending finally made sense after the umpteenth gazillionth time of hearing it. But some touches are deliberate, so please allow me to acknowledge a token few.

The Yaysayers. My goodness what shiny star did I sleep under to have chanced upon your sisterhood. I'm real good at finding the straight-edged pieces, of framing the picture, but you, you come along with your truly God-gifts and find every.single.missing.interior.piece. Blessed by Shelly Dippel, Jenny Spinola, Karen Schravemade and Jenn Fromke. Blessed, blessed, blessed.

Two individuals made the book smarter than its writer's contributions. Dr. Ken Rainer, author of *First Do No Harm Reflections on Becoming a Neurosurgeon* and current attorney and many other things which require a lot of school and an IQ off the charts, helped me craft the initial plot line. Who knew an early Saturday morning on a screened-in porch would yield the words on these pages? And Christine Dean, my friend and attorney who shows up at Upward basketball games in stilettos and hip-babies. She carefully scoured each page for believability and accuracy. If any legal minds find flaws in the writing, they're mine alone.

I'm grateful to serve a Lord who's gifted me with writing. I say this with absolutely no pride or sense of self. Each word, each sentence, everything for His glory. If you don't know Him, if you've chanced upon this book from a recommendation, contact me through my writing page on Facebook, Christy K. Truitt, The Write Purpose. I'd like to introduce you to the last love of your life.

AUTHOR BIO

Christy Kyser Truitt is a child of the Deep South, raised at the junction of the Tombigee/Black Warrior Rivers in West Alabama. She is a graduate of Auburn University and lives in Auburn, Alabama, with her husband and three children. For more information on Christy's writing and appearances, please visit www.christytruitt.com or join her Facebook page at Christy K. Truitt, The Write Purpose.

CPSIA information can be obtained at www.ICGtesting.com
Printed in the USA
LVOW12s0419150414

381723LV00003B/3/P

9 781939 447241